September Wind
Book Two

Kathleen Janz-Anderson

Publisher's Note
This is a work of fiction. All
names, characters, places, and events
are the work of the author's imagination.
Any resemblance to real persons, places or
events is coincidental.

MY TAKE ON AI
AI has its place in novel-writing if someone
cares to use it; if so, AI should be credited.
As far as writing my novels,
I use minimal Grammarly help,
thesauruses, and research for authenticity.
I am open to using AI for trailers,
book covers, and other marketing,
and will give AI credit.

Copyright © 2025 Kathleen Janz-Anderson
ISBN: 979-8-9872130-3-2
Mary Wright ~ Graphic Designer
www.fiverr.com/mary_k_wright

Cover photo by Sophie Engstrom
https://www.instagram.com/sophiaengstromart/

Other books by Kathleen

September Wind ~ book I
Knapsack Journey Home
Scrooge & the Romance Effect
Poems of Glass
October Will Never be the Same (2024)

Until we meet in Heaven.... Always missing you, Chaddieboy—every day all day long ~

To all the devoted writers who struggle with their craft. Best wishes. Writing truly is a labor of love.

CHAPTER ONE

1960

*E*mily tried to ignore her uneasiness as she stood on her tiptoes and gazed out the window in search of Shayne's car. He said he'd park across the street next to the cypress tree. But after the second hour of waiting for the man who promised to marry her and take her away from *The Palace*, she decided to look for him.

She pulled herself from the window, went to stand next to the bed, and gazed down at two cloth sacks that held all of her worldly goods. Lifting the strap of the blue bag over her left shoulder, she hefted the pillowcase with the gifted Tom Sawyer and Huck Finn books over the other, switched off the light, and stepped into the hallway. Her plan had been to ask Miss Bea for the money owed her on the way out. Now, all at once, she was in a hurry to slip away unnoticed.

This urgency followed her to the stairway with visions of the first day she arrived at *The Palace,* when Michael, the handsome resident doctor she met on the train, was still fresh on her mind. A rush of pleasure spread across her shoulders as she thought of his beautiful, dark eyes gazing at her in the vestibule where she so ungraciously ran into him.

What am I thinking? Shayne is the one who asked me to marry him. Michael is the one who led me on. She saw it right out of the train window when he missed a breakfast date with her, departed unexpectedly, and welcomed a woman into his arms.

Emily pushed back the painful memory and tiptoed down the steps, cringing when the pillowcase holding the books brushed against the wall. As she reached the bottom, Miss Bea's brooding voice came from her office.

"Is that you, Emily?"

"Y-yes. It's me."

"Well? Get in here! And hurry it up!"

Letting her bags slip to the floor, Emily headed to the madam's office, wishing that just once, she wasn't hoovering like some wily edition of a mother duckling. Thankfully, for the most part, Miss Bea had let the dark of the night lead by its own design, otherwise who knows what kind of a state she would be in by now.

Emily stepped through the doorway where Miss Bea was sitting at her desk, looking like she was ready to explode. When she latched the door, the woman dropped what she was doing and glared up at her.

"You certainly took me for a ride, young lady."

She stood and walked around the desk. "By the way. Shayne's no longer allowed at *The Palace*."

"Wh-what do you mean?"

Miss Bea leaned back against the desk, folding her arms.

"Did you know he's married?'

"Well, I—"

"There's a baby on the way. Did you know that?

Emily sank to a chair, tears brimming.

"But... He's living with his parents. He's not... *with her*. Just last night, he—"

"Oh, sheesh... Naive as ever.

"For your information. I had an interesting talk with Moose this morning. He informed me that Shayne's wife was planning a lawsuit against *The Palace*. Thank goodness he was able to put a stop to that nonsense."

Miss Bea pushed herself from the desk and stood over Emily. "Imagine what kind of mess that would've been."

She walked around to sit again. "Lucky for you. Those two are working things out.

"Now… Let's get to what's at hand. Like you pulling a fast one on me... And our customers, too."

"Miss Bea… I—"

"If you want to dance, the men seem to be smitten by you. But you're going to do just what I hired you for those other nights. You owe me. You owe me big time."

"It's just that since my dancing brought in customers. I…I was hoping for the pay I'm owed."

"You mean the money you tried to swindle by not doing your job?"

Emily had put a lot of work into her dance routines. And she wished Miss Bea would consider that in the long run, *The Palace* lost nothing. But that would never happen. And if she wanted any mercy, she would have to show remorse.

"Working here hasn't come easy. But still, I... I should've done my job the way you intended."

"Well…I'll leave it at that. Now go on up and wash away those tears."

Emily closed the door as she left, angry with herself as much as with anyone. Moose had warned her that Shayne was fickle and that he was a yellow-belly, impulsive dreamer. That concerned her at first. But because he was such a kind and generous man, she decided those traits weren't as bad as Moose portrayed.

She picked up her things at the bottom of the staircase and shuffled back to her room. Dropping everything on the bed, she lay across the spread with an arm around her belongings, her books spilling from the pillowcase. The scent of the bag she fashioned from a flour sack back at the farm made her long for home and all the things she missed. She groaned, remembering those things she fought to forget.

Her engagement to Shayne was probably the shortest one in history. She admitted that it had been exciting, thinking she was free of *The Palace*. But he had never been hers in the first place. She chuckled at her own fickleness, knowing she wasn't *in love* with him, not when she was still pining for Michael.

Raising to an elbow, she reached for one of the Twain novels. As she opened to the first page, a piece of paper fell out. Setting the book aside, she picked it up.

> *Dear Emily,*
>
> *I want you to know how grateful I am that someone will enjoy what was once a big part of my son's life. He was such a blessing to me. Even though my heart will forever be broken, I'm grateful for the twenty-three years I had with Samuel. All I ask is that you think of him when you read the books he treasured.*
>
> *Ruby*

"What in the…?"

Emily scanned through the note, confirming that her mother's friend Samuel would be at least eighteen years older than Ruby's son. She fell back on the bed and picked up the Huck book again, flicking through the pages.

"So, you're not the Samuel I was looking for after all."

Her heart soared with renewed hope. But a jolt of sadness washed over her when she thought of what young Samuel's mother still faced. *Oh, Ruby, I'm so sorry. And I'll think of your son when I read his books. I'll read them in his honor. I promise.* How could she not think of him as she held the same books that his fingers had eagerly turned through each page with anticipation for what was to come.

Late afternoon, Emily went downstairs and warmed leftover soup. Miss Bea had a standing dinner and movie date each Sunday evening. And except for the weekend house mom in the back room, she was alone at *The Palace.*

Taking her dinner to the table, she gazed out the bay window, wondering what her chances were of meeting the real Samuel Dimsmoore. She had sent him a letter while at Mack's House of Food and set up three potential dates to meet at the restaurant. Thinking back, she realized November ninth, December first, and the nineteenth, each between one and two o'clock, were all still in play. He was back in the picture. And she was more determined than ever to meet him.

After washing, drying, and putting away the dishes, Emily checked the calendar on the wall. The ninth was three days away. Monday wasn't a workday, so that only left her one more night of dancing before the meeting.

*T*here had been talk that changes were coming to *The Palace.* And after two days off, the place was buzzing with excitement. A round, two-level stage sat at the far side of the waterfall, just short of the grand piano. Miss Bea had hired additional dancers, which meant more money coming in and more young women to help fulfill her dreams.

Emily felt the energy as she strolled up the strip in a yellow strapless cocktail dress. Gabe had her usual drink ready when she walked over and sat at the bar. She had barely taken a few sips when her theme song *Poetry in Motion* began to play.

Slipping off the chair, she ran up on stage, trying to hold onto the excitement that had always been part of her dance. By now, her routines were down pat, with fresh steps and moves, some of which brought chuckles, and others, wide-eyed smiles and whistles.

At times like this, or when she was upstairs in the attic working on dance routines or reading in her room, it was easy to brush aside the dark undertone in this posh, secretive club. Even with the downside, she believed many of the customers and some of *The Palace* workers were probably ordinary people, most likely in transition, like herself, and like Toni, Gabe, and a few others who frequented the scene and found their way, whether by mistake or otherwise, like Shayne. But no matter how much energy she put into her dance, worked to keep positive, and tried to ignore the rest, Emily knew this was not where she belonged. She dreaded the thought of what her grandmother would've thought of where she ended up. And partly because of her, now that the days of avoiding her duties were over, her departure was even more urgent.

*W*ednesday the ninth, Emily arose in anticipation of going into town to meet Samuel. At first, she stubbornly resisted wearing anything from Miss Bea. But after looking over the faded clothes she brought from the farm, she put on a chiffon petticoat, a pastel-colored hoop skirt, and a matching pullover sweater. Her first meeting with Samuel was far too important to allow a grudge to get in the way.

Setting off for town, she took a bus to the pier and walked the streets, stopping at restaurants to see if they were hiring. One said openings were coming soon, another that a dishwashing job would open the following month, and for her to check back. Her last stop was a diner that required experience. They all asked for her telephone number, and because Miss Bea occasionally took the calls, unless Emily's address changed, that wouldn't work.

Fifteen minutes before the set time to meet Samuel, Emily walked into Mack's House of Food. Thankfully, Maxine, the brazen waitress who set her up at *The Palace*, was off duty.

She took the empty spot at the end of the counter and sat with a coke and fries, turning expectantly each time the door opened. An hour later, she ordered more fries and a refill of coke.

By two-thirty, it was obvious that Samuel wasn't coming. From what Maxine said, it was possible he hadn't picked up her letter yet. And there was a chance he never would.

Returning to *The Palace* with a heavy heart, she started up the hallway when Miss Bea called from the parlor.

"Just to let you know, Donald Schillings is taking you out to dinner tomorrow night."

Emily stepped back and peered through the doorway.

"Me? But…why?"

"He didn't say. And I didn't ask."

Now even more disappointed, Emily continued up the hallway. Deciding she needed a lift, she stopped by the lounge. A maid glanced up, nodded, and went about her cleaning while Emily picked up a bottle of vodka and a shot glass. Noticing the photos Abe had taken while she was on stage and had put aside for her, she picked them up and started to put them back but thought twice and took them to her room.

She dropped the photos on the bed and went to stand at the table, gazing out the window as she opened the bottle and took a shot of vodka. Pouring another half shot, she drank it down, set the bottle beneath one of the end tables next to the couch, and went into her closet.

Pulling her journal from a shelf, she went to lay across her bed and tucked the photos inside the cover pocket. She lifted the white goose feather from her last entry and took out the pen and begun to write — *Things changed so quickly. One minute I'm engaged, and the next it's over. I'm back where I started. I thought Donald Schillings initial interest in me was over. But now he wants to take me to dinner. I'm uneasy around*

him and in a quandary as to what he wants with me. I must leave
this place. The sooner, the better.

She was considering when, where, and how she would
leave when she heard someone outside her door.

"Hold on a minute," she hollered, slipping into her
shoes. When she opened the door, no one was there.

She checked the hallway and listened for footsteps, but
it was eerily quiet. Having lost her train of thought and
feeling restless, she replaced the feather and returned her
journal to its spot on a closet shelf, making sure it sat
squarely against the wall and out of sight.

Wandering back into the bedroom, she brushed a hand
across the bedcovers, tucked them in, and fluffed the
pillows. She glanced at the clock and saw that it was still
an hour before she needed to be in the lounge but decided
a few cocktails before work sounded good. After
showering, she put on the black dress she had worn the first
night at *The Palace* and headed down.

On her way up the strip, her gaze wandered to the table
where she first saw Shayne. No matter what had taken
place, and no matter how imperfect he turned out to be, she
missed him.

She took her favorite seat at the bar and watched Gabe
mix her drink, her mouth watering with the same
anticipation she had back home waiting in the kitchen for
cookies to come out of the oven.

"Here you go," he said, placing her drink on a coaster.

"Thanks, Abe."

Several customers bought rounds, and she was
finishing her second vodka sour when someone turned up
the Jukebox. Already feeling the effects of the alcohol, she
started on another drink while listening to a song called *I*
Put a Spell on You, a most unusual song with words and a
rhythm that were hard to ignore. Emily wasn't aware of
when the song ended and played again, only that the
alcohol was no longer an ember but smoldering along with

the intoxicating beat of the music that swept through her like a furnace. When the song played yet again, she stood and moved onto the dance floor, her body and the beat becoming one, she and the room spinning with the pulsing wail of the saxophone.

Someone came up behind her, hands sliding across her hips.

Shayne.

She swung around to embrace him, ready to forgive.

"Hello sweetie," Moose brayed in her ear. "So, you like my music, huh?"

She stepped around him, and he followed her back to the counter.

"I'm here to collect on the promise."

"Well, I dance tonight, so…."

Moose glanced to where the new dancers were checking out the layered stage.

"That may be true. But I see you have backups. Plus, you owe me."

Emily picked up her cocktail and took several drinks. When she set the glass down, Moose grabbed her wrist.

"I've never stopped thinking about you. Can't you see that? And now that Shayne's out of the picture, I decided you're going to be my number one girl at *The Palace*."

Emily yanked from his grip, planning to move down several chairs. But before she could rise, he came in like a cheetah with his hands around her shoulders and neck. Sliding his thumbs up her cheeks, he forced her to look at him.

"It's time to make good on your promise."

He stared into her eyes as the song played again, smiling and playfully rubbing her chin. All at once he dropped his hold, picked up his drink, took her by a hand, and led her down the strip, signaling to the woman behind the council window as they passed into the hallway. When they reached the foot of the staircase, he released his hold on her.

"Go on."

"Mm?"

"Up the stairs. Go."

She gripped the handrail and started up the steps feeling his eyes move up her legs. It was as if Claude was breathing at the back of her neck, ready with his arms like sheets of steel and massive shoulders like boulders ready to crush her. At the landing she rushed up the stairs to her room.

Footsteps approached and she froze as Moose reached around her and opened the door.

Inside, he shoved his glass at her. "Drink up."

She wanted to scream that no amount of alcohol could force her to give him what he wanted. But she did as he wished and finished it off. She set the glass on the nightstand and looked down at the bedspread she had tucked in so neatly.

His hands moved up her arms, slipped beneath the straps of her dress, and pulled them down over her shoulders.

CHAPTER TWO

For the flower plucked by a gust of wind
and dropped to the ground
it's already too late for nature's way
but for the tender hand that
lifts the bloom from its grave.

Kathleen Janz-Anderson

*M*oose dropped a fifty-dollar bill on the nightstand.

"You're a jewel, Emily, enticing. Everything a man could want." He reached down and lifted her chin. "But next time, I expect you to bring your dance moves."

In a moment of anger, Emily almost ripped the money into pieces and threw it at him. When he left, she snatched up the bill and went to open the bottom chest drawer. She dug into her bag, pulled out the pouch, now bulging with cash, and stuffed it inside.

Slipping into a bathrobe, she went up the hall to the shower, turned the water to hot, and scoured herself raw. When her skin stung from the heat and the scrubbing, she turned the water all the way to cold, pressed a washcloth over her mouth and screamed as tears ran down her cheeks.

Still recovering from the shock, she returned to her room and dressed, pulled her damp hair into a tight bun, and headed back to the lounge, swearing with every breath and ounce of blood that rushed through her veins, that the streets would be her home before Moose touched her again.

*D*elilah knocked on Emily's door, reminding her that she agreed to help her find a dress for the opera.

"Sorry. But I can't go."

"You've gotta come. I need your keen eye. Besides, everybody's left for town but you."

Emily rolled her eyes, glancing back into her room. "I don't know, it's just that…."

Delilah slid a foot against the doorframe. "Guess what… I just bought a brand-new red Chevrolet convertible. So, come on. Let's take a ride."

"A convertible. Hmm. Oh, all right.

"But I can't stay long," Emily added, as she headed to the closet to find something to wear.

She noticed her worn clothes had been washed and patched. Knowing it was Toni's doing, she silently thanked her for what Miss Bea said would be a waste of time. She pushed the new clothes to the side and pulled down the blouse and skirt she wore on the train. They felt comfortable—like home, and Grandmother.

On the way out the door, she took a twenty-dollar bill from her pouch and stuffed it into a pocket.

Riding in Delilah's car was exhilarating. It gave Emily a taste of what real freedom felt like. They took the long way into town, gliding along the coast for a time before turning back to their destination.

The experience left Emily on a high and made her wish for things she had never dared to dream about before. Later, after Delilah found a dress for the opera, they sat for lunch.

"You know, Emily," Delilah said, as they ate, "you've surprised me since you came to *The Palace*." She laughed. "And no major blowouts with any of the girls. That doesn't happen too often."

"Maybe not. But there's been some tension between Layla and me."

"Considering the source, that's not surprising. You wanna know what that's about? Moose. She's madly in love with him."

Emily nearly choked on her food. "Wow! I never would've guessed."

"The fact being, Moose was dazzled by Layla until Angellee showed up. But since their relationship has started to cool off, Layla's been expecting Moose would return to her. That's until you came along. You see. He has a habit of falling for the new girls. And I think she sees you as her ultimate threat."

Emily was relieved Layla's problem with her was a simple one. She would be gone soon, glad to leave this foolishness behind, with no desire to respond and rile her up even more.

"So... I bet you're excited that the opera's just around the corner."

"I am. Although it's been built into this huge event. Hopefully, I won't be disappointed."

"I doubt that. Just take it all in."

The two continued their lunch in lighthearted conversation about the opera, a subject Emily found fascinating. It felt good to be chumming in this manner like the first time they shopped with Miss Bea. Once again, Emily wanted to open up, but something stopped her. As quarrelsome as Delilah and Miss Bea were with each other, the two were bonded. This was apparent, not only with them, but with many of *The Palace* girls. No matter how mischievous they became, there was a bond that Emily would never be part of. Not that she cared. It was easy to accept that her friendship with Miss Bea and the girls was superficial. And she knew it was best to watch who she trusted.

When they left the restaurant, Delilah dropped her off at *The Palace* and sped away to meet a friend. Emily hurried up the front steps, considering whether or not to pack her things and leave. From what Delilah said, she figured there was enough money in her pouch to buy a used car; a very simple process if one had the cash. Delilah may have been bragging. But it made sense. She could probably pay rent on a place for several months. Although with a car, whether or not she had a job, at least she would have a place to sleep without being obligated to anyone.

As Emily started up the stairway, Miss Bea came from the kitchen with a broad smile.

"You wouldn't believe what happened this morning," she said, motioning Emily into her office.

Emily stepped down and traipsed in behind her.

"Oh, and…don't forget. Donald Schillings will be here at four."

She scooped up a pitcher and watered several plants as she spoke.

"When you're out with him, keep in mind who you're dealing with."

Emily gaped at Miss Bea's twinkling eyes and flushed cheeks, wondering why she was lit up like a Christmas tree.

The woman set the pitcher aside and turned to her.

"So, it's official," she said with a gloating smile. "Donald Schillings has granted a new home for *The Palace* right there on his estate. It's the most gorgeous property you can imagine, several thousand acres, at least, that will be used to grow and expand his empire. No private club in the world compares to what he'll be able to offer."

Well… There it was. The source of Miss Bea's ecstasy. It was obvious she was buttering up because of Donald's sudden interest in her. And Emily thought it was best to play along.

"Sounds like good news."

"Oh my, yes, it certainly is. And with all the additional amenities, it'll bring a plethora of customers from all over the world."

Miss Bea reached for a drawing and rolled it out on her desk.

This is just a preliminary plan and I'm sure the final will be even more spectacular. Oh, and see, here's what *The Palace* will look like."

Emily stepped over and looked at a building that sat on a hilltop. There were archways, private balconies, and varied sizes of windows along three floors. Below, across the valley, were hundreds of immaculately kept acreages set around a mansion partially hidden behind trees. To the north was a horse arena, and to the west, set within a forest was a long driveway, maybe a mile long. On both sides of the forested way, were drawings of beautiful buildings set amongst the trees.

"He's waiting on a few circumstances to change before he begins construction on the road that'll lead up the hill to where *The Palace* will sit. When that's finished, it'll be the first building to go up. Just think, a beautiful view of the valley from the lounge. Can't you just imagine how magnificent it will be?"

"Yeah. It's quite something."

The older woman's spark fizzled. She rolled up the drawing, moved it to the side, and leaned back on the desk.

"Anyway, listen here. When you're having dinner tonight, whatever he needs from you, tell him, yes. You see... Mr. Schillings is a very powerful man, if you don't already know."

Emily couldn't get to her room fast enough. She opened the bottom chest drawer and dug her money pouch from her bag. When she saw that it was empty, she dropped it and opened the top drawer where she kept her jewelry. Everything was there except for her necklace. Even though she knew it was futile, she did a double check, trying to come up with something that made sense. But it made no sense.

Closing the drawers, she raked her fingers through her hair, walking in circles and trying to rationalize why someone would have done this. It would be unlikely that any of the girls would take her things for cash when none of it would compare to what they made working for *The Palace*. Her necklace couldn't be worth much more, although she had a feeling it had been a mistake to wear it to the lounge and especially reveal that it was a beloved heirloom.

Recalling the twenty she took from her pouch that morning, she checked her pocket to make sure the change was still there. It was, but it wouldn't pay rent, buy a car or do much else.

Peter came to mind, and she rushed back to the dresser to get his card—to no avail. She hadn't even bothered to look at his last name. *How could things have gone so wrong?* She was worse off than when she arrived in San Francisco. And now someone made certain that leaving *The Palace* would be almost as impossible as staying.

That's when the full impact of her loss hit, and her shock and frustration turned to anger. She rushed from her room and to the stairway, holding onto both banisters as she took the steps down in search of Miss Bea. Her office was empty. When she checked the kitchen, Toni said she came in for coffee and left ten minutes earlier. After a look in the lounge, Emily headed to the parlor, where she found her talking with a young woman.

Miss Bea spun around with a scowl, although her voice didn't reflect the irritation on her face. "Would you please wait in the kitchen, dear? I'm busy *as you can see*."

Emily was tempted to warn the girl. Although, by her plunging neckline, heavy makeup, and dress that barely covered her undergarments, it looked as if she was already aware of what she was getting into.

Exasperated, Emily went back to the kitchen.

"What's got you so worked up?" Toni asked, preparing to leave for the night.

Emily took a seat at the table, thinking about telling her what had happened. But she was afraid that, in the end, it could ruin what Toni had going for her at *The Palace*, certain that she wasn't the only one that this kind woman had helped.

"It's nothing I can't handle.

"Mm. What'd you have baking in the oven?"

"Chicken casserole. And make sure you have some."

If Emily had her way, she would be gone before the casserole finished baking, although she assured Toni that she would have a double helping.

Toni left for the night, and a few minutes later, Miss Bea walked in and headed to the stove for coffee. "Want some?" she asked as if nothing was wrong.

"Nope."

"So, what's up?"

"Someone went into my room and stole my money. They took my necklace too. Remember? I wore it to the lounge one night."

Miss Bea stirred sugar into her coffee and went to sit at the table.

Emily searched her eyes for clues of guilt. "Why would someone take my things?"

"Maybe you met up with a pickpocket."

"No. I just said they went into my room."

"Oh, stop fretting over the measly bit of cash you lost. Or most likely mishandled. And as far as that necklace, the clip probably broke and it's lying on a sidewalk somewhere."

"There was no pickpocket. And the clip didn't break."

Emily stood, shoved a hand into a pocket, and clutched the last of her money.

"I'm going to find out who did this."

"Don't do that! You'll stir things up. It'll scare off the new girls.

"Listen...I'll check around myself. So, keep still about this… You hear?"

Miss Bea glanced at the clock on the wall. "Say, you'd better go up and change. Donald will be here soon. I'm sure he'll take you to a nice place for dinner."

Reluctantly resigned to the idea of having dinner with Donald Schillings, Emily headed back to her room. She went to her closet. And as she reached for her journal, she hesitated, thinking it seemed slightly askew. *Nah*, she thought, pulling it down. She flipped through the pages, coming across her sizzling purge as she rode on the bus after fleeing from her grandfather's farm, remembering how desperate she had been that day.

Samuel Dimsmoore seemed further away from her than ever. But he was her only hope. Maxine said he was probably a kook, or something worse. Although, as far as she was concerned, there was a better chance he was as normal as anyone else, and exactly what she needed. And as discouraged as she was, she couldn't give up on him.

In the meantime, the best thing she could do for herself was to stay calm and find a way through this mess. Not only that, but she would keep her ears and eyes open for signs that would lead her to the culprit who invaded her privacy, stole her livelihood, and her necklace. Someone knew where it was and why it was taken. Now all she had to do was find out who and why.

*A*s much as Emily dreaded having dinner with Donald Schillings, she rummaged through the closet and chose a white dress with black polka dots. Pulling her hair into a ponytail, she applied red lipstick, rouge, and stepped into a pair of black heels.

On the way downstairs, she heard laughter from the gathering room and leaned over the railing as Angellee and Felice were walking out the back door.

"Wait up, guys!"

She hurried down the last few steps and approached the girls as they poked their heads back inside.

"Do either of you know a man who comes in by the name of Peter? I'm looking to find his last name."

"Well, let's see," Angellee said, thoughtfully, "I know several Peters who come in."

"This guy is tall. And he wears his hair long and tied back."

"Oh, that Peter. Well, I've talked with him, but I don't know his last name. We usually don't."

She turned to Felice. "How about you?"

"Nope, me either."

"Can't help you," Angellee said, ready to leave until Emily stopped her again.

"Say, how well do you know Donald Schillings?"

Angellee smiled as she stepped inside.

"Mr. Schillings? Mmm. He's the king around here."

She leaned back, dreamily, with a foot against the wall. "You see, he's what you'd call a... well, an enigma, in a beguiling sort of way. You might have noticed how everyone stands at attention whenever he comes around. Oh, but he doesn't mess with any of the girls that I know of. Which is a disappointment to some and peculiar to others. But then I guess it keeps the suspense. Probably makes him more interesting and mysterious."

"I see. Well, thank you."

Angellee stepped back outside, and Emily went to meet Donald, wondering how she could have been so wrong about him. When she reached the parlor, he was puffing on a cigarette like a man with a lot on his mind.

He noticed her standing in the doorway. "Good evening, Emily."

She returned his greeting and watched him put out his cigarette and walk into the hallway where she stood. He didn't seem as serious as the last time she saw him. Still, she couldn't squeeze into that good feeling Angellee had about him.

After they settled in the limousine, he poured two glasses of champagne and handed one to Emily. He took several drinks before turning to her.

"I know you're in a spot. And for your own good, I'm going to be blunt with you. I've lived around here for many years. And I speak from experience when I say that the life of many a-young-woman in your situation has come to a tragic end."

He gazed at her. And she wanted to trust and find compassion in him. But when she looked into his eyes, she saw neither.

"Now, as for you," he continued, "it's simple. All you have to do is relax and let me help you. As I see it, you don't have any other viable options."

The limousine rounded a bend and turned into a restaurant parking lot that overlooked the Pacific Ocean. Emily gazed at the beauty, leaning toward the window, wanting to feel the ocean breeze whip across her face. When they stopped, she stepped from the car and went to the lookout, gaping in awe at the mass of water that spread out as far as the eye could see. As she watched the waves rush to shore and explode into the rocks below, she thought of Michael's wish to share these moments with her. She imagined that if she stayed there long enough, he would come up beside her, and they would find their way down and stroll along the shore.

"Let's go inside," Donald said, calling to her.

The restaurant was luxurious, with wall-to-wall windows that overlooked the ocean. They were immediately seated, and a waiter came with a bottle of wine.

"Would you like to start with the usual, Mr. Schillings?" he asked.

Donald nodded, and the waiter uncorked the bottle and poured a small amount for him. After a swirl, a sniff, and a taste of the wine, Donald motioned his approval, and the young man filled their glasses and left.

Emily sipped wine and mulled over the gourmet menu until Donald noticed her hesitation.

"Would you like me to order for you?"

"That's probably a good idea," she said, setting the menu aside.

A waiter came to take their orders, and several more waiters approached. One filled their glasses of wine, another brought a cocktail for Donald, and two more served plates of appetizers. Emily thought the restaurant at *The Palace* topped them all, but this was a world in itself.

When Donald was called away for a phone call and stopped to chat with someone on his way back, Emily watched him in his element, wondering what in the world he wanted with her. She had doubts that he intended to do her a favor.

Soft music played as flames from candles flickered and glistened across willowy glasses and pricey-looking tableware. Emily sat back and took it all in until she felt Schillings beside her.

"I have a proposition for you," he said, taking a seat.

"A proposition?"

"Yes, an offer."

He finished his cocktail and set it aside, motioning to a waiter.

"You see, I lost my wife a while back. She left me with two young children. I'd like you to be their nanny."

Emily might have been thrilled with his offer, although she couldn't help but wonder why he chose someone he thought of as naïve and inexperienced, and, for that matter, someone who worked for *The Palace,* an impoverished orphan, forced to become a woman of the night.

Dinner was served on warm plates with creative garnishing and hot rolls. After a waiter served Donald a fresh cocktail and left, Emily turned to him.

"Have the children started school yet? Or are they even old enough?"

"They're old enough. However, after my wife left—uh, died...in such a sad way. I thought of sending them to a boarding school. But until my uncle—"

Donald cleared his throat. "Well...he and I have different opinions."

"Your uncle doesn't want them in boarding school?"

"No, that's not it."

He looked irritated, and Emily wished she hadn't asked.

"I'm sorry. It's none of my business."

He seemed satisfied with that and continued.

"Like I was about to say, I found a tutor. No bureaucratic bull. And no snoopy staff to contend with."

"So... If you don't mind me asking. Who's been taking care of the children since their mother died?"

"Pearl, the cook, usually fills in when there isn't a nanny. But eventually, she'll be leaving.

"You know, I've tried out a number of young women. More than I care to remember. And, well...it's hard to find help now days. Someone who isn't *stuck* in their ways.

"The pay is two hundred a month, plus room and board. Since all your needs will be met, the payout is once a year, or until you leave your position."

Emily thought the setup seemed unusual and wondered if that was customary. But if everything was supplied, receiving pay on the way out wasn't such a bad idea. Hopefully, he didn't dock pay for bad behavior like Miss Bea did.

As night fell, floodlights reflected a glimmering iciness that flowed across the lawn and over the cliffs toward the sea. The scene was breathtaking. Emily tried to imagine the excitement of living in a home with children. She wondered why she couldn't just come out and say, yes, to his offer, and why it was easier to focus out the window.

"I don't think I could ever get used to such a beautiful sight." she said, fascinated by how quickly the fog was rolling in.

He glanced out for a moment. "I see the ocean more as a resource."

She thought it was interesting how he talked as if they were looking at two different views.

"I'll pick you up tomorrow morning," he said, standing, preparing to leave.

She sensed sudden impatience in his voice, knowing that the job would not be an ordinary one. All the warning signs were there. And it was apparent that there was a lot more to Donald Schillings than what he allowed her to see.

When they arrived back at *The Palace*, there were echoes of music and laughter coming from the lounge as he walked her to the staircase.

"The car will be here at nine a.m.

"Goodnight," he said, and turned to leave.

She went up to the landing and waited around the corner. When she heard the door to the lounge close, she headed down and went inside to see if, by chance, Peter had come in. She slipped past the pond and peered from behind the layered dancing stages. Peter wasn't there, but she noticed Donald Schillings heading to the poker room.

CHAPTER THREE

A dim glow lit the northeastern skies as Emily went to sit by the window, still undecided if she would accept the nanny position from a man she wasn't sure was trustworthy. The way she saw it, she had three options: *the Palace* filled with deception and those who took advantage of others; the streets without hope and filled with certain danger; or a place where two young children longed for their mother.

Finally, with her head resting in her arms across the table, she found sleep, knowing that when the sun came up, she would leave with Donald Schillings.

Emily woke a few hours later, went down for a cup of coffee and said goodbye to Toni. She showered and dressed. And at ten minutes to nine, she picked up her bags and headed downstairs, nervous but with expectancy and surprising excitement. Ever since waking, she had imagined herself and the children together like a real family, with her being the big sister. They would look up to her and treat her with respect. This was exactly what she needed.

So, what're you going to do, find yourself happiness and forget what you did to Claude? If you recall. You, were, holding the pitchfork.

There was that pesky voice again trying to ruin the day. She stopped at the bottom of the stairs, closed her eyes, inhaled, and slowly released her breath before continuing up the hallway.

When she reached the parlor, she saw that instead of Donald Schillings waiting for her, it was the man who drove them to the restaurant the night before. His only words had been, yes, sir, and no, sir. And even now, he spoke with reserve as he introduced himself as Bruce. He was a mild-mannered, elderly man who wore a uniform hat that cast a shadow across his eyes and didn't quite cover his bald head. His shoulders squared his blue jacket, and his round clean-shaven face was almost milky except for a touch of pink on each cheek. She wondered if he had pinched them like her grandmother used to when she was expecting company.

They headed up highway 101, Emily feeling cozy on the cushioned leather seat, still surprised by the extravagance of her new life, but making a point of enjoying every moment. When they made a right turn at what looked like a traveler's attraction area and headed into a forest, she began to count the turns Bruce made, her way of keeping directions in rural areas. Not more than twenty five minutes and five turns later, two right and three left, they pulled onto Schillings' property.

Bruce bolted the dark green, iron gate behind them, and they proceeded up a long, narrow road. Giant trees towered on either side, with ferns and various flowers along the road. Emily held her bags close, taking in the mysterious but beautiful sight, glancing at the driver every so often, wondering if he was always so quiet.

Without warning, the car slowed as they reached another gate. This one sat wide open. As they drove through, the shadows of the forest gave way to rolling acres of pristine grounds of velvety green grass, trees, plants, and an array of flowers set around a three-story mansion made of white rock. There were black shutters at each window, and a row of sturdy white pillars along the front porch.

Emily positioned herself for a better look at a sculpture of a man in the middle of the circular driveway. Water poured from the sphere of the globe held above his head, flowing down his outstretched arm and off the tips of his fingers into a pond below.

"There's Otto," Bruce said as he pulled up to the front entrance and stopped.

Emily noticed a tall, thin man with graying hair, gazing down at them from the porch. He was standing between two pillars with his hands behind his back and an air of importance etched on his handsome face.

Bruce shifted into park and went around to open her door. Emily stepped from the car and made her way up to where Otto stood. He extended a hand, offering to take her bags as she climbed the last step. Thinking it made no sense, she handed them over anyway.

"Your room is on the second floor," he said as they stepped inside.

They walked through a bright, welcoming corridor that opened into a great hallway where swirls of black and white marble tiles covered the floor. Walls were filled with stunning art. And there were statues, vases, and finely crafted doors holding the promise of exquisite furnishings beyond. Her gaze followed a staircase that wound gracefully to the second floor. She couldn't believe such beauty would be hers to behold each day.

"It's like I'm in a dream," she said, more to herself than to Otto.

The corners of his mouth turned slightly, giving her the impression that his stuffy manner was, at least, in part, his job. He moved to the foot of the staircase and stood aside, allowing her to lead the way.

She slid a hand along the railing as she moved up the steps taking in the scene from a lofty perspective. The second floor had a large open area with a waterfall in the center, scattered cushioned benches, plants, and trees lining the walls, and a solid wood railing that looked down onto the first floor.

Her bedroom was the second to the right, around a corner. Otto opened the door for her, and she took her belongings from him and stepped inside.

"Have you had breakfast?"

Emily surveyed the room, only partially aware of him.

"I'll have a snack sent up if you like. Maybe some fruit and cookies?"

She pulled her gaze back to him. "Oh, sure, thanks."

When he closed the door and left, she set her bags next to the bedstand and looked around at the elegant furnishings, polished hardwood floors with plush rugs overtop, and three front windows with floral paneled curtains. She wrapped an arm around one of the tall bedposts and ran a hand over the silk spread that had the same hues of green as the wallpaper.

Setting out across the room, she opened a door, expecting a closet, but instead found a large bathroom with tile flooring so shiny she could see the reflection of the green marble sink. There was a dressing table, a walk-in shower, and a tub around a corner below three narrow stained-glass windows. The luxury stunned and excited her.

Moving back into the bedroom, she opened the closet door and explored the spacious area. At the far end was a small wardrobe in various sizes, which included two simple but lovely gowns. She checked the sizes and felt the cool satin material of the white gown, imagining how perfectly it would fit, smiling at the absurdity of a nanny finding an opportunity to wear it.

Checking out a rack with several pairs of shoes, she lifted a box from a shelf where she found jeans, slacks, pajamas, a robe, and various other items. She presumed that everything was left behind by nannies and possibly unwanted clothing that Mrs. Schillings had donated throughout the years.

Stepping from the closet, she made her way across the room to an alcove with soft-pillowed benches, a window on either side, and a glass exit door that led to a small porch. She looked outside to a serene setting with a table, two chairs, flowering plants, and surrounding trees for privacy.

Wandering back inside, she stepped to a window, her gaze following a flat-stone sidewalk running alongside the mansion to the backyard, where she could make out a playground beyond a row of trees. Further out, rising above the plush grounds, was a forest of stately fir trees.

Emily couldn't wait to start exploring. The thought of children playing about stirred hopeful images. She wondered when she would meet them.

When there was a knock on the door a few minutes later, she expected it to be her charges and hurried over. Instead of the children, it was a maid holding a tray.

"For you, ma'am," she said as Emily stood back and let her in.

She was a frail, freckled-faced girl, at least a foot shorter than Emily, wearing a gray, cotton dress, the same color as the tray she held. Her long, sand-colored hair was pulled back and clipped at the nape of her neck. She seemed very young, maybe fifteen or sixteen, yet her hazel eyes had dark circles beneath and seemed worn and suspicious.

Emily followed the young lady as she scurried across the room. She set the tray on a table and swung around in such a hurry that the two nearly collided. The maid flinched, obviously expecting a scolding.

"Sorry," Emily said. She glanced down at the tray that held fruit, cookies, and a pot of tea.

"I'm Emily, by the way. And thanks for the snack."

"My name's Gabriel. I hope the tea is okay. I...I wasn't sure."

The maid started back across the room. "Dinner's at six."

She stopped at the door and turned a shoulder to Emily. "Pearl says you'd best be on time.

34

"I-I was supposed to tell you that," she added, seeming embarrassed by her bluntness.

Emily stepped closer, keeping a comfortable distance.

"Thanks for letting me know. Oh, and I normally drink coffee, but I like tea as well."

"H-have you been to the formal dining room yet?" Gabriel asked.

"Oh no. Otto brought me straight up."

"If you want. There's a buzzer at the foot of the stairs. Press that, and Otto will come."

"Then that's what I'll do. Thank you."

Emily watched Gabriel disappear around the corner, curious to know what made her so jumpy. She closed the door and finished checking out her room as she snacked on cookies, apple wedges, and sipped on the tea.

After sitting on her private porch, enjoying a book and the sounds of a breeze ruffling through the trees, she freshened up and headed to dinner. She expected the children would burst from their hiding at any moment. And when she reached the first floor, she rang the bell and looked back up just in case they were peeking through the railing.

She was relieved that Otto didn't make her wait too long. He escorted her beneath the balcony and around several turns, stopping to point out a sunken living room behind a row of ivory columns.

"This was always the children's favorite room," he said with tempered emotion.

The open space was welcoming, filled with beautiful modern furnishings throughout, with white couches and chairs in front of a black stone fireplace. Two French doors opened to a courtyard. Emily imagined this was where they spent memorable time with their mother.

Further up the hallway, just beyond the last column, a left turn took them through a set of double doors. Donald Schillings looked at home in the striking room with colors of autumn browns and trims of orange. He stood at a corner bar pouring a cocktail mix into a crystal goblet.

Otto led her to a long dining table with an orange lace fabric running up the center. A petal-shaped vase brimming with orange roses sat in the middle. He pulled out a chair and waited for her to sit before moving around to the other side of the table. Emily was disappointed there were only settings for two.

When her boss settled in his chair, she gazed over the centerpiece. "I was looking forward to meeting the children."

Donald picked up a fork and knife and watched Otto set a plate in front of him before glancing up.

"Maria and Nathan? You'll meet them for breakfast. If you don't already know, the kitchen is just down the hall to your left and up the foyer. I presume you've already seen your bedroom?"

"Oh, yes. Otto took me up. It's beautiful." She glanced around again. "Everything is."

Lifting his glass, he took a generous drink and set it aside. "Well, it's here to enjoy for as long as you're with us."

"You mentioned your travels. Are there any particular duties I'll have when you're gone? Any extra chores?"

"Chores?" he said, chuckling. "No, there'll be no chores. Besides the regular help, there's a crew that comes in. Your job is to keep the children out of trouble. And I should probably warn you that the little rascals will run you over if you let them."

Although it sounded like they might've run off a few nannies, she couldn't imagine they were that bad.

"How old are the children?"

"Let's see. Nathan's eight. And Maria's ten."

"Sir," Otto said, holding the pitcher of mix, "would you like your cocktail freshened?"

Donald reached for his drink and slowly polished it off. Carefully, almost tenderly, he set the glass on the table and sat back. He looked handsome sitting there patiently waiting for his refill. Emily wondered if this was the side of him Angellee and some of the other girls saw when they looked at him.

Whether it had been a fleeting thought of days gone by, that side of him didn't last. She sensed a mood change, seeming distracted as he picked up his cocktail and drank it down. He finished his meal in silence, wiped his mouth with a napkin, and folded it onto his plate. When he looked up at her, it was as if a shade had been pulled over his eyes.

"I have business to attend to, but there are some things I need to go over with you. Meet me in the library in thirty minutes. It's down the hall across from the front staircase."

*W*hen Emily stepped into the library, she was delighted to see that all four walls were filled with bookcases. She searched through titles until Donald walked in.

"How long did it take you to collect these?" she asked, returning a book to the shelf.

"Oh, the books," he said with a brush of a hand, "they were part of the purchase, some of them from nearly a century ago."

She was amazed he didn't seem more enthused about all the knowledge and entertainment surrounding him.

"We'll sit over here," he said, taking a seat on one of two large, brown, leather couches slightly angled in front of a massive rock fireplace. She sat across from him. They had barely settled in when Otto came with dessert.

Donald took a bite of cake and picked up his coffee. "I should mention that because of the struggle it's been to find the right person for this job. And because of security breaches and other misconduct, I've found it necessary to tighten my reins. As you can see, I'm a wealthy man. And with two young children, I can't be too careful."

He took a sip of coffee, placed the cup in the saucer, and leaned forward with his elbows on his knees.

"There are some things I want to make perfectly clear. First of all. Your only job is to take care of Maria and Nathan. Since you're their nanny, you'll live under the same rules as they do. Do what's expected, and you have nothing to worry about."

It was as if a cold wind swept into the room and settled around them. Emily wondered what would happen if she made a couple of mistakes.

He sat back and lit a cigarette, moving an ashtray from the end table to the armrest. "Rule number one is that the children are forbidden to leave the property without my permission. Rule number two is that the telephone is off limits. If necessary, a phone is available to you in the downstairs den. But you'll need Pearl to let you in.

"Rule number three. My private quarters on the north wing of the second floor are off-limits. And let me just say." He made a point of catching her eye. "There are no exceptions."

Emily shivered to think what the consequences would be for that one.

"Now, for rule number four. What goes on in my house is my business. I forbid you to repeat anything you see or hear. My employees are hired to work, not socialize, gossip, or snoop where they don't belong. That means as long as you're the children's nanny, they will be your only concern. Is that clear?"

"Yes, i-it is."

Donald was about to begin on rule number five when Otto tapped on the door and peeked inside.

"Harold is waiting in the den, sir. He said it's urgent."

"Tell him I'll be right there."

"Yes, sir."

Otto held the door open for his boss.

"I'll be busy for the rest of the evening," Donald said as he picked up his coffee and stood. "We'll finish our talk later."

He left in a hurry, Otto right behind him. Emily stared at the door in disbelief, ready to burst into tears. She stood, went to poke at the fire, and turned everything he said over and over in her mind.

It was unsettling the way he came on with the rules so quickly. Considering the alternatives, she had hoped being the nanny for his children was the right choice. But as she thought through all that had happened at *The Palace*, she was almost sure that Layla was the thief who stole her money and necklace, and Delilah may have even been used as her accomplice; no better way to get her out of *The Palace*, and out of the arms of Moose. Furthermore, Emily had a feeling that her boss was involved in some way. Although, why he would get wrangled into something so insane was beyond her.

Emily realized that she could walk out that very minute. That's if someone didn't stop her. *Or... Or what?* She gazed at the hundreds if not thousands of books on the shelves and thought of the beautiful bedroom waiting for her upstairs. They looked much better than the dark lonesome road she would have to take, and where things could end up even worse. Her heart sank, resigned, feeling like a willing prisoner, free, but not really free.

When Emily left the library with an arm full of books, she noticed a man leaving out the front entrance. The door to the den was ajar. All at once, Mr. Schillings' voice drifted out into the hallway. Still debating on whether she should or not, she approached the door.

"Dammit. How'd you get my new number?"

There was a pause, and it was obvious he was talking on the phone.

"Fine, don't tell me. But believe me I'll make sure this doesn't happen again."

Another pause.

"Now, how in the world do I get one of those?"

He listened again, sighing, "I don't know, maybe. Just don't hound me about it. Oh, and one more thing. Remind Kenneth I'm well aware of how to reach any airline he may work for.

"From here on out. No more calls. And stick to our deal…or else!"

With that, he slammed the receiver down.

When his chair creaked, Emily hurried for the staircase and up to her room. She dropped the books onto the bed and curled up beside them. Sound sleep had eluded her the previous night, and she drifted off.

As the approaching dawn brought hints of light at the sides of each curtain, Emily was awakened by a low, vibrating rumble. She sat up, scooted off the bed, and went to the back window in the alcove. By then the strange noise had stopped. Whatever had caused the rumbling, it seemed to have awakened a pack of wild dogs. Although their squawks and yowls came from a distance, she had been around animals her whole life, but they had never sounded so ferocious.

The sudden invasion of her sleep was unnerving, as were Schillings' threats, odd tactics, and unbending rules. She wandered back to bed and sat, moving the books to the nightstand. Her gaze dropped to her blue bag sitting on the floor. Reaching in, she pulled out a bottle of vodka, took a couple of sips, and corked it up. Setting it on the stand, she pulled a throw blanket over her as she curled up on the bed.

CHAPTER FOUR

*T*he next morning brought Emily hope that things weren't as bad as they seemed. After dressing, she started for the door when she noticed the vodka on the nightstand. Heading over, she secured the cork, and placed the bottle, inside the cabinet, below.

Padding down the stairs, she made her way up the same hallway that she traveled the night before, past the living room, and formal dining room door, past the foyer that led to the kitchen, past a staircase, and out the back door.

She took steps down onto a sweeping stone terrace. Approximately twenty feet to her left were steps leading up to a spacious porch. To her far right was the play area.

Beyond the terrace, a green lawn spread out into a beautifully landscaped yard with the giant fir trees she had seen from her bedroom window, looming in the far background. She took a path made of large, flat rocks across the lawn, through a grove of red maple, althea, and weeping cherry trees, to where it opened into an area with a waterfall, a pond, and a bridge to cross over. Circling the pond were life-size statues made of marble and stone, benches of cement, and a plethora of colorful shrubs and perennials.

Making her way out the other side of the grove, where the rock pathway continued and wound around the forest of fir trees, she noticed three dirt paths leading through the forest. She took the path that veered to the left and wound up and down and around bends.

It was tranquil deep within the forest, with the citrusy aroma of bark, ferns, moss, and sounds of birds and small animals waking to a crisp sunny day. Recalling the dogs from the previous night, Emily hesitated, but she decided they would surely be kept behind a fence and possibly belonged to a neighbor. Moving further up the path, she found herself standing beneath an arbor of rosebushes. Beyond the arbor was a colorful flower garden with statues of little men and women holding baskets of flowers. Within this lovely, tranquil garden, a bench sat beneath another arbor.

Something caught her eye, and she looked to where a young girl with long blond curls was kneeling beneath a tree.

Maria.

Emily felt like an intruder, and when she attempted a quick exit, she tripped over a weather-beaten stick horse. She regained her balance and looked back at Maria as she scrambled to her feet. Her pale, oval face was angelic-like, even though her blue eyes looked on crossly.

"Sorry for bothering you," Emily said, watching her walk over. "I'm such an oaf, sometimes."

The little girl approached, yanked a rope that was tangled in a bush, freeing her stick horse. She swung a leg over and examined her new nanny.

"You make that skirt?"

Emily glanced down. "Yeah. How could you tell?"

Maria raised her brows and started up the path.

"At least you're not bossy like the last one.

"You hungry?" she added happily, as if they had known each other for a while. "I'll bet Pearl has the pancakes on by now."

"Pancakes. Yum," Emily said, hurrying after her, not sure what to think of this beautiful but strange little creature.

"You'll meet Nathan, too," Maria said, looking up as Emily came up beside her. "Sometimes he's such a brat, though. How 'bout later, us three have lunch outside."

"Like a picnic? Under a tree?"

"Yes, under a tree."

"Sounds like fun."

When they reached the house, Maria tossed her stick horse onto a bush.

Emily had to force herself not to laugh. "You've had that for a while, huh?"

"Since I was seven. My uncle Bud bought it for me."

"So, is your father going to buy you a real horse?"

"I wish."

Maria pushed the door open, and Emily followed her inside, up the hallway, and to the right into a foyer. There was a fancy door entry, right forefront, but the rest of the area was a display of the children's colorful, framed artwork set against light gray walls.

Emily stopped and admired them as they walked.

"These are wonderful, Maria."

"Mommy had them framed and hung. So, it's kinda cool."

At the end of the foyer, they walked through double doors and into a huge open space with off-white walls, black molding, and dark hardwood floors, stretching ahead at least forty feet, to a side exit, then circling around to the right revealing the family room with an oversized couch, a TV, and a game table. Continuing around was a breakfast nook in front of a picture window, a back exit, and to the right of that, a large open kitchen. Emily noticed that beyond the kitchen, behind a divide, was a dining area with a long white table and matching high-backed chairs that sat in front of a fireplace.

Pearl was at the stove ladling pancake mix into a frying pan. Bacon sizzled on a back burner.

"Here she is," Maria said, taking Emily's hand and pulling her over to the woman.

Emily gazed down at the stout woman who didn't look much over four feet tall. Her gray hair was braided and twisted around the top of her head, and her full face was flushed from the heat.

"Hi, Pearl."

The woman looked up at Emily with fading blue eyes slanted like the shape of half-moons. "Hi yourself."

She dropped a wooden spatula into the bowl and motioned.

"You two go on and take a seat.

"Where's that brother of yours, Maria? I've got pancakes warming in the oven and more cooking."

The two sat at the breakfast nook overlooking the porch that was lined with potted trees, plants, and flowers. Pearl brought pancakes and bacon to the table as Nathan barreled into the room.

"Stop running," Maria, scolded. "You're gonna fall and break another tooth."

Nathan stood with his hands on the back of his chair, wagging his tongue. "Can't make me."

Pearl forked pancakes and bacon onto his plate. "Sit, young man, and eat."

The boy took a seat, and Pearl moved the platter in front of Emily. Shoving a container of jelly over to Maria, she wandered off to clean the kitchen.

Emily noticed that Nathan took after his father with his dark hair and eyes, although the lines of his nose and chin were softer.

"Hi Nathan."

He reached for the syrup, glancing over with a mischievous smile. "Hi."

Maria smeared jelly onto her pancake. "Guess what Nathan. We're going on a picnic."

"We are?"

Emily caught Pearl watching them over the counter. "If that's all right with you."

"Fine with me. Long as you let me know when so I can put everything out on the porch."

"Today, Pearl," Maria announced. "Only we're sitting under a tree. So, we'll need a sack lunch and a blanket."

"You can just as well get your own blanket."

"Whoopee," Nathan squealed, kicking his legs so they hit the bottom of the table.

Maria covered her ears. "If you stop screeching, you weirdo. And stop kicking the table."

She slid down in her chair and aimed a kick at him.

"Stop it, you creep! Pearl! Maria's kicking me!"

"Well… Nathan called me a creep!"

"They're all yours," Pearl said with a chuckle.

The room became silent as the children's eyes turned to their new nanny.

"I… Uh," Emily began. She cleared her throat and bore down for the challenge. "S-stop the bickering…or. Or no picnic."

The children looked more amused than threatened, and Emily narrowed her eyes so they would know she meant business.

After breakfast, they went out to the backyard to find the tree where they would have lunch.

"Maria?" Emily said as they walked. "I heard some dogs early this morning."

"They belong to Harold. A guy who works for Father. He lives out in the brush."

Nathan growled and scratched the air with a claw-like hand. "Yeah, and they're killer dogs."

Maria nudged him. "Who told you that?"

He bent his knees and leaped, grabbed a tree branch, and swung back and forth. "I just know. And Harold's mean as they are."

"That's because you bug him like you do everyone else!"

"Come on, Nathan. Your father wouldn't allow killer dogs so close."

The little boy dropped to the ground. "Yoou'll see."

He slugged Maria on the shoulder and ran off.

"You brat," she squealed, starting after him.

"Hey. Let him go."

Maria turned back with a pout. "I hate him."

"Aah. I doubt that."

"Well, he's mean as the dogs are. Only they don't come over and bug me."

Emily realized that having the children under her care wouldn't be easy. Although they would certainly distract her from her own troubles.

Later that day, the children took Emily to each of their bedrooms. She noticed that, on their bedstands, was a photo taken of them with their mother, who looked so much like Maria. There was a glimmer of sadness in the children's eyes for a moment when their attention was drawn to the photos. But they rebounded quickly and reverted to almost continual harassment toward each other that reminded her of how Steven and Timothy had bickered back and forth.

Emily wanted to know the children better. And during the next days, she asked questions and requested them to show her their favorite pastimes. For Maria it was her dolls and playing with her dollhouse, and Nathan loved his building blocks, toy cars, and his many gadgets. They both loved to play in the forest, but it was apparent that it was a special place for Maria as she and her mother used to spend a lot of time in the flower garden.

Every so often, Maria and Nathan became quiet and thoughtful. They seldom mentioned their mother, but Emily knew they were still grieving and that some of their mood swings had to do with their loss. What had her just as concerned was the strain between them and their father. It was easy to see that his non-stop preoccupation with his business was part of the problem, although it was obvious that he had a difficult time connecting with them. Pearl wasn't the most pleasant person to be around, but at least it was gratifying to know that she seemed to care about the children.

The tutor, Miss Hutcheon, came in four days a week. She was a slender woman with dark hair worn in a proper bun, always in heels, suits made of cotton, and rayon blouses. Her dedication was solid, but whenever Emily tried to talk to her about the children, she was evasive and rushed. With Emily's refusal to give up, she finally admitted that Mr. Schillings insisted he was the one to notify if there were any problems. That sounded like him, considering he didn't seem to want his help collaborating with each other. On the other hand, because he was too busy to spend time with Maria and Nathan, and from things she had witnessed, it seemed rather unlike him.

CHAPTER FIVE

*I*t wasn't even eight yet, and the children were at one another's throats. Emily stepped from the shower, drying off as she rushed into her bedroom, hearing Maria cursing at her brother. She pulled on a robe, tying the belt as she burst into the hallway and around the corner to the open area.

Nathan had a world globe under an arm, and he was darting back and forth so Maria couldn't take it away.

"Give it to me, you brat!" she screamed.

He shuffled the globe around to his back and grabbed her hair with the other hand.

"Ouch. Let go of me. Ooouch!"

"Stop this nonsense!" Donald bellowed, rushing around the corner. He set his suitcase down, grabbed them each by an arm, and shoved them at Emily.

Nathan landed at her feet as the atlas spun across the floor. He looked up at her through a tuft of dark locks and gave her an impish smile. When she realized he was enjoying himself, she scrunched her eyes at him, hooked an arm around one of his and pulled him to his feet.

Donald wasn't amused. "What did I hire you for anyway, young lady?"

He picked up his luggage and brushed past them.

"By the time I return next week, I want these... *Hooligans* straightened out."

"Yes, Mr. Schillings. I'll do my best."

He stopped for a moment, giving a sweeping glare at the three before heading down the steps.

Maria and Nathan knew each time they messed up. And Emily appreciated that after a heated brawl, they tried to put their best foot forward, for several days, anyway.

She enjoyed helping them with homework and getting them to bed with enough time to read stories. An early morning rise, making sure the children made it to breakfast on time, and that their teeth were brushed after meals was normally entertainment for them all.

Consoling the children came easy. But some of their arguments left Emily shaken. What troubled her almost as much was the discipline she was forced to give. And if they did something wrong, as far as their father was concerned, she was at fault as much as they were. Like the day Nathan snuck a baby skunk into his room and Maria tattled. Donald was so upset he hollered at Emily and sent Nathan to his room without dinner. A week passed without a squabble after that one, but the next Monday morning, the fight was back on.

Emily hadn't touched the vodka since the first night she arrived, although, after scolding the children that day, she went to her room and had several shots. Returning the bottle to its spot on the bottom shelf of the nightstand, she closed the door with a solid click.

Feeling revived, she fell back onto the bed, recalling how, at *The Palace,* she had learned to erase a wound in minutes with just a few sips of a cocktail, almost like a paintbrush brightening a dark sky with a sun. There was no harm in that. She took her responsibilities as a nanny seriously and would never allow a little drink to interfere.

The next day, Maria and Nathan were with their tutor when Emily went to the library and found books on child-rearing and the psychology of childhood. What she learned gave her courage to put muscle behind her words, and at the same time, show them that she cared. Tough love is what they called it.

*W*hile the children were in class, Emily began to explore the forest in the back yard. Her favorite spot was the flower garden where she first met Maria. That's where she ended up most days, sitting on the bench with her feet up, reading. In no time, she went through all of young Samuel's favorite books.

Not that she ever needed a break from reading, but sometimes she sprawled across the grass, gazed through the trees at the sky and daydreamed. She thought of Michael and Samuel and wondered if there would be a future with them. Sometimes she reminisced about the days in school with Haiti, and, of course, Daniel. It didn't hurt so much any longer to think about him as long as she didn't linger. Her grandmother, who raised her from the moment she was born until the day she died when Emily was seven, was never far from her mind.

As much as Emily enjoyed daydreaming, she wasn't used to having so much free time and had to force herself not to feel guilty. One afternoon, she decided to take the outer path around the forest of fir trees before making her way to the flower garden. She had been out meandering around for a while when she heard Maria talking to someone. Moving closer, she saw her visiting what she now thought of as the kneeling tree.

"And God," the little girl was saying, "if my mommy is there with you, can you let me know? You can whisper in my ear if you want."

Emily clamped a hand over her mouth. The sad little scene made her angry. And in desperation she looked up to the heavens. *If you won't come down and talk to her, will you at least give her…something?*

After the prayer of her own, Emily tried to sneak back to the mansion, but she happened upon Maria anyway. The little girl was holding the stick horse by the mane, dragging it behind her, looking distraught.

"Hey, Maria. I was just thinking about you," she said, coming up beside her.

"What about?"

"Well... I realize it's been hard on you since your mother died. And I want you to know that...um, any time you want to talk, I'm here to listen."

Maria stopped and glowered up at her. "Where were you just now?"

"Over yonder, around the bend," Emily said, pointing.

"You heard me in the garden, didn't you."

"Uh... I didn't intend to. Sorry."

Maria mounted her stick horse and started up the path again.

"Well, don't tell my father."

"Of course, I won't."

Emily followed after her. "But...why not?"

"He doesn't believe in God."

"Oh."

"He made me stop going to Sunday school with one of my friends. Said it was a fairytale." She stroked the fake hair on her horse and turned to gaze up at Emily. "Do you think it's a fairytale?"

"No. No, I don't."

"But how do you know for sure?"

Emily thought for a moment. "Being here and looking up at the stars at night is proof enough for me. But, you see, for a while I had a hard time understanding how God had no beginning and no end. Then one day it became clear."

"How'd that happen?"

"I saw infinity."

Emily knew she had to say something. *Please, God...don't let me mess up.*

"You see, Maria...since I was young, well, especially when I was young, I've studied the stars and imagined myself flying through the universe. One night, it occurred to me that space goes on forever. It's impossible to comprehend such greatness, but once I came to terms with a reality I couldn't fully understand, it was easy to see that God was and is to infinity."

Maria wrinkled her nose. "But space has to end somewhere."

"What would be at the end?"

"Um…nothing?"

"But space is nothing, it isn't created, and yet it holds everything that exists. If it ended, there would have to be something there. And that something would need space to hold it. So, you see, it's impossible for space to end."

Emily stroked Maria's hair back. "I know. It's not an easy thing to fathom."

The little girl gazed up at a patch of sky through the trees. "It makes perfect sense to me."

She skipped up ahead with the tail end of the play horse scraping along the walk. "Maybe that's why space is so big. To make room for God."

Emily laughed. "I think you might have something there."

CHAPTER SIX

A bond began to grow between Emily and the children. And she found herself caring about them more each day. The problem was that Maria and Nathan still fought like they were enemies.

Everything came to a head one Saturday morning when Nathan put salt into the sugar bowl. Maria took a bite of her cereal and threw a fit. They carried on until Emily had enough.

"Ok. That's it. No playing outside today. We're going to spend the day in the library."

They sulked all the way there. But once inside, she was surprised how fast the children came upon books of interest and promptly found spots where they sat and read. She watched them as she searched for books of her own. It was like a miracle. And to make things even better, she found The Adventures of Sherlock Holmes and other books of Arthur Conan Doyle's novels.

The children came to appreciate the library. And each day, as Emily read through articles and books on human behavior, she learned more about them, herself, and even the men back home.

After struggling for weeks on end to find answers, it occurred to her that maybe everything she endured was so that she would end up with the children. The thought that she had a purpose made her shiver—as if somewhere in time she had chosen to give herself up to self-sacrifice. She smile. *Or... Maybe it's merely justification, making sense out of chaos.*

◇◁▷◇

*O*ne afternoon, Emily found Maria sitting on the front steps gazing anxiously up the driveway.

"Hey, what're you doing?" she asked, taking a seat beside her.

"Watching for the mailman."

"So, you're expecting a letter, huh?"

"Mm-hmm."

Maria plucked a leaf from one of the plants that lined the steps. "I'm not supposed to tell," she said, picking the leaf apart and tossing it aside. She brushed off her skirt and turned to Emily. "Promise you won't say anything?"

"Of course, I won't."

"So, um... I have a pen pal."

"Oh, really."

"Yep, and her name's Elsie. Starting this week, she's sending me a letter the second Monday of each month. If it doesn't arrive Monday, it should come the next day. Bruce gave me the first letter. He doesn't always pick the mail up. That's why I'm waiting."

Emily wondered why she seemed to wait in secrecy. But she saw how important it was that she kept it that way.

"I'm excited for you, Maria."

As they talked, the limo came up the driveway, passed the mansion, and continued around the corner. More times than not, Donald took the steps at the side entrance to his private quarters, although today he came around the front as the mailman pulled up. He took the bundle and shuffled through the envelopes, freezing for an instant before tucking everything under an arm and coming up beside them.

"Nowhere better to sit?"

When he had taken the steps up and went inside, tears were streaming down Maria's cheeks.

Emily put an arm around her. "I'm sorry."

The little girl pulled away and ran around the side of the building. Emily wished there was a way to help her. She couldn't understand why Mr. Schillings couldn't see that his daughter was in pain over losing her mother and her friends. Something had to be done.

Emily's own misfortunes had followed her up the dirt road away from the farmhouse and to that very moment. No matter what brought her to that place and time, she knew that being with the children gave her purpose. She would find a way to make this up to Maria.

CHAPTER SEVEN

*U*ncle Bud came from Texas early one morning and took Maria and Nathan to Disneyland. The children had talked so well of their great uncle that Emily was disappointed she missed him.

Five nights later, she was in the library when he walked in.

"Why hello," he said. He sailed across the room, and she stood as he took her hand. "It's a pleasure to finally meet you."

"You must be the Uncle Bud the children were raving about."

"I am. And I'm sorry I missed you the other morning."

"Are the children coming in?" she asked, looking past him.

"I just put them to bed. They had a long day."

"So, how was the trip?"

"Oh, we had a fabulous time."

Emily sat, and he took the couch across from her.

"They sure were excited to see you."

"Well, the feeling is quite mutual. And they couldn't stop talking about you."

"Oh, really. Nothing bad, I hope."

He laughed. "No. They're very fond of you. In fact, Maria confessed you were the first nanny they didn't want their father to get rid of so they could live with me."

"Those little rascals," Emily said, jokingly. "I have to admit they have their moments. But they're great kids. And I try to keep in mind that they've been through some difficult times."

"That's thoughtful of you. And honestly, I know you've had a positive impact around here."

He considered for a moment, seeming to weigh his next words.

"You know, Emily. I questioned whether I should bring this up. But after my conversations with the children, and now that I've met you, I'd be remiss if I didn't say something."

He took a breath and straightened his shoulders. "I'd like to ask a favor of you if I could."

"Yes…of course. Anything."

"As you can see, I'm getting on in years. And…if something should happen to me, it would be of great comfort to know that the children have someone they can turn to. Someone who will make certain they get the best care possible. I realize things can change quickly. And no matter what happens, I'd like you to be aware of my concerns, even if it's just to pass them along."

"Of course, I'll do everything I can to insure that happens."

"Thank you, Emily. I appreciate that."

"So then… Are there relatives I should be aware of?"

"There's an aunt. Agnes Pitts. As far as I know, she's living in Europe."

"Bud? Is everything okay? You're... You're not sick or anything, are you?"

"No. I'm healthy as anyone could expect at my age. It's just that. Well… Don't get me wrong. I love Donald, and I hate to say this about my own nephew. But I'm afraid he doesn't always have his priorities straight."

Bud gazed at Emily intently as if questioning whether to go on.

"I want to hear what you have to say. It's important. For the children's sake."

"Yes, yes. I'm sure you're right." He folded his hands in his lap and gathered his thoughts. "You see… Donald was an only child. A little spoiled but a nice kid. His father deserted him and his mother when he was ten. Although his leaving left its mark on Donald. What was even more devastating was that his mother, my sister Eleanor, died less than two years later. All he had was me and my late wife, Sarah.

We were living here at the time, only because I had the best business partner one could wish for at our Texas headquarters. Anyway. When Donald returned with us after his mother's funeral, we saw that he had become more serious and closed off, at least to us. Strangely enough, it wasn't long before he found something in San Francisco that drew him in and gave him what he craved. It seemed for each heartbreak, he became tougher, as if he were trying to forget his past."

Bud motioned toward the section of books Emily had been reading through. "Thanks to my wife for that collection, we were able to search for help from experts."

"I read through a number of those myself," Emily offered, "You know…for the children."

"Now that's great to hear."

"I'm still reading, but it's already done some good.

"It's too bad about Donald, though. About his parents."

"Yes, it was a heartbreak even before his mother died. But after…his outlook on life took a drastic turn."

"That might explain why he's… Well. Sometimes he can be…."

"I understand. And don't feel ashamed for your thoughts, my dear. The children have probably said the same. It's an odd thing. But when some feel they've lost control over their lives, they start demanding control over others. Whether it's a habit or a character flaw it's hard to say. Nevertheless, Donald's losses were devastating. And it's too bad he couldn't have found healthier ways to maneuver through his challenges.

"When he was sixteen, he started to take narcotics, and we moved back to Texas. We took him to a well-known counselor who brought him back from a dark time. He went back to school, received his high school diploma and seemed ready to start anew. I talked him into working for me. But after a while, he became tired of the hours spent sitting at a desk and taking care of clients. When he was offered a position as manager of a popular nightclub, he accepted without hesitation. After that, things changed for him. He was truly happy for the first time in years and seemed to care about life again. Not long after, he told me about his dream to one day open an exclusive, private club. Let's see. What was it now? Oh, yes...a club for the exuberant rich, with his eyes on the wealthy oil countries."

"Really. That's interesting."

"I'm sure some of it came from working at the club. But... He's like his father in some ways. And I can't help but to wonder if some of that rubbed off.

"Nevertheless, he married and settled down. We were thrilled he had fallen for such a lovely woman. May God rest her soul. It was wonderful to see them together. And things got even better after Maria was born. Nathan came along, and all seemed well for a time. Donald has his good points, you know. Some reputable qualities, a sense of style and charm. I counted on that to continue. But after a few years, he began to slip.

"The bottom line is that I'm concerned about the children. I offered to take them in, though he won't hear of it. And I have several businesses that keep me going. But I'd find a way to care for them if he'd let me."

"I'm surprised he didn't take you up on the offer."

"Oh, me too. With all that's happened, it's puzzling."

"Well...young lady, I wish we had more time to talk," he said, standing, "but I have an early flight to catch, so I think I'll turn in for the night."

Emily stood, and he took her by a hand and held it in both of his. "I try to visit at least two or three times a year. And I'll look forward to seeing you again."

She watched Bud leave, knowing he was a good man, and wishing she could have been completely straight with him. Everything she told him was from her heart. And most days the children were perfect in her eyes. But, besides their battles she had to untangle, there were things from her past that, as much as she fought to keep hidden, at times these memories flashed without cause, and there were days when she wasn't at her best.

*T*he children didn't argue for several weeks after Bud left. Emily knew it was too good to be true when Nathan dropped a water-filled balloon over the upstairs railing as Maria passed below.

The little girl stomped up the stairs declaring revenge. While she was in her bedroom changing her wet clothes, Nathan went into hiding. When Maria stormed back out and couldn't find him, she went to his room and gathered up a set of building blocks, his football cards, a container of his cars, and dropped everything over the railing.

Hoping no one would see the mess, Emily was helping the children clean up when Otto stepped from the ballroom. She tried to explain what they were doing. But it sounded weak and didn't come out right. It was embarrassing, almost as if she had thrown everything off the balcony herself.

The hallway was finally back in order, and with the children still arguing, Emily sent them to bed and went to her room for some solace. As she closed the door, her eyes drifted to where the vodka was stored in the bedstand. She went over, pulled out the bottle, and took a seat in the alcove. Planning to have just enough for the spark of relief it would bring, she emptied the bottle.

Disappointed, and not wanting anything more than to keep the high, she recalled the cabinet where Donald kept his liquor. Before she knew it, she was out the door and down in the formal dining room. With the alcohol rushing through her veins, it seemed like a perfectly normal thing to do.

There were seven containers of vodka. She grabbed the half-empty bottle, a glass, and some mix. By the time she finished the first drink, the high she had felt back at *The Palace* pulsed through her like a train. She went to the record player, put on music, and in between drinks, she danced.

As much fun as she was having, eventually, something began to change. And right in the middle of a turn, she almost lost her balance. Wandering back to the bar counter, she took several more sips and waited for the excitement to return. But that carefree feeling was gone. In fact, she was having a hard time keeping upright. Once she admitted that she had gone overboard on the drink, she carefully put everything away and headed back to her room.

The steps seemed steeper and longer than normal. And the alcohol was threatening to come back up. When she reached the top, Maria was peeking around the corner.

"Where've you been?" she demanded, hurrying over and glowering up at Emily. "You've been *drinking,* haven't you. Are you even old enough?"

Emily didn't like her tone and that accusing look on her little face.

"Infact, I had sevro drinkss."

She placed a hand on the wall to steady herself. "And whass it to you if I have a lil drink. You guys runnin' round figh-in' like a bunch of hoooliginss. Whadoyou expec me to do?"

Emily saw the pain on Maria's face and watched in horror as the little girl ran off around the corner to her bedroom, hating herself for what she had just done, and realizing, at that moment, she wasn't any better than the men back home. She longed to follow Maria. But her stomach was churning, and she rushed into her room and to the bathroom just in time to heave some of that miserable drink.

Washing her face with cold water, she brushed her teeth, and sat out on the porch, taking in long breaths. When she felt like herself again, she went to Maria's room, knocked on the door and peeped inside.

Maria was in bed with her dolls piled around her.

Emily stepped inside and leaned against the wall.

"I just want to say, sorry... And I'm not gonna drink no more."

"Promise?"

"I promise."

"Emily?"

"Mm?"

"How come people drink?"

"To feel good. Sometimes to forget."

"And how do you feel now?"

"Well... Not great."

Maria smiled. "Hmm."

"Smarty pants."

Emily turned to leave and looked back. "I really am sorry."

Maria hugged one of her dolls. "And I'm sorry Nathan and I fight so much. I'll try harder."

Emily left the room feeling a whole lot better than when she walked up the steps. And she hoped with all of her heart that she could live up to the promises she had been making.

*M*ore than ever, Emily realized the children needed her. Uncle Bud was right to open up to her about their father. Her wish was to get to know Mr. Schillings better and be able to discuss the concerns she had about his children.

One evening, when she went to the kitchen for a snack, she got part of her wish, but not in the way she had hoped. She had just picked up an orange and was about to head back upstairs when she heard voices coming from the side entryway. Being unusual for that time of night, she tiptoed alongside the family room and listened at the door to the voice of a young man.

"Do you want to be obligated to him for life? This'll get you out of here?"

"Erwin, please. Whatever you're planning, don't do it. It's not worth it."

Emily gasped when she realized the girl's voice was that of the maid, Gabriel.

"I'm already obligated, remember?" She sounded like she was in tears. "I thought you were going to do the right thing."

"I am. Can't you see this is my big chance?"

"No, I can't. Please Erwin, stop before it's too late."

"I will as soon as I... Oh, never mind. I don't know why you're being so...."

The young man's voice drifted. Emily imagined he was looking out the window. As she leaned closer and peeled an ear, someone came up behind her.

"Uuh! Mr. Schillings," she said, stumbling back.

The outside door closed, and Gabriel and Erwin were gone.

"What's going on?" Donald hissed.

"Uh... Nothing. I-I heard voices, and—"

"Remember what I told you about doing your job and minding your own business?"

"Mr. Schillings, I have no idea what that conversation was about. Or even who Gabriel was talking to."

She wished she hadn't mentioned Gabriel's name.

He placed a hand on the doorknob and looked back. "I'd watch myself if I were you, young lady."

She stared after him as he left, in shock, and for the first time, truly afraid of him.

CHAPTER EIGHT

If Emily could make it to Mack's House of Food by one o'clock, this could be the day that everything changed for her.

Once she got to know Bruce, when his demure personality was less cautious and sunlight revealed soft brown eyes, she dared to ask him for a ride to San Francisco. To her relief, he agreed to take her. Although it looked like she may have lost her ride because he and Mr. Schillings left three days earlier and hadn't returned.

From the moment she rolled out of bed at the break of dawn, there wasn't an hour that passed when she wouldn't look out a window or step onto the porch off of her bedroom or the one out the front door to check for the limousine. Finally, she went to find Pearl.

The woman was at the side entryway, talking with a deliveryman, regarding Donald Schillings' run for mayor of San Francisco.

Emily went to the kitchen to wait, surprised by the news, as much as she was by the, normally sullen, Pearl's enthusiasm.

"What is it?" Pearl asked as she stepped on a stool and opened a cupboard door.

"I was just wondering if, by chance, you're going into town this morning?"

Pearl gave a how-dare-you-bother-me look and set a couple of jars on the counter, poking again for more.

"No, I'm not. What're you asking for, anyway? You have children to watch."

She set another jar on the counter and stepped from the stool. "You've got something up your sleeve."

"No, it's nothing like that. If I could just use the phone…."

"Well…there's a call coming in a few hours. Until then I'm staying put."

Pearl straightened and gave the stool a shove against the wall. "And don't go asking for the key because I've got strict orders not to leave sight of it. I learned my lesson on that one."

The scowl on Pearl's face didn't give Emily much hope of changing her mind, so she left in search of Otto. About this time, he usually went from room to room with a basket of dusting tools. She caught up with him in the ballroom.

"Excuse me, Otto. If it's not too much trouble. Would you mind unlocking the den so I can use the phone? Pearl would've, but—"

"Is this an emergency?"

"Yes, it is."

He finished dusting a candleholder and returned it to the mantel. "Come along then. I'll unlock it for you."

"Otto?" Emily said as they walked. "Is there a reason Mr. Schillings restricts use of the phone?"

He gave her a look that made her regret bringing it up. "I don't intend to sound disrespectful. It's just—"

"I suppose it's something you've heard," he said, giving her a sideways glance. "I don't know what exactly you've been told. But just to clear Mr. Schillings of any rumors you might've heard, I'll tell you why. But keep it to yourself if you will."

"Oh, of course."

With that, he revealed more than she ever expected to hear.

"It all started when Mrs. Schillings vanished. She went to bed one night and never came down to breakfast. The only thing that seemed out of place was a pair of her special-order slippers she left outside Maria's bedroom door. That, and one of the cars was gone. Rumors started flying until a maid found a suicide note."

Emily stopped and clutched her chest. "She killed herself? But... That's awful. Do the children know?"

Otto set the basket on a table and continued across the room. "I'm not sure."

He glanced back as she caught up with him. "Sadly, her car was found a few weeks later. Fifty miles up the coast. In the ocean."

"But, how?"

"They say she drove herself off a cliff."

Emily shivered, thinking of the beautiful view over the rocks that had taken her breath away.

"The rumors stopped after that. But then Mr. Schillings caught the... Well...he caught one of his employees on the telephone, badmouthing him. That's when he laid down the law."

"But I'm not planning anything like that."

"I should hope not."

"One more thing," Emily said, unable to resist. "Is there a reason Maria isn't able to receive her mail?"

Otto hesitated and headed off again. "Listen, I can't say why Mr. Schillings handles things the way he does, but I assure you he has his reasons. And it's not up to me to question him."

As they approached the ballroom exit, he reached for a brass knob, gave it a turn and offered Emily entrance into the hallway, closing the door behind them.

"Come to think of it, a while back he mentioned there are those trying to take advantage of the children because of their wealth. And, well... For some time now, he's counted on me to size up the help. But... I'm no expert."

Otto glanced down at Emily. "Although something tells me you're one to be trusted. Even Mr. Schillings is well aware that if you leave, his exhausted searches for a stalwart nanny of his liking are over.

"You know what? You, remind me a lot of my youngest sister.... When she was young, that is."

Emily felt the heat rise on her cheeks. If she was to Schillings liking, she would hate to think if he really disliked her.

"How old are you? Still in your teens I bet."

"Nineteen. I just turned nineteen in September."

"A very good age as I recall.

"Anyway... To my point. You have to understand that Mr. Schillings is just trying to protect the children."

"I'm sure you're right. Although his tactics are a little confusing, especially with the help, who can be a little standoffish. Not you and Bruce, though... Pearl. She's not so easy to understand."

"She does speak her mind," Otto said with a slight chuckle. "I think the difference with Bruce and myself is that we've been here for many years, even before Mr. Schillings came into the picture, and, then later, took over. I know his uncle Bud well. A wonderful man. And as far as the other employees, sometimes a steady flow, coming and going... Well...the boss isn't keen on his help chumming. Thinks too many problems arise when they get caught up in each other's business. I have to say, having had assignments all over the world, I agree with him for the most part."

The two passed the library and continued to Schillings office where Otto turned the key and pushed the door open.

"It's over on the desk. The phonebook is in the top left drawer."

Emily hoped he would leave her alone. But he seemed compelled to stay and busy himself while she looked up the number and dialed. It rang several times before someone picked up.

"Mack's," came a voice over the noise in the background.

Emily couldn't tell if it was Maxine or not. She glanced at Otto, turned her back to him and cupped a hand over the mouthpiece, keeping her voice down while attempting a disguise.

"I was wondering if you would get a message to a customer. I'm supposed to meet him there at one."

"What's he look like?"

Emily winced. It was Maxine all right.

"I-I don't know. I've never seen him. I told him I'd meet him at the end counter seat, next to the wall. And if I don't make it...."

Emily turned the pages of the phonebook, looking for his number, realizing it wasn't listed. Glancing at Otto, she searched the desktop and noticed an envelope.

"Could you tell him I tried to make it there? And would you mind letting him know where to find me?"

"What's this fella's name?"

Emily thought for a moment, considering if Maxine would know Donald Schillings.

"Come on. I don't have all day."

"Well, um." Emily took another peek at Otto, lowering her voice even more. "It's Don. Don Schillin—"

"Donald Schillings? Ha. Is that you, Emily?"

"....It's me."

"I had a hunch all along. You'd better have a bowl of chicken broth or something. You sound awful. So, Miss Bea already got rid of you, huh?"

Emily could hear the smile in her voice. "No, that's not what happened."

"Remember what I said about wasting your time with that P.O. Box address? I see you haven't learned a thing."

"Oh...just forget it. I'm on the way. Tell him I'm on the way."

Emily hung up, wondering how she was going to pull this off, but determined as ever. No telling what Maxine would say to Samuel if he showed up.

"Say, Otto? Do you drive?"

"Never did. There's really been no need. Besides, Mr. Schillings doesn't like his help cluttering up his place with cars."

He finished straightening a curtain and looked over.

"Why do you ask?"

"Oh, just wondering. Thanks for letting me use the phone."

The children were in class, so Emily left a note on Maria's pillow saying she had an appointment and that she would be back before dinner.

There was only one thing left for her to do. She would walk to the highway and flag down a ride. Steven had picked up several hitchhikers on the way to Watseka. It seemed easy enough.

By quarter of ten, Emily was heading up the long driveway feeling like an ant beneath the giant trees. Whenever she was tempted to turn back, she thought of Samuel waiting at the restaurant. She could just see Maxine standing over him with her mouth going like a thrashing machine. The vision made her move faster.

When she reached the highway, she pulled her skirt up into a knot and scaled the fence. Once over, she positioned herself next to the pavement and held out an arm to her first potential ride coming up the road. The closer the car came, the further she stretched her arm. A moment later, it shot past, nearly knocking her over with the wind. She held her skirt down, pulling her hair out of her face as she watched it disappear up the road.

Another car approached minutes later. The driver slowed for a look and sped off. This went on for about twenty minutes until something caught her eye. It was more of a hunch to start with, but soon it was clear that her boss's limousine was coming up the road.

"Oh, shoot."

Darting into the trees and to the fence, Emily bunched up her skirt and scaled back over, watching from behind a tree as Bruce pulled into the driveway and opened the gate. Once the gate was closed and the car disappeared up the drive, she hightailed-it back to the house.

Emily knew the children were on a break as she approached the kitchen.

Maria was concocting a story for Pearl. "Emily was a little sick last night too."

"Now that's a crock, young lady. Because she came in here not that long ago wanting to use the telephone. And she didn't look sick to me."

"But she—" Maria tried again, although the woman wasn't having it.

"No, something's up with that girl."

Emily cringed, put on a smile, and walked around the corner. "Hello everyone," she trilled.

"Well, there she is. Where've you been, anyway?"

Pearl dropped a basket of apples onto the counter and glared up at Emily. "I've been wanting to talk to you."

"I'm sorry. What do you need?"

"Turns out I've got urgent matters to take care of and there's a taxi on the way to pick me up. Gabriel isn't around for the next few days so you're going to have to do some cooking."

She pulled a pad from a drawer and dropped it on the counter.

"Here's the lunch and dinner menus. And there's a casserole in the fridge ready to pop in the oven. Think you can handle that?"

"Absolutely."

Pearl pulled a knife from a drawer and set it next to the apples.

"There's dough in the fridge for pie crusts. Make sure to save a piece of pie in case Mr. Schillings comes down for a snack. And don't forget that Otto will be around to take up his meals. Have a tray ready at 5:50, sharp. One for Otto and Bruce as well."

Pearl went up the short hallway into her bedroom, locked up, and returned with a suitcase.

"Oh, and I'll be going home for Christmas. I already gave Otto a gift list. So, if you want him to pick something up, you'd better let him know right quick."

She started for the exit and stopped next to the children. "You kids behave yourselves."

"We will," Maria promised in her sweetest voice.

Pearl looked at the two a moment longer, pulled a bag off the counter, draped it over a free shoulder and walked out.

"Oh, good," Nathan said, heading for the refrigerator. He took a bottle of Root Beer and darted out the patio door.

"Uh. Emily. Today isn't pop day," Maria piped.

"Nathan! Get back here with that!"

Emily sighed and picked up a knife and an apple.

"Okay. That means none tomorrow. Don't let me forget."

"I won't."

Maria pulled up a chair and hopped on the counter. "Guess what? We picked out a gift for you."

"Oh, that's nice," Emily said, although she was disappointed because the children had mentioned they went shopping with Pearl a week before Christmas. She had hoped, not only to buy a gift for the children, but also drop a letter in the mail for Samuel.

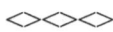

*f*or the next several days, with the kitchen to herself, pretending it was hers, Emily frolicked in a state of whimsical fantasy without interruption or belligerent demands.

While putting together a chicken dinner with all the trimmings, and a chocolate cake for dessert, she imagined Michael was on his way home. They would have a lovely dinner at the long white table with romantic music playing, candlelight, and a crackling fire as they reminisced about their time on the train. Afterward, they would stroll through the flower garden where a kiss would follow. Her mind lingered there, remembering that first kiss on the train, and after, his boyish apology.

Her fantasy ended with the vision of a woman sweeping into his arms one stop short of his assigned departure. The children rushed into the kitchen just in time to soften her disappointment, excited to see the white table set in the family dining room with a fire blazing in the fireplace.

There wasn't a harsh word exchanged between the children throughout the meal. Emily gleaned from their conversations that it wasn't about Pearl not being there, but rather the memories of their mother in that room laughing and talking with them.

As they lingered with their dessert, it was decided, upon Pearl's approval, that this would be an ongoing Friday night occasion.

Pearl came back three days later in the same mood she left in. Emily put it off to her frustration about not being able to pack up and go home for good. She was amazed that as much as Pearl wanted to leave, her loyalty to her boss was paramount.

<><><>

Chances were that Samuel had never received Emily's message from Maxine, and she couldn't just stand by and hope. So, she wrote him another letter, not even sure the first one reached him. Since Mr. Schillings recently stopped mail delivery to the house, she would give it to Bruce to mail.

A few days later, Emily noticed Bruce was waiting in the limousine and ran upstairs to get the letter.

"Sure am glad I caught you before you left," Emily said, catching her breath and handing it to him. "Oh, and...um. It's rather personal."

"I promise I won't open it," he said, with a wink.

"Is there a problem?" Donald asked as he approached.

Emily moved back as Bruce stepped from the car and opened the door for their boss.

"Just bidding a good day. Good day, Bruce. Good day Mr. Schillings."

Emily watched them disappear up the drive and went for a stroll, trying not to think the worst.

The weather had been mild with little rain, although it was muggy with clouds moving in. The signs were there, but when she heard a low rumble in the distance, it took her by surprise as thunderstorms weren't common in that area like they were back home. Still, she didn't take it too seriously—until it came again.

Those fierce Illinois storms had left their mark on her since she could remember. Her grandmother described a storm that came through in the early morning of her birth, and Emily had always wondered if that's when it began.

She stopped to study the clouds. And with another rumble even closer, she turned back to the house and to the library where the sounds would be dimmed.

Maria and Nathan came in after class, as they did so often now, bringing their homework to the library instead of up to their rooms. Later, Otto brought in dinner and set it on the coffee table next to the fireplace.

When it was time for bed, Emily settled the children in, read them each a story, and retired for the night. The storm seemed to have passed. Although as Emily began to drift, she heard rumblings in the distance.

Soon, crashing thunder and bolts of lightning lit up the skies. She pulled the covers over her head and hugged her pillow, drifting in and out of sleep through the ebb and flow of the storm.

All at once, she was at the hearth, at the farmhouse, looking into the kitchen watching her grandmother put a loaf of bread into the oven. She stood and walked to the table. Her grandmother came, and they sat with hot chocolate and cookies, talking, just like old times with the crackling fire at their backs.

An eerie calm filled the air, and she was twelve again. She was walking in the early evening with a book in hand, heading toward the tree house. Climbing up, she snuggled into a blanket and read. Soon, her eyes became heavy.

Night was falling when she awoke to sounds of rain and branches beating at the walls and roof of her little bungalow. A flash of lightening and a crack of thunder hit as s*he scrambled down the tree and ran for the house. With another crack of thunder, she tripped and hit the ground. Wet and soiled, she pulled herself up and hurried through the grass and crossed over the sodden earth of the driveway. She looked up, and Claude stood before her with rain dripping off his chin. A woman wobbled up behind him and giggled drunkenly.*

"This must be the maiden you got hid here. And what is your name, youngin?"

"Mud," Claude hooted, "Her name's Mud, look at her."

The two howled with laughter and climbed into his pickup.

"And you're nothing but crap," Emily called as they drove away. You're crap. You hear? Crap, crap, crap....

CHAPTER NINE

Sunlight poured through the windows. And the scent of flowers and wet grass should have been enough to roust Emily out of bed. But the night had been long, and her dreams had left her shaken—dreams that were as it happened.

She rolled over and reached for the knob on the nightstand. Her hand dropped and she fell back against the pillow remembering the bottle was empty. Tears filled her eyes, disappointed that it was gone, and hating that she would have broken her promise to Maria.

The urge to curl up and sleep was tempting, but she had never been one to lay around and sulk for long. She flung back the covers and sprang out of bed, yanking off her pajamas on the way to the shower.

Maria and Nathan had slept through the storm and were feeling chipper. By the time they ate breakfast and left for class, Emily had pushed aside the troubled images in her dream.

Donald was on a trip and wasn't due back for at least a week. The children were still with their tutor when Emily decided to explore more of the sprawling estate. She rummaged through the boxes of clothes and searched through the jeans. Finding a pair that fit, she pulled on a shirt, slipped into a pair of shoes and went out through the backyard and followed the rock pathway that circled the fir trees. Cutting away, she crossed a broad section of lawn and strolled through another grove of trees to where bushes and creeping vines grew alongside a fence.

She was picking flowers when she noticed an old oak tree several feet beyond the fence. When she stopped to check it out, her gaze dropped to a gate used as a passageway into the dense forest. She went over and pulled away leaves and branches, just enough so the gate could be pushed open. Still debating on whether to go in, Nathan scrambled over.

"Hey, how come you're out early?"

"Miss Hutcheon had an appointment."

His face lit up as he peered around the gate and up a path that was nearly overgrown. "Can we go down to the water?"

"Is that your property over there?"

"Yes. So can we go?"

"Well, maybe we could—"

"Oh boy!" he said, slipping through an opening before she had a chance to change her mind.

She placed the flowers on the ground next to the fence and stepped to the other side.

"Wait, Nathan, not so fast!"

Starting after him, the oak tree caught her eye again and she made a quick stop, digging through fallen leaves and twigs for a handful of acorns. Stuffing them into a pocket, she hurried after the young boy.

Deeper into the forest, there was a strong odor of bark, vegetation, and undergrowth more intense than in the trees closer to the house. The path was rugged and the atmosphere raw and exhilarating. Each time Emily called for Nathan to wait up, he stopped and waved before disappearing around another corner. She was starting to worry that he might run into trouble.

"Watch where you're going. And don't go in the water Nathan, you hear? Nathan!"

She picked up her pace until she stepped on a shoelace and stooped to give it a quick tie. Moments later, pounding hooves were upon her. Expecting the dogs had found them, she yanked the loops of the shoelace, bolted upright, and grabbed a branch. Before she could pull herself up, three deer shot by.

Shaken but relieved, she dropped to the ground and charged up the path. "Nathan! Nathan, where are you! Naathan!"

She was about to call out again when she rounded a bend and the ground sloped to a sandy beach where he was skipping rocks across the water.

"There you are. You scared me half to death."

She made her way down the slope, noticing a wire fence that wound around several hundred feet to the left.

"Do the dogs ever come over the fence?"

"Not unless Harold brings them," he said, reaching down for more rocks.

He angled his wrist and flicked a rock so that it bounced several times before sinking.

"Hey, that was a good one," Emily said as she reached the bottom of the hill and collapsed onto a moss-covered log.

She leaned back on her elbows, thinking what a peaceful setting it was with the sun shimmering off water and a gentle breeze rustling through the trees.

Nathan gave up spinning rocks and picked up a stick, pretending to spear fish.

"Woo… Got one," he said each time he made another jab.

Tired of the stick, he flung it aside and went to gather small branches to build a ramp alongside the water. It was heartwarming for Emily to see him have so much fun.

"You've never talked about this place before. It's fantastic."

He didn't answer.

"Nathan? Why haven't we come here before?"

He stopped what he was doing and looked out across the water.

"You've come here to swim, haven't you?"

Still no answer.

"Nathan. Answer me!"

"A long time ago!" he said, sounding irritated.

She sat up, wondering what had come over him.

"Who brought you here?"

"....Mommy."

He picked up more rocks and threw them into the water one after the other.

"Oh, Nathan," she said, sliding off the log. She went to him and put an arm around his shoulders, "I'm sorry."

He dropped the rest of the rocks on the ground and wandered into the trees that ran alongside the water. She caught up with him and they walked in silence.

The forest was full of life, and the tension lifted when a raccoon ran toward them, stopped with a startled look, and scampered off.

Nathan laughed. And when something caught his eye, he pulled her over to observe an army of ants.

As they huddled around the mound of dirt, watching the little creatures with packs on their backs scurrying about, there was a low, thump-thump-thumping sound. It was the same noise that had awakened Emily that first morning.

She grabbed his arm. "Shhh... Listen."

"Haven't you ever seen a helicopter before?"

"Just in photos."

He leaped to his feet and ran to the riverbank, she right behind him.

The helicopter came over the trees and landed across the lake next to a building. A few moments later, two men left the aircraft and began to carry boxes inside.

"What's over there?" Emily asked.

"Father's business."

She noticed half a truckload of logs to the side of the building and a dozen or so logs floating in the water.

"Have you ever been inside?"

"Nope."

"Ever asked your father if you could?"

He wrinkled his nose. "Nah, no use. He wouldn't let me anyway."

Noticing a bridge a short distance upstream, Emily realized this was where his father went sometimes when he wasn't traveling. On several occasions, she had seen him drive out of the yard in a Model T, which was most likely the same car he snuck off in as a teenager. He made a right turn into the trees while Nathan looked on. She had wondered at the time why he didn't take his son along.

There was movement across the water again, and she noticed the men come from the building and head back to the aircraft. Nathan jumped on a stump as the helicopter lifted.

Emily went to stand beside him. "You ever ride on one of those?"

"No. Maybe when I grow up, I will. I'll probably be a pilot."

The helicopter disappeared over the trees and the drum of the engines melted into the distance. They were preparing to leave when pandemonium broke as the dogs came through the brush and clawed up the wire fence.

Nathan leaped from the stump.

"Let's get out of here," he shrieked, already scrambling through the trees and up the slope with Emily right behind him.

When she reached the top, she stopped and looked back. There was a man standing under a tree looking up at her. He called to the dogs, and they followed him back into the brush.

Emily caught up with Nathan at the gate, squatting beside him. He stood wringing his hands refusing to look at her.

"What's going on? We weren't supposed to go down to the water, were we. Why's that?"

He squirmed but kept silent. She sighed, frustrated that he couldn't see she was trying to help.

Poor boy, she thought. *He was so excited earlier, and now this.*

"I saw a man down there. Was that Harold?"

He nodded, keeping his head down.

"I'm not going to force you to do it now, but you need to tell me what that was about before your father gets back from his trip. You hear?"

He gave another nod and tried to pull away, obviously intending to make a beeline for the house.

"Wait," she said, taking his hand. "Please don't worry. We'll work it out. You know I'd never do anything to hurt you."

He looked up with a spark returning to his eyes. "Can I go watch *Leave it to Beaver*?"

"Go on," she said, letting go of his hand.

She closed the gate, gathered up the flowers, and hurried after him. When she returned to the mansion, she dumped the acorns into water and tossed out the ones that floated. Drying the others in a towel, she stored them in the closet where it was cool.

Stepping into the alcove, she gazed out the window and watched Maria take one of the swings up, knowing that whatever happened down by the water, there would be a price to pay.

CHAPTER TEN

*I*n two days, Emily had one final chance to meet Samuel Dimsmoore. She already talked to Bruce about taking her to San Francisco. But because it hadn't worked out the last time, she wanted to be sure he would be around on Friday.

She walked through the kitchen to pick up a snack on the way out. Pearl was mixing a batter of biscuits as Gabriel came from the pantry with a jar of jelly in each hand. She gave Emily a timid smile, set the jars on the table, and headed for the basement, glancing back as she stepped through the door. "How many potatoes?"

Pearl used her apron to wipe flour off her hands. "At least a dozen. Same as usual."

The maid headed down the steps and Pearl kicked the basement door shut on her way to the refrigerator. "Stupid girl. Can't remember to close a door."

Emily reached for an orange and yanked back the peel. She was tempted to tell the moody woman not to treat Gabriel so mean but guessed that would only make things worse.

"Hey, Pearl, do you know where I might find Bruce?"

"Probably fiddling with the Model T. You'd think he'd find better ways to use his time.

"Men and their toys."

She glowered up at Emily. "What do you want with him, anyway?"

"I have a question, that's all."

"I hope you're not—"

"Just a simple question," Emily said, ready to bite her tongue so as not to say more. Her tone got Pearl out of sorts long enough for her to slip out the side door.

Like all the other areas of the estate, the garages and other quaint buildings were kept inside a fenced-in area bordered by various flowering trees and shrubs. Emily made her way over and through the gate. She picked out the most conspicuous building and walked inside. Sure enough, there was Bruce polishing the old car.

"Hi, Bruce."

He looked up. "Kids too much for you?"

"No...not at the moment," Emily said, chuckling. "I was just wondering if you're still available to run me into San Francisco on Friday. Remember, I mentioned it a few weeks back?"

"Sure, I remember. Well... Let's see, today's Wednesday. Mr. Schillings isn't do back until Sunday, so I think we're set.

What time do you have in mind?"

"I have an appointment at one."

"Okay, then I'll be out front, let's say, around eleven thirty?"

"You're a lifesaver, Bruce."

She lingered, trying to get up enough nerve to ask him about the letter.

"Is there something else I can help you with?"

"I was just wondering if the letter I gave you to mail went out okay."

"Oh, yes... Well, actually, Mr. Schillings noticed it and offered to mail it for me."

A chill swept across Emily's face and down her bare arms.

"Is something the matter?"

"Um...no, everything's fine. I was just thinking about my appointment." She gave her left cheek a pat. "Dentists always make me nervous."

"Ha, you and me both. So then, we'll see you on Friday."

*A*s much as Emily didn't want to cast a cloud over the leisurely lunch the children and she were having on the porch, Mr. Schillings was to arrive home in a few days, and they still hadn't talked about the water incident.

"There's something we should discuss, Maria. It's about a trip Nathan and I took down to the water. Harold saw us."

Maria looked aghast.

"Nathan. You know we're not allowed down there. Not ever!"

Emily looked back and forth between the two.

The little girl was almost in tears. "The last time we went to the water we got a scolding I'll never forget. And we were grounded to our rooms for two whole days."

She leaped from her chair and went around to give her brother a good shaking. "You really messed up this time. You brat! I bet you're gonna get it good."

"I'll decide who gets what around here."

Emily had already heard the footsteps, but the sound of his voice confirmed what she suspected. Donald Schillings had arrived home early.

"Go on, get out of here!" he bellowed, shooing the children off the porch.

When they scrambled down the steps, he swung around to face Emily. The veins on his neck swelled from under his collar and the darks of his eyes pierced into hers.

"How dare you go behind my back and try something so stupid!"

"I'm sorry, but...I-I didn't realize we weren't to go down to the water."

"Then why'd you run from one of my men?"

"I don't know. The dogs. And, I-I guess I was following Nathan."

Donald glanced over a shoulder. "I'll deal with him later."

Emily realized what she had just done and pleaded on Nathan's behalf. "Oh, but Mr. Schillings, it wasn't his fault. At the time I—"

"I'm not interested in excuses. Your duties are to keep the children out of mischief, not get into it yourself."

He gripped the back of a chair and leaned forward.

"By the way? Bruce won't be taking you into town tomorrow. He won't be mailing your letters either. And I've let Pearl know that the phone is off limits for the next several months. And coercing Otto into such matters won't work next time."

He straightened and walked back and forth, rubbing the back of his neck.

"Dang-it. There's too much going on for me to deal with this right now."

He glared at her, sighed, and headed back inside.

Yes, she took Nathan down to the water, but the rest, the way he had taken away all of her rights, was wrong. It seemed that he was trying to keep her insecure and believing he was the only one she could count on. The more she thought about how he had ruined her chance of finding Samuel, the angrier she became. She considered jail as an option but knew she couldn't just desert the children.

There was a knock on Emily's door and Pearl poked her head in the doorway.

"Mr. Schillings wants to see you in the library. I wouldn't make him wait too long."

Emily put the book she was reading aside. "I'll be right down."

When she walked into the library, Donald was standing in front of the fireplace puffing on a cigarette. He put out the stub, motioning for her to sit before taking a seat across from her.

He didn't seem like the wild, angry man from the day before. Instead, he looked distinguished, dressed in a fancy suit and tie with his face cleanshaven and his hair fashionably in place. It struck her that with him in a better frame of mind, maybe they could have a real discussion. Of course, one never knew when his mood would change.

"First… You break my rules, wander through the deep forest with Nathan, and down to the water. You know how many kids drown each year?"

"I'm sorry. That will never happen again."

"And the letter you tried to send. There's no such person at that P.O. Box."

"But, how—"

"I turned it over to a friend at the post office. Like I said that first night you arrived, I can't be too careful. You do remember that don't you?"

"Yes. But I promise he wasn't a threat. Th-the guy I wrote to. He was an old friend of my mother's. And he probably moved ages ago. I knew it was a long shot, but I had hoped to learn more about my mother through him. I never got a chance to know her. You see… My mother died just hours after I was born."

Donald listened thoughtfully, taking in what she said as if he heard every word. She wondered if he was remembering his own mother.

"All I've asked of you is to respect my rules and keep the children content. Nothing more."

"And I'll do that. But if I want to do it right, there's something I need to discuss with you."

"Oh? And what's that?"

"It's about Maria and Nathan. I'm seeing problems on the horizon. I've heard them talk. And I've noticed signs that concern me. They're missing something in their lives, and—"

"How dare you! They have more than most kids ever dream of having!"

"Yes, you're right. But they miss their mother and their friends. And it's not just that. Maybe this doesn't alarm you now. But Maria and Nathan are growing up. They're changing. It's been documented how children go through different stages in life. You know…when adults become old fashion and incompetent."

She had come across those very words in her reading and hoped he was recalling his own youth.

"Basically, if they don't have events that stimulate their imagination and satisfy a need for adventure, it won't be long before they're out looking for excitement."

Donald thought for a moment. He stood and went to the fireplace, tapping his fingers on the mantel.

"Pearl's anxious to leave. Then there's Otto. He's as reliable as one gets. But the children unnerve him when they're left in his care."

Donald lifted a cigarette from a box and lit up. "I need someone that'll keep an eye on them. Someone who minds their own business. And someone I can trust."

He gazed at her thoughtfully. "Well, we'll see," he said.

There wasn't much else to say after that, and she stood to leave. "I'll be on my way, then. But I'm glad we had this talk."

He nodded. And she left his office, relieved he had taken her seriously and was able to plant some seeds.

CHAPTER ELEVEN

*O*ne week before Christmas, Maria and Nathan were wondering where Bruce was and why he hadn't put up the tree. When Emily went to Otto for answers, he said Bruce already left for the holidays. That took her by surprise, and she thought it was very odd he didn't say goodbye.

The children were about to be dismissed from their studies, and Emily gathered their jackets and waited at the back staircase.

"What's this about?" Maria asked when they walked out of their classroom.

Nathan grabbed his jacket, digging his arms into the sleeves. "A walk, dodo bird. Whadoya think?"

"Not just a walk. We're going to cut down a Christmas tree. It looks like Bruce left for the holidays, so it's up to us. And guess what? At this very moment, Otto is taking the decorations to the living room."

Nathan squealed and sped up the hallway. "I'll get the saw."

"We'll have to keep an eye on him," Maria said, sounding so mature Emily had to laugh. She took her hand, and they started after him.

"Nathan, don't you dare touch that saw you little rascal!"

They caught up with the boy at the garages and gathered supplies before searching the forest for the perfect tree. The children helped Emily take it down and carry it to the house. As Otto promised, there was a tree stand, numerous boxes of lights, decorations, and a ladder set up next to the fireplace.

After they put up the tree and finished stringing the lights, Maria picked out a box.

"Can we put these up first, Emily?"

"Of course."

Each of the ornaments were carefully stacked and wrapped in cellophane.

Emily unwrapped one and held it up.

"Wow, these are beautiful. I have a feeling this is a special box you have here."

"Yep, it is," Maria said, holding a silver, diamond-shaped ornament. It was painted with mistletoe and had Maria's name down the side.

"Every year Mommy made Nathan and me an ornament. And we made one for her."

Nathan finished hanging his ornament then dug for another.

"It was our, tree-dition."

"It's tradition, not tree-dition, silly," Maria said, making sure her ornament hung just right.

"So, I like tree-dition better."

Emily stood back and marveled at their creations. "Well, if you ask me, I like it pronounced both ways."

When the boxes were emptied and put away, and with the tree lit up and brimming with decorations, they went to the kitchen where Helen, Pearl's substitute, had pasta and salad waiting for them. She was easier to work with than Pearl. And they decided to linger after dinner, make cookies, fudge, and play a game of Monopoly in the family room.

*W*hen Christmas Eve arrived, Emily and the children decided to sleep in the living room. After changing into pajamas, they brought down blankets. Emily loaded record albums on the turntable. And they were sitting next to the tree listening to Christmas music when Donald walked in.

He looked out of place, holding two large packages, one in each arm, and several smaller boxes on top.

"Here's some presents," he said to the children. "These on top are from Uncle Bud."

Emily went over and helped him place the gifts next to the tree.

When they finished, he looked as if he might bolt but took a seat instead. "Beautiful tree," he said, stiffly.

"We helped Emily saw it down," Nathan said. He rose to his knees from where he sat on the floor and scooted closer to his father.

Maria picked up a plate of various desserts from the coffee table and brought it to him. "We made treats. Want one?"

He looked over the selection, deciding on a sugar cookie.

"My favorite too," she said, taking one for herself as she returned the plate to the table.

Donald held the cookie in the palm of his hand, gazing at the tree. "I was just thinking about the race bike my mother gave me."

His voice came unexpectedly, and everyone waited for his next words.

"That was," he began, clearing his throat, "a year before she died. It was black with silver trim."

"I'll bet it was very nice," Emily said, hoping to encourage him. She wondered if he was turning a new leaf, maybe feeling guilty because the children had lost their mother too. Her grandmother used to say there was good in everyone. That night, Donald Schillings didn't sound like himself. And maybe this was it for him. Whether that was by drink or guilt, at least he made an effort.

Then just like that, he stood.

"Well, I'm expected somewhere in an hour, so I'll be going now."

Maria sat up and watched him walk away. "Merry Christmas, Father."

He took the steps up and turned back, the cookie sitting like an orphan in his hand. Emily thought of the moment in the same way that she pictured her grandfather in church, awkward and wanting a quick exit.

"Merry Christmas," he replied, moving his gaze from Maria to Nathan, nodding to Emily then turning up the hallway.

Chestnuts Roasting on an Open Fire played as the three listened in silence.

"You know he loves you," Emily said as the song ended.

Her comment surprised her as much as it did the children. Nathan's eyes were on one of the presents his father left, and she couldn't resist.

"So, you guys want to open one of the presents from your father, tonight?"

Nathan jumped up and dashed for the tree. He shoved the large box to Maria and sat with his arms around his.

"Opening gifts, already?" Otto said as he walked in and set three more boxes under the tree.

"Just one from Father," Nathan said, waiting for Emily's final okay. "We got you some plaques, Otto."

Emily chuckled and rose, handing Otto his presents.

"Might as well join in.

"Go on, kids, start opening."

Nathan dug his fingernails into the wrap and had his present open before Maria finished taking the ribbon off hers. When he saw what was inside, his eyes looked like saucers.

"I got it! Maria, I got my train. Remember? Just what Mommy promised."

Maria glanced over. "Yep, it's a Lionel, all right. Just like she said."

Nathan was pulling out the railroad tracks from the box as his sister lifted the lid off a square container.

"Oh, Emily, look! A new playhouse. It's exactly the one I wanted. Can you help me put it together?"

"Of course. We'll set it up in your bedroom right after Christmas dinner."

Otto held up his plaques, each decorated with a bird perched on a branch. "These are marvelous. Thank you, children."

Nathan looked up from his track-building. "There's hooks on the back so you can hang them."

"Oh, yes, I see," Otto said, turning them over. "And I've got the perfect spot." He sat back, looking pleased as he watched the children enjoying their gifts.

After Otto left, the three curled up in their makeshift beds.

"Emily," Maria said, as *Rudolf the Red-Nosed Reindeer* began to play. "This is the best, don't you think?"

"It is. It's the best Christmas I've had in a whole lot of years."

Maria thought for a moment. "Now that Mommy's not here. I'm glad you are."

Nathan pulled his blanket under his chin. "Mine's even better since I got the train she promised."

*E*mily rose bright and early the next morning, stoked the fire in the fireplace, and woke the children as Helen brought in breakfast. After eating scones and berries, and opening more gifts, which included lovely earrings and a matching necklace for Emily, they cleaned up the wrappings, bundled up and took a long walk through the grounds of the estate.

When they returned, it was time to dress for Christmas dinner. On the way up to their rooms, Emily kept an eye out for signs that Donald would join them. He had acted differently the night before, and the children were pleased. But she had doubts his attitude would hold over into another day. She was right. When they entered the formal dining room, the table was set for three.

Helen was carving a turkey, and when they had taken their seats, Gabriel started around the table, filling glasses with punch.

Emily noticed Maria glance at her father's empty spot at the table with a flicker of sadness then turn away with defiance. She was watching Abigail fill her glass with punch when her gaze dropped to an ornament sitting beside her plate.

"What's this?"

"Hm. Looks like a Christmas ornament."

Maria reached over and picked it up. "I know what it is, but...how'd it get here?"

Helen was dishing out the turkey by then and glanced up.

"Wasn't me."

"Hey Nathan. Look! You've got one, too," Maria chirped.

"Oh, Emily," she said, "see how beautiful it is. It's like the ornaments Mommy made with us." She set it down carefully, moving it so it sat, just right.

Nathan picked up his ornament, checked it out, and set it back down. "Maybe and angel brought them."

"Do you think so?" Maria asked Emily.

"Well... I don't know about that. Maybe. Although Otto could have brought them in before he left for the day. No matter what. I believe your mother knows you have these."

Nathan couldn't wait to get back to his train and spoke of it all through dinner, as Maria examined her ornament thoughtfully, eyeing it now and then with sparkle in her eyes.

Emily knew the little girl was fantasizing and thought if that's what it took to bring her joy there was something good in that, and maybe was part of the plan. The most important thing was that the symbol of these ornaments and the memory of their mother brought the children hope, just as the children had brought her hope. That's all any of them needed at the moment.

CHAPTER TWELVE

*A*lthough winter had been gentle in contrast to what Emily was used to back in Illinois, the final bite of the season came with lissome wind sweeping through the clouds as birds were fattening up for their migration north.

Spring was on the way. And it looked like a typical day in February, except for another kind of migration taking place on the front lawn of Donald Schillings' estate. Emily wasn't fully awake when a racket filtered in through her bedroom windows. For a moment she thought she was back at the farm.

She sat up, shaking her head to clear the fuzz. Scooting off the bed, she went to a window and pushed it open all the way, gazing upon a dozen or so cows enjoying the acres of endless green grass. From the far distance, a Belgian Sheppard came like a bullet, across the lawn and over to the grazing cows.

"Look at all the cows!" Nathan hollered over the sounds of the makeshift barnyard below.

All at once, his precarious position from his bedroom window was more of a threat than the mess the animals were making.

Their bedrooms were set in an L-shape and Emily could see straight across to his window.

"Nathan, get back from the window before you fall. Hey! What happened to your screen?"

"I'm going down," he said and promptly disappeared.

Emily pulled on a robe, a pair of slippers, and went after him. She made a quick stop to ring for Otto. As she reached the front steps, two people on horseback, and a shaggy-haired dog that was no more than a pup, came from beneath the trees beyond the entrance of the property.

Nathan was standing on the grass at the corner of the porch, excited as any young boy would be in that position.

"You don't budge from there young man. You hear? And make sure to tell Otto about your screen."

He nodded, glancing up at her with a smile.

Emily gazed back out across the grass. There was a young man around Emily's age, and a boy looking to be about twelve or thirteen.

The boy wound his way across the lawn with the shaggy-haired dog by his side. When Emily saw the young man ride toward the mansion, she tightened the belt on her robe and made her way down the steps to meet him.

"Sorry about this," he said as he approached. "We'll have 'em out of here in no time."

"That'll be good. Thank you."

Emily wasn't sure if she should just stand back and let it happen or demand an explanation.

"Well, I'll get busy. Just wanted to let you know," the young man said before heading off.

Maria ran out onto the porch and climbed the wood railing, dangling her legs.

Otto was right behind her, stopping just outside the doorway. "For heaven's sakes. What in the world...."

"Isn't this something?" the little girl said, turning to smile up at him.

He sighed, looking about, shaking his head. "Well...I'd better start making calls."

Emily walked back to the steps and sat until the cows were nearing the outskirts of the yard. When she saw the young man walk over, she went to meet him.

"My name's George. George Trutman. The youngster helping is my brother Jeramie Dean. But unless he's in trouble, it's JD. And that long-haired pup running wild alongside him is Rusty."

Emily and George turned their attention to the Belgian. "That's Gracie. By the time she slows down, Rusty will be at his best."

George pointed to an area where the land gradually elevated up a hillside. "We live that-a-way, about two miles."

He turned back to Emily. "Say, it's nice to meet you, auh...."

"I'm Emily. The nanny."

"I thought as much."

The introductions were over, and they stood looking at the mess. Emily sensed there was something more troubling him. He pulled in his breath and began to tell her exactly what that was.

"Wish I could say Schillings is getting what he deserves...but, what a jacka...."

He stopped, red-faced.

Emily held back a chuckle and couldn't wait to hear more.

"Go on, I'm listening."

He flashed a smile, pushing back his cowboy hat. With his blue eyes grinning, along with his smile, and his blond hair curling around his ears, he looked rather pretty for an almost full-grown man. His boyish looks reminded her a bit of Daniel.

"The point is that I'm sure this *mess* Schillings caused will somehow work to his advantage."

"Um, George. I'm not meaning to take sides here. But to be honest, I mean, the cows are yours... In his yard."

George gave a half-hearted laugh that was more of a smirk. "Yeah, I see what you're saying, but you've got it wrong."

He pointed to where the back ends of the cows were moseying back into the tree line, the German shepherd, and young boy guiding them. "See the fence that's been dismantled? Well, Schillings brought it down. It wasn't us."

Emily shaded her eyes with a hand, gazing to the far end of the property. "Yes, I see. So, he just up and tore it down? But...why? When?"

"Most likely yesterday afternoon. A while back he claimed the surveyor made a mistake. Even had his lawyer send us documents to back it up. But without waiting until we could investigate, he had it taken down. I'm sure it was Harold who did the deed. My grandfather told us all about that guy. You'll see. Within the next couple of days, he'll be putting up a new fence further onto our property. As if that'll make it official."

The young man folded his arms, working trampled grass back up with the tips of his boot.

"We own at least a fourth of that hillside." He pointed to the fence running up. "He's going to tear that down too and claim our portion.

"Oh, and over there?" He nodded in the direction of the back yard. "In the last two years, several neighbors moved within months of each other. I wouldn't be surprised if he coerced them out or at the very least, bribed them."

"Really."

"Yep. And when we refused his offer to sell our place, he started this...*bull*."

George glowered at the mansion, his nose twitching. With his boots on, he was about an inch taller than Emily, and nearly as thin. She thought it was amusing how much he reminded her of an over-zealous pup trying to protect its ground.

"The guy gets me so dang worked up I can't think straight."

She saw visions of Donald Schillings grabbing him by the neck as George continued to egg him on.

"So, what does your family think about what's going on?"

"Oh, my mother feels like I do. Now, as for my father, well...I guess his cushy nature doesn't help us any. It makes Schillings even bolder."

Emily recalled Miss Bea telling her that *The Palace* was going to be built on top of a hill. She gazed onto the neighbor's property. Her eyes followed the tree line to the top of the beautiful mountain, and back down again, contemplating on whether to tell George about the building plans. She gazed at the young man, thinking that when he wasn't growling or twitching his nose, he looked so innocent. Knowing that the information may get him more worked up, there was no need going into detail just yet. She rather liked him.

"You see, Emily," he continued, "once the neighbors, across the water, moved, that's when he started a logging business. Maybe I'm wrong, but it all seems strange to me.

"Anyway, I should go help my brother. I'm glad we got a chance to meet. If you ever need anything, don't hesitate to come by."

"I'll keep that in mind. Thank you."

As he disappeared, Emily studied the fence, the section that was down, and the section further up the hillside that would soon be taken down, troubled by what she knew and confused about what she should reveal.

*B*y the time Donald arrived home, the yard was back in order. If he found out about the cows, he decided not to make a big deal of it. Emily guessed this was because he had more important things on his mind.

She was expecting to meet the children for their Friday night dinner next to the fireplace. While they went to their rooms to change, Emily sat on the porch with a book. When she came in for dinner, she found Gabriel still there and a few others helping out.

"Where're Maria and Nathan?" she asked Pearl.

"In the formal dining room having dinner with Mr. Schillings and some important guests."

The woman was flushed and hurried about putting out orders to a waiter in a tuxedo, a waitress in black and white, and a lank backup cook with a bandana tied around her head.

Emily recalled the attention Donald gave to his children on Christmas Eve, and the initial disappointment, at least, from Maria, on Christmas Day. It seemed, once again, that he was trying to make an effort.

Yet, Emily's hopeful theory only lasted a day or two. Nothing had changed. Within days, it became apparent that the children were invited to the dinner to impress a California State Senator and his wife, hoping that they would support his run for mayor.

CHAPTER THIRTEEN

*E*ven as a young child, Emily could sense things more astutely than most. She remembered being in the kitchen with her grandmother, laughing and dancing to the beat of music playing on the radio. The outside door would open. And when her grandfather walked in, more times than not, the look on his face killed her joy. Her grandmother let her know that his frown was not about her. But it was because his precious daughter died, and it ate at his soul. And that each time he looked at his beautiful little granddaughter, it reminded him that his girl was never coming back.

Grandfather's rejection of Emily and the offenses she endured from Claude were not in vain. As time passed, their abuses became distant, strengthening her resolve, and taught her to listen to her intuition.

She didn't know exactly what drove Mr. Schillings. And if it weren't for Maria and Nathan, none of it would matter. But for the way it was, she was invested in the children's well-being. And it was time to take advantage of an opportunity.

When she approached Donald's den and found the door ajar, she knocked and poked her head in the doorway. He was sitting at his desk.

"Excuse me, Mr. Schillings?"

He turned in his chair. "What is it?"

She pushed the door open, stepped inside and moved across the room, determined not to let this opportunity slip by.

"Do you have a minute?"

She took the seat next to his desk, watching for signs of his mood.

"I was wondering whatever happened to Bruce. Is he coming back?"

"Your last concern should be what happened to the old guy. Now, is that all? Because I've got a plane to catch."

"The children were asking about him."

"They could've talked to me and I would've told them, no, he's not coming back."

Emily wanted to tell him that if he had given the children a chance, they might've asked. But she would stick to her original plan, with something that might do them some good.

"The reason I stopped by was because Maria's birthday is coming up in a few months. And I'd like to invite her friends over for a party. She said she hasn't seen them for nearly a year."

"I'll have you know. There's a reason they haven't been around. The little devils ended up where they didn't belong, one too many times."

"And that's why I'm here. I have an idea that will help keep the children occupied and out of mischief."

"So…what's this plan of yours?"

"You've probably seen how Maria is still clinging to that battered stick horse. And… What I thought was, if you bought her a pony for her birthday, and, of course, as an early birthday present, one for Nathan, it would do wonders for them."

"Well…I've heard enough."

Donald leaped to his feet, collected papers from his desk, and dropped them into a briefcase.

"For your information… Pearl saw that Maria was getting too old for that stick horse and tried to throw it out several times, but Maria dug it out of the garbage."

Emily knew she had to do something quickly and moved forward in her chair.

"Just my point. It's a love-hate thing for her. And let me remind you, Mr. Schillings, of when Nathan brought the skunk up to his bedroom. And there was the lake incident, remember? He was just bored. And I don't have to tell you about their squabbles. But the real problems will begin when they start sneaking around to find excitement. I've taken advantage of your library. And I've been reading up on this and learned some important facts that'll make things a lot easier on you."

"Oh? Now what could that be?" he said, sarcastically.

"You see, as they get older, they're misbehaving will most likely become bolder. It won't be too long before they're sneaking out or bringing friends home when you're out of town. Remember when you were young?"

Donald slammed the lid of his briefcase and sat.

"You're getting too big for your britches, young lady. But you might have a point."

He tapped his fingers on his desk, seeming to consider his options, and possibly the follies of his youth.

"You know. Putting up that stable and bringing in some ponies may not be such a bad idea. From what I've been told, it seems to be a big deal now days."

"Oh... Mr. Schillings. That would make them very happy, sir."

He secured his briefcase, clutched the handle and stood, walking to where she sat.

"You may have brought something to my attention," he said, giving her a look that had run chills through her at one time, "but don't think I don't know what goes on around here. In fact, I'm seriously considering hiring help in that department. One can't be too careful now days."

Motioning her from the den, she followed him out. He locked up and rushed out the front door as Emily went to see Maria.

The little girl was sitting on the floor rearranging furniture in her new playhouse. Emily sat beside her.

"Say. You were telling me about your best friends."

"That would be Audrey and Nora."

"So…was there anything in particular that happened the last time they were here?"

"Did father say something?"

"A little. I gather you guys got into some mischief."

"Mm... That's the night they came over for a slumber party."

She pointed to the closet. "It's covered now, but I was on a stool looking for costumes when Audrey noticed an entryway into the ceiling. She said it was just like her grandmother's. And if we got it open, we'd find a secret room up there. We were so excited that we snuck a ladder from maintenance. Audrey was on her way up when Father walked in."

Maria scrunched her nose. "One of the maids ratted on us."

"Yikes, I'll bet your father was angry."

"Oh, boy, was he ever. Audrey hurried down the ladder so fast she missed the last few steps and twisted an ankle. The maid wrapped her foot, and Father had Bruce take them both home. Audrey's mother came over later, threatening to call the police on Father for assaulting her daughter. After she left, he told Nathan and me we were lucky he finally got her calmed down. That was the last time we were allowed to have friends over, and when he brought Miss Hutcheon in."

Emily understood why Donald had been upset with the girls. But he went way too far with his punishment by not allowing his children to experience what is most important for any child—spending time with friends.

Something told her there was more to it than just the misbehaving. And that it wasn't only about keeping Maria and Nathan out of mischief by not allowing them to have friends, but it was also to keep them from the outside. What worried Emily was why.

CHAPTER FOURTEEN

*F*amily man was not something that would have been associated with Mr. Schillings, at least not with those who spent time with his children.

Nevertheless... A month after Emily's talk with him regarding Maria's eleventh birthday, a crew of men began construction on a stable. When it was completed, a bunkhouse was added. Next, they fenced a large arena with sand at one end, and further out, paths that cut through trees for a unique riding experience. Emily was shocked by the extravagance.

The purpose of the activity wasn't always easy to keep from Maria and Nathan, although they obediently stayed away from the work area when told their father was doing this for them as a surprise. It didn't take much recall from the day Miss Bea showed Emily the new plans for *The Palace* for her to realize that everything had already been in the works as part of Mr. Schillings forthcoming business adventure. Although he sped things up in order to keep his children out of his hair, they were much happier believing their father was going through all this trouble just for them. Whatever the case, Emily didn't lose hope that somewhere deep inside, he was thinking of them.

*T*he best time to catch Mr. Schillings was as he was about to leave on a trip. Emily had been waiting at the overlook when she saw him step from his office. She rushed down the stairs, up the entrance hallway, and came up beside him, thrilled he was in an unusually good mood and didn't shut her down. He seemed caught up in her enthusiasm when she revealed her utmost desire to be the children's riding instructor. She explained the extent of her experience with horses, and that even finding herself ankle deep in dung was no problem for her. Surprised by her candor, and, slightly embarrassed, she hurried on with the speech she had prepared, reminding him how much free time she had on her hands when the children were in class. She pointed out that the bunkhouse would come in handy when extra help was needed, but that it was a waste of time to go through the hassle of finding another riding instructor for the children when she had the qualifications needed. He seemed to listen with an attentive ear and nodded in agreement several times. From his response, there was no doubt in Emily's mind that everything was settled. She would be the children's instructor in charge of everything, the horses, cleaning the stable, and keeping up on the riding arena.

Emily couldn't wait for the excitement to begin. To prepare the children without revealing the surprise, the next time she went to the library, she found several books on the subject of riding horses and put them out where they would be sure to see them.

Otto let her know that the horses would arrive the day before Maria's birthday and assured her that everything was being arranged to the very last grain of feed. When that day finally came, Emily heard the vehicles approaching early that morning. She rushed Maria and Nathan to class and sat waiting with them until Miss Hutcheon arrived. That evening, she was tempted to go to the stable but decided it would be more exciting to wait and enjoy the surprise along with the children.

*F*ollowing breakfast on Maria's birthday, Emily began to decorate the back porch with balloons and crepe paper. Maria's friends from school weren't invited, although after some goading from Pearl, Donald had a couple of his business associates send over several of their children. They arrived just as the last of the decorations were being put in place. Even though the guests were strangers when they walked in, soon they were all in the back yard playing games.

Pearl brought out peanut butter and jelly sandwiches and a chocolate cake with fluffy white icing topped with eleven candles. After lunch, the children went on a scavenger hunt and played pin the tail to the donkey. To top the excitement, there was a game of pinata that held enough prizes to go around several times over. The party ended with Maria opening her gifts and Pearl making sure the guests left with a piece of cake and a sack of prizes.

Emily saw how disappointed Maria and Nathan were after everyone left. And she couldn't wait to take them to their ponies.

"Guess what you two? There's one more surprise."

Bouncing back from post-party blues, the children squealed with delight as Emily pulled two blindfolds from a pocket. Covering their eyes, she took them each by a hand, led them around the side of the mansion, up a pathway, through a grove of trees, and to a beautiful, red barn. She slid the door open, guided them inside, and closed it behind them.

Maria sniffed the air. "Where *are* we anyway?"

"Wait right there," Emily said, starting off to open the stall doors until she noticed they were already open, and the children's ponies were secured with a pink and a blue rope.

Turning back, she took the children by their shoulders and led them in front of their ponies.

"Okay. Take off your blindfolds."

Nathan ripped his off, *wooing*, as he flung it aside and cautiously went to his pony. Maria, on the other hand, pulled off her blindfold and stood gaping.

Emily gave her a nudge. "Go on. She's yours."

The little girl set the blindfold on the floor and walked around to the side of her pony. "Happy. I'm calling you Happy," she said, placing a gentle hand on her.

Nathan spoke to his pony, smiling at Emily. "Is he a boy?"

"Yes, he's a boy," she said with a chuckle.

Emily went over and handed Nathan a brush. "Let him get used to you. And don't go around to his backside just yet."

"Oh, I won't. And guess what. His name is Mr. Ed," he announced as if it had been decided months earlier.

Emily watched the children with satisfaction, seeing how comfortable they were with their ponies and how calm the ponies were with them.

"Hey guys... I'm giving you some time with Happy and Mr. Ed. Then comes the real fun."

The stall partitions were slanted enough to where Emily could see her horse in the stall next to Maria's. She walked over, picked up a brush and moved it over the black silky coat.

"Hey, pretty lady. How do you like the name, Startoo?"

Emily knew they were going to have so much fun and couldn't wait to begin their adventure. Not since the day she was nine and proudly walked downstairs wearing the dress her aunt Francine had sewn for her first day of school had she been so excited. Nothing could break her spirits.

There was movement in the next stall, and she walked around, surprised to see another horse.

"Well... I'll be. Ha."

There wasn't much of a chance that it was Mr. Schillings'. She smiled at the thought of Pearl attempting a graceful mount. Visions of Otto and the new driver were nearly as comical.

Still perplexed, she heard the barn door slide open. Stepping back, she looked around a post at a tall strapping Black man whose shadow nearly filled the doorway.

Whether it was the shock of seeing him show up out of nowhere or how he seemed to be forcing himself on them with his sudden presence, she knew her plans were ruined. The extra horse was obviously for him. And she had just lost what would have been a dream come true for her.

Nathan hadn't noticed the visitor yet and called to Emily. "Can we take our ponies out now?"

The stranger swept into the barn and over to the children.

"No riding just yet," he said, in a burly thunder. "Not until I've gone over some things."

Nathan came around his pony's stall, and the stranger began to joke with the children, explaining that he was their riding instructor. Their connection was instant.

When his gaze turned to Emily, his grin faded, and he gave her a greeting that left her unsettled.

He wasn't making it easy on her. But she knew nothing about him and didn't want to be rude.

"Hello," she said.

It seemed he might say something more, but Nathan, in his eagerness to get started on the lessons, pulled him away.

Emily turned back to her horse, keeping an ear and an eye on the three.

The stranger reached for a bridle from Maria's stall partition and placed it around his shoulders.

"Ready to get started?"

"Oh, boy," Nathan said, doing a little dance.

Emily's gaze wandered over again, and she watched the stranger bridle the pony then pull down a pad and show the children how it was done. *Just be happy for them,* she thought, with a sigh, and a reprimand to herself. *Let the man do his job.*

"By the way, my name's Paul," he said, pulling the saddle from its spot. "Once I ready the ponies we'll start the lessons. But first, I need to go over safety procedures and relay orders from the top."

Orders? Emily's heart sank.

By then Maria was in high spirits. "What kind of orders, Paul?"

"Well, for one," he said, placing the saddle onto Happy, "you don't ride alone, certainly not until you're experienced. And more importantly…."

Paul's voice cut off, and Emily turned to the silence, meeting his gaze for an instant.

"More importantly," he repeated, "are the strict orders from Mr. Schillings that no one is to ride outside the arena. And no riding after dark."

Emily sensed the change in Paul's tone was about her. She had hoped Mr. Schillings trusted her at that point. And that she hadn't yet proven herself to him, well, it was disappointing. She had been delighted, imagining the experience of a lifetime with her being the children's personal instructor with full charge. The letdown was harsh. So, of course, it would take time to adjust and try to understand why this stranger was hired when she had plenty of time and ability to give the children riding lessons, clean the stable, and do it all for that matter. It would seem like a lot of work. But looking back at her experience on the farm, being a stablewoman at the estate would be a cinch—two, or maybe three hours a day at the most.

Wanting it so much, Emily thought about offering to work with Paul. Almost convinced, something occurred to her that jolted her back to her senses.

What had seemed like a warning, Mr. Schillings told her he knew what went on around his estate and that he was thinking about hiring help in that department. Otto alluded to that as well when he mentioned several employees had been caught gossiping about their boss.

Mr. Schillings had the right to protect his property. But it was his demands and the way he put fear into his employees that bothered Emily.

All the more she thought about it, all the more it seemed that he hired Paul, not only as the stableman, but essentially a spy; a well-built man, nice-looking, yes, but on the rugged side, enough to intimidate the help. Although she admitted there had to be a lot more going on than she understood, she had been scrutinized and rebuked by Schillings enough. He didn't even trust her to take a perfectly healthy, normal young boy to enjoy an afternoon by the water. That told her all she needed to know about his intentions.

Emily did her best to hold back her irritation as Paul finished saddling the ponies and turned to her.

"Need some help?"

Placing a hand on the saddle, she yanked the leather strap. "No, thank you. I'm doing just fine."

Paul had come on like a bull. And although his voice had softened as he continued with safety procedures and saddled the ponies, she couldn't forget why he was there.

While the children had their first lesson, Emily road around the arena, took a trip through the trees, then dismounted Startoo and slow walked her back to the barn.

On their way back to the mansion, Maria and Nathan raved about Paul and asked Emily what she thought of him.

"Well… He seems like a very nice man. And he sure knows his horses, doesn't he."

The children agreed.

Several days later, as Emily stood at the library entry, she watched the children head for their lessons and cross paths with their father. She was amused when she noticed that Maria and Nathan's excitement and a thank you from each to their father got to him a little. Although soon he was off on another trip and life went on as usual.

*T*he children were so happy, Emily scolded herself for judging Paul. He was only doing what he was hired to do. And each time she went into the barn to saddle her horse, everything was in perfect order as was the riding arena.

What got to her was her lack of privacy. It seemed, when she was playing basketball with Nathan, Paul might show up out of the blue to work on the porch, do touch-up painting, or adjust something. He would joke with Nathan. But when she happened to catch his gaze, there was that look again. At times, when Emily took a walk, somewhere in the distance, Paul was pulling up weeds or pruning shrubs somewhere along the line, something the gardeners would normally do. One day, when the children were in class and she was sitting on the bench with her feet up, reading in the flower garden, she heard what sounded like someone walking through the brush. After sitting up and looking around, not seeing anything, she still couldn't shake the feeling that she was being watched. It was downright odd. Why her? She wasn't a threat, at least not at the time.

CHAPTER FIFTEEN

Nearly, a year had passed since Emily left the farm. The children seemed to rely more on Paul than on her of late, and her thoughts had been drifting to the future. But that was more frightening than comforting. She wasn't ready for a big change, or at least the one waiting for her.

Even though there wasn't much hope of finding Samuel Dimsmoore, Emily wasn't ready to give up on the idea. He had been a good friend of her mothers, which made him part of her life too. As her time of reckoning neared, she was reminded of days gone by and found herself thinking about the event that sent her fleeing from the farm. Although she seldom had visions or dreams of what happened to Claude, when they hit, she was grieved by the guilt.

The support she received from Shayne had given her temporary peace to fall back on. His words had come to her just at the right moment. But she wasn't flippant on the subject like he was and didn't agree with him about not turning herself in. From things she heard, prison was the last place she wanted to be, but she couldn't think about that. The truth was, she was guilty on some level. And one day she would surrender herself to the police. The moment hadn't arrived just yet. But when the time came, she would know.

Ever since meeting George, Emily wished she was free to saddle Startoo and ride over to the Trutman farm. One night, the opportunity came in a way that left her no choice.

She was standing on her private porch, looking up at the stars, when she heard the cry of an animal. At first, she thought it was an injured coyote, or a fox. Once she got it into her head that it sounded more like a dog, she couldn't let it go.

With a flashlight in hand, she ran across the sprawling grounds toward the, by then, whimpering animal. Climbing over the new fence that looked to be at least a hundred feet further onto the Trutman property, she rushed to where the neighbor's dog, Rusty, whom she saw during the cow invasion, was caught in a trap.

"You poor thing," she said, releasing his long, shaggy hair. She checked the area for an injury, and though there were a few drops of blood, she knew he was okay and lifted him into her arms.

"What're you doing out here by yourself, little guy?"

Her answer came a moment later with a rustling sound. Spinning around, she saw a cow pulling up clumps of grass, relieved it wasn't Paul or Harold.

She carried the young dog to the stable and cleaned the superficial wound on his hind leg with disinfectant and wrapped it with gauze that was stored in a cabinet with the rest of the animal care products. Thankful it was only his long shaggy hair that held him to the trap, she went to the house and brought back leftover hamburger gravy. When the pup finished eating, she set out water and wrapped him in a blanket. She would take him home in the morning before anyone was up.

A whisper of light filtered through the mist as Emily made her way to the stable. Saddling Startoo, she gathered the pup into a sling and anchored it around one of her shoulders. She led the horse behind the bunkhouse and followed a line of maple trees and flowering shrubs that ran alongside the fence. When she reached the gate at the end of the circular driveway, she looked back at the house that was draped in early morning fog. There was a dim light from her bedroom window, and she could only hope she had forgotten to turn off a lamp.

Mounting the horse, she left out the gate and took the road a few feet before turning south into the trees, through a field, and made her way up the hillside. By the rugged terrain, it was obvious why her boss wanted the portion of the hill that George said belonged to his family.

When she reached the crest, she came out of the haze into an amazing vista where patches of fog hovered below. She stopped to take in the splendor, knowing this was the view Miss Bea had been so excited about.

Once Emily made her way down the other side, she followed the old section of fence until she came upon a gate. Reaching through the fence, she tugged on a latch that was corroded and obviously hadn't been used in years. After a few good hits with a rock and a couple of yanks, it broke open. Replacing the latch as good as possible, she continued for a mile or so before reaching the Trutman farm. George's brother, JD, answered the door.

"Rusty. You found Rusty," he cried, pulling the dog into his arms.

"What happened to his leg?"

"Don't worry. It's nothing serious."

Mrs. Trutman appeared at the doorway, fumbling with a wire hair roller. She wiped her hands on a flour-speckled apron and shook Emily's hand.

"I'm Greta. You must be Emily. George mentioned you met."

"We did. And I'm sure glad I found your place."

Greta leaned over for a peek at the pup and motioned the two into the kitchen. "Go on and take the little guy in where I've got a morning fire going."

She grabbed a pillow from the couch, followed them into the kitchen, and dropped it on the floor in front of a wood stove. The boy made sure Rusty was comfortable in his usual spot and curled up beside him. Emily sank to the pillow.

Greta took a chair next to the stove. "Now...tell me. What happened?"

Emily recounted hearing Rusty in distress. And how she found him just over the fence from Schillings.

"I think he was frightened more than anything," she added as she ended the story.

The older woman leaned toward the pup and scratched the top of his head. "Poor fella.

"I'm sure Schillings is involved. And he knows Pa gives into things like this."

She sat back, repositioning a bobby pin in her hair.

"My father used to trap years ago, him and some friend of Schillings. And I have a feeling Schillings will turn that back on us if we bring it up."

Reaching over, she pulled a latch on the stove and stuffed a log into the fire.

"I don't know if you realize this, Mrs. Trutman, but the new fence is already up."

Greta closed the steel door. "It is. Well, there's your answer."

She sighed, turning to Rusty. "So, you don't think he needs a vet?"

"Nah. I'm certain it didn't touch a bone. Last night I used disinfectant. The gauze can probably come off by tomorrow. And if you've got something that'll fight infection, that's all I'd worry about."

"That we've got."

"Oh, by the way, he was there with a cow of yours."

"Ha, just like the little guy. I'll bet he's going to be one of the best herding dogs we've ever had."

When someone shuffled up the back steps, everyone turned as the door opened, and George poked his head in.

"Emily," he said, stepping inside, "what a surprise."

He noticed the dog, wiped his feet, and walked over.

"Where'd you find Rusty?"

"With his shaggy locks caught in a trap. He was just short of the fence, next to Schillings, with one of your cows."

"That's it. I'm gonna kill that man."

Greta got up and went to the stove. "Well, you need to eat first. How 'bout you two sit over here and I'll dish up some oatmeal. There's biscuits and honey too."

"Just a small bowl for me," Emily said as she took a seat at the table. "Oh, and maybe a biscuit with a bit of honey would be nice."

Greta dished the food and went to the sink to start washing up.

George leaned over his bowl, took several bites of oatmeal, and clenched a fist. "We can't allow him to get away with this, Ma. You know how it is. Give him an inch, and he'll take a mile.

"Think I'll ride back with you," he said to Emily. "I'd better fetch the cow. And if that trap is still there I'll bring it back for evidence."

His eyes narrowed so only the blue showed. "When I'm done with that, I'm goin' over to wring that man's...neck!"

Emily couldn't help but to smile. "You think that'll do any good?"

"Damn right it will."

117

He dropped the spoon and pushed himself from the table.

Greta rinsed a plate under the tap and set it on the draining rack. "Son. I want you to be careful. You're probably right. But where's the proof."

George took his bowl and spoon to his mother. He grabbed a biscuit off the stove, leaning back against the counter. "I got all the proof I need right here in my head. What we need is a good lawyer."

"Yes. And if there's a shady one out there, you know Schillings already hired em."

The young man dusted his hands off, went to the door, and put on his cowboy hat while Emily brought her dishes to Greta. After saying their goodbyes, the two set out.

They rode across the stubble of harvested fields and followed a trail through a grove of pear and apple trees. Emily could see why the land meant so much to George.

"We sure appreciate you bringing Rusty home," he said as they made their way through a patch of rocky grassland. "I can't thank you enough."

"No need for that. You would've done the same.

"Say. I sure hope Donald Schillings gives you guys a break."

"Yeah. What a joke. Just wish more people knew what a thug he is. It's hard to believe he works alone.

"Oh, did you hear? It sounds like he has political ambitions."

"You're kidding."

"Nope. And there's a senator who's already backing him."

George laughed so hard he nearly fell off his horse.

"Where does that man get his nerve, I wonder.

"You know. I'm working on some things that may put a stop to his ambitions. Make sure to drop by sometime soon."

"I'm not always able to get away. But I'll try my best.

"Well, here's my exit," Emily said as they arrive at the gate.

She slipped off her horse, pulled on the worn latch, then walked Startoo through the opening, watching George wander away, letting out hoots of laughter as he went to fetch the cow.

Emily closed the gate, set the latch in place, and mounted Startoo. While heading back to the estate, she felt for George and wondered where fate would lead him and his family. As much as she believed in the Trutman's plight, she hoped she wouldn't regret collaborating with them.

*W*hen Emily reached the barn, she was relieved Paul wasn't there. It was still early, and she hoped he hadn't noticed that she took Startoo off the property. As she led her horse inside, she thought again about how good Paul was with the children. *Why should I care if he makes sure the help follows Schillings' stupid rules, or whatever else he's doing to satisfy the boss.*

Recently, she had a decent conversation with Paul. This change in their rapport made her wonder if he could be trusted enough to be told about Rusty, where she had been, and just how bad it could have turned out for the dog. If he had a heart, he would make sure it didn't happen again.

Emily put everything away, snooping around, and thinking that she had been a little hard on him. That was until she came upon four traps sitting in the corner of one of the supply closets.

"Well, that miserable, rat!"

She was so furious she went to find Paul and let him know what she thought about his horrible actions.

When she saw him, he was coming from the island of trees in back. And he didn't look happy.

"Emily," he said, yanking off a pair of gloves with that miserable look and accusing tone he had given her at times.

"Where've you been? We need to talk."

Her need to talk to him had vanished. She backed away and fled to the house, rushing in through the back entrance. Otto stepped in front of her, folding his arms as he checked out her soiled clothes and muddy shoes.

"Do you often traipse the halls dressed like that?"

He was serious by nature but sounded unusually stern.

She looked down at the stains on her shirt and pants, and the tracks on the floor. "Sorry. I'll get a mop and clean it up."

"No, don't bother. Just take off your shoes from now on after you've been...." His gazed returned to her shoes. "Well, wherever you've been."

She took her shoes off and carried them up the back stairs. At the top, she looked down over the railing. Otto had taken out his hanky and was wiping the floor.

"Sorry," she said again, feeling ashamed when she thought of all the times back home when the men had come in and muddied her polished floors. She had been furious with them.

*O*nce the riding lessons for Maria and Nathan had moved to the advanced stage, it became routine for Emily and the children to take an afternoon outing. They spent much of their time riding through the forested area which was like a land of fairytales for them. But their ride wasn't over until they stopped to climb their favorite tree.

Each of them looked forward to these outings, Emily particularly because Paul had other duties during that time period, and she wouldn't have to face him after what he had done to the Trutman dog. To make sure that would never happen again, when they returned from their rides, as the children took care of their ponies, she would play detective and take a look around to see if the traps were still in the supply closet and not where they would do harm. She thought of trying to talk to Paul again. But that would do no good. Traps were set to kill. And he did what his boss wanted. Although… Now that it seemed Mr. Schillings was able to extend his property line, hopefully, there may not be a reason for him to cause more trouble for his neighbors.

CHAPTER SIXTEEN

*F*lying leaves and twigs tapped against the windows with each gust of wind. Something about the length of the gusts and the melodious sounds made Emily think of her grandmother's messages of foresight and caution. She was beginning to understand the full meaning behind her words:

> *'After every dark season comes light.*
> *So don't get discouraged, my little*
> *Bella Bambina when the only way to*
> *the good is through the bad.'*

Like her grandmother, Emily relished the newness of each season, whether it was the first snow of winter when the moon reflected off blankets of white frozen crystals, or when a tempered breeze swept across her face in early spring, or the first warm summer day when it was impossible not to dig her bare feet into cool dirt. But nothing filled her with more joy than a walk through a breeze in late Autumn with leaves crunching beneath her feet.

She got up, opened all the windows in her bedroom, the windows in the children's rooms, and beckoned them out for an early morning ride. Maria and Nathan were becoming proficient at riding. Life had made a complete turnaround for them. She couldn't remember their last fight. And some days it was plain easy to keep a positive attitude.

Now that the children were doing so well, and as sad as it would be to leave them, she knew that soon she would turn herself in.

Following dinner that evening, and an hour of television that Emily allowed the children, they were reading in the library when she decided to take advantage of the time she had left and take Startoo out before nightfall.

Emily rode around the arena several times before heading into the trees. When she reached the far end, she slid to the ground, took a handful of grain from a pocket, and fed it to Startoo. She was standing next to the tree that the children and she had been climbing and couldn't resist going up.

While enjoying the view from a branch, Emily imagined how excited Maria and Nathan would be to have a treehouse up there. She was considering how that might happen when she noticed movement a good distance beyond the fence. At first, she didn't think anything of it. Animals wandered through the forest all the time.

In spots, the density of the terrain hindered clear definition, but within a minute or two, she realized it was a man, not an animal. As uneventful as it would normally be, she couldn't pull her eyes away. The man wore a cap with a long beak and thick earflaps similar to what her uncles used to wear when they hunted. But something seemed strangely odd as this man trudged along, struggling with a heavy object. When he moved out of focus, she leaned for a better look.

"Auhhh!"

This can't be. It just can't be.

Ready for a quick exit, she hesitated when he moved in her direction and stopped several hundred feet from the fence. Her perched view put him in a straight line to his back as he bent and made thrashing movements. Straining her neck once again, she pulled back in horror then grabbed a branch and swung from the tree.

<><><>

*H*urrying through the children's nighttime routine, Emily walked the halls searching for Otto's room. She stopped at several doors and listened, each time, doubting her move even more, questioning what she had seen, and finally giving up and going to her room.

As she lay in bed, she recalled her boss's words, '*What goes on around my house is none of your business.*' She thought that sounded like a good idea by then. And she came up with a logical explanation that the man in the woods was burying deer-carcass remains as her uncles had done back home. When she looked at it that way, she felt silly for allowing her imagination to get out of hand.

CHAPTER SEVENTEEN

*T*he household was bustling over a ball Donald Schillings was giving to establish his political career. Pearl was on fire, gushing to deliverymen about his donations to the needy as she tipped them and asked that they vote for her reputable boss.

When the big night arrived, Emily tucked the children in and decided to take a walk before going to bed. There was *The Adventures of Sherlock Holmes* waiting for her on the nightstand, and she didn't plan on being long. Although she hadn't planned on running into Peter.

"Emily?"

"Peter! It's nice to see you."

"You too. So… What're you doing here?"

"I'm the nanny for Mr. Schillings' children."

"You're the last person I expected to see here."

"Why's that?"

"Well. When I returned to *The Palace.* I asked Miss Bea about you. She said you broke into her office, stole cash, and ran off."

"Wow. I hope you didn't believe her."

"I knew there was another side to the story."

"The truth is, I was the one who was robbed. Someone went into my room, took all my cash, and a necklace. An heirloom."

"Now that's a shame. I'm sorry."

Peter thought for a moment. "You know…just in case. Why don't you give me a description of the necklace. I can't promise you anything, but I'll keep an eye out for it."

"Oh, thank you. Thank you so much. My hands have been tied. And I've all but put aside hope of finding it."

Emily described the necklace in detail. She was about to ask if he knew about the building plans for *The Palace* when Donald came up the path.

"Uh… It's Mr. Schillings. I'd better go," she said with a warning nod.

Emily ducked into the thickets. And Peter left in the opposite direction. She had already started toward the mansion when Donald hurried past and caught up to Peter. Alarmed, she turn back and made her way to where they were talking.

"Of all people," Mr. Schillings was saying. "I thought you were back in LA."

"I was."

"Funny you should show up here tonight. I've wanted to ask you about your visit to Las Vegas. Mainly, how the meeting with Detective Righetti went."

Emily noticed that Peter was taken off guard for a moment.

"You see, Donald, there wasn't a meeting per se. Of course, I'd heard his name, knowing he's one of your biggest adversaries. But I had never actually laid eyes on the guy. I had no idea who he was until he introduced himself. And then, well, that was the end of our conversation."

"You expect me to believe that?"

The two made a few jabs at each other. And Peter left. Moments later, one of the police officers Emily had seen at the estate on occasion, approached her boss.

Donald took a drag from his cigarette and dropped it onto a rock slab. "Get rid of him."

He put out the cigarette with a heel and hurried up the walk.

<><><>

*D*etermined to find Peter and warn him, Emily rushed through the back entrance, up to her room, into her closet, and pulled the satin gown from a hanger. Holding it next to her, she looked down at her shoes, then to the three pairs on a rack, and knew that none of them would do. Not wanting to settle on white socks, she recalled the slippers Mrs. Schillings left at Maria's bedroom door just before she disappeared. Emily had noticed them in the little girl's closet and was almost certain they would fit. She had reservations about asking if she could wear them. But Peter's life was at stake, and she hurried to Maria's room, relieved to find her still awake.

"Say, um. Those shoes your mother left for you?"

"Mm? Oh…you mean, the princes slippers?"

"Yes, those. Do you mind if I borrow them? I'd like to go to the ball for a bit."

"You can wear them all you want. But don't let Pearl catch you down there. Nathan tried that once and she pulled him back upstairs by an ear."

The young girl went to her closet and brought back soft white slippers that had a row of pearls set around each opening.

"Oh, Maria. I forgot how beautiful they are."

"Mommy had three or four of them made in different colors. I used to sneak a pair from her closet. But I don't play dress up anymore. So, you might as well make use of them." Taking off her shoes, Emily stepped into the slippers. They were slightly snug, but soft and pliable. Thanking Maria, she picked up her shoes and hurried back to her room to change.

Emily pulled the gown over her shoulders, raised her arms, and let it slide down over her hips. She zipped it up the back, and pinned her hair into a quick updo, applied rouge and lipstick, then took the stairs down to the ballroom.

Knowing how serious the matter was, she ducked into the shadows of a pillar and began to scan the room for Peter. As she looked around the cold marble, Donald walked in. He stopped at a group of people for a chat, and she crossed the room in the opposite direction. She glanced over her shoulder to check on him. And when she turned back, she came face to face with a man who was transfixed on her. He introduced himself as Gregory Lancaster the Second. She was about to make an exit, but realized that with a man by her side, it would be less likely Donald would notice her.

"May I ask your name, Miss?"

She turned back, spilling out, "E-Emmie."

"So. Where've you been all my life, Emmie?"

"Uh… Traveling abroad…."

"How exciting. I do a bit of traveling myself. Which countries have you visited of late?"

"Let's see. There's France, Germany, Paris… Well, ha, you know…Paris…as in France."

When a waiter came over with drinks. Emily recognized him as someone who had helped during one of Donald's dinner parties. She thought it was best to give him a confident smile.

The young man held the tray as Gregory picked up two glasses of champagne and handed one to her. He glanced at her as he moved on to other guests, and she flashed him a smile, hoping he wasn't one for idle gossip.

With Gregory at her side, they headed to the far side of the room, sipping champagne, while she looked for Peter. When they reached the wall, she rolled to her toes and gave a thorough scan of the crowd.

"This reminds me of my trip to Greece," Gregory said.

"Oh, really."

Emily dropped to her heels, and they continued to stroll the circumference of the room; she, sipping her drink and keeping her eyes peeled for Peter while Gregory talked of parties in Athens.

By the time they reached the other side of the room, her second glass of champagne was near empty, and the alcohol was bubbling through her like old times. That pleasant feeling was interrupted when Maria's hurtful expression, and her vow to the young girl, jarred Emily's conscience.

"You, okay?" Gregory asked, bringing her from her thoughts. "How about taking a turn outside."

Convinced that Peter hadn't come in, or had gone out for another breath of air, she agreed to step out with Gregory. They started to leave when she spotted Layla, thankfully without Moose. Unlike Peter, Emily wasn't surprised to see her at Schillings. And her presence confirmed more of what she suspected.

Emily and Gregory moved outside, following the walkway to the back yard to where the pond and waterfall were located. It had become a popular place, with a group of violinists entertaining on the bridge. She kept her search for Peter as they found a spot amongst the guests listening to the music. Sure that Mr. Schillings would be stepping out again, she watched for both men. At the same time, she wondered how to make a polite exit.

"Is anything wrong?" Gregory asked.

"No. Not really. Well…besides needing to um…." She leaned closer. "To use the *john*. You know… The drink?"

Gregory placed an arm around her shoulders. She wondered what exactly compelled him to do that, considering she just told him her bladder was ready to burst.

Curious about another group of people heading their way, she peered around the couple next to them. Well, she knew where Donald was.

"Sorry, Gregory. I've got to run."

She handed her glass to him, slipped through the tall willowy shrubs, and made her way back to the ballroom for one more search.

The lights were dimmed. And the band played a ballad as Emily circled the room looking for Peter. She was about to give up when she saw him with a woman off in a corner and rushed over, pulling him aside.

"Peter, I have to talk to you."

"My goodness, Emily. Look at you. All you need is a pair of glass slippers and you could be Cinderella."

He glanced at her feet. "Oh, but those have to be more comfortable."

Emily couldn't decide if he'd had one too many drinks or if he was playing a role. "Listen Peter, you've got to get out of here."

She started to explain when two men appeared on either side of him. They casually locked arms around each of his elbows. One of the men whispered in his ear, and he was promptly ushered from the room.

Emily watched them leave, wondering what to do. She searched out the woman Peter had been talking with and saw her conversing with a lady as if nothing had happened. Looking around, no one else seemed to have noticed either. She walked over to the woman.

"Ma'am. Did you see the men leave—"

"Are you okay, young lady?"

"It's Peter. I'm worried—"

"Peter can take care of himself. No need to worry about him."

She patted Emily's arm, smiled, and turned back to the conversation with the other woman.

Emily went to her room, wondering if she was losing her mind. She went to a window and searched the grounds, although fading daylight made it difficult to see much past the post lamps lining the driveway.

It occurred to her that Peter hadn't seemed concerned. And no one else was alarmed by his quick exit. She wondered if Donald's threatening remark was only meant for the men to make sure he left. That made sense. *Of course, that has to be it. It's settled then....* Anyway... George wasn't far away.

Sherlock Holmes forgotten, Emily prepared for bed and drifted into an exhaustive slumber.

CHAPTER EIGHTEEN

*E*arly the next morning, Emily managed to sneak away with Startoo once again to see George, not able to get the nightmare she had about Peter off her mind.

When George saw the look on her face, he stepped outside and closed the door.

"What happened?"

"I'm not sure. Maybe nothing. But... I...I think one of Donald's men harmed a friend of mine, or maybe even worse."

George marched down the steps. "Let's go," he said, turning across the yard.

"Wait. You can't go over, now."

"I know. We're going to his logging company. I've been snooping over there on Sundays for several months. Today, I'm going inside."

"Oh," she said, feeling a spark of excitement.

George was saddling his horse when his father showed up.

"Where to, so early, son?"

"Hello, Pa. We're checking on something. We'll talk later.

"Say, this is my pal, Emily. She's the replacement nanny over yonder. Emily, this is Pa. His friends call him Chatty."

Emily nodded at the slightly husky man thinking he looked much different from how he had been described.

The two young people mounted their horses and headed into the trees and to the water. George reached up, snapped a twig from a branch, and tossed it into the stream.

131

"It used to be a nice-sized creek. But the geezer made himself a private lake and ruined our swimming hole for a dam that no one's allowed to go near."

"I know. I took Nathan down to the water and found out the hard way."

"You took him to the forbidden area?"

"I did. Of course, Donald blew his stack."

George laughed. "What a little stinker for not warning you."

"Can you blame him? I remember a time when nothing felt better than a swim in the creek. Of course, Nathan didn't get a chance to swim, but he sure enjoyed himself."

"You know... I went to see Schillings after he dammed up the creek. That's when he told me Pa okayed the move for a bit of money. Turns out we owed back taxes. So, I asked if we could swim in the lake he created. The guy refused. Said it was meant for his logging company. I guess they knock down a few trees, saw them up, and hall them off. But from what I've seen, unless Schillings has bigger plans, this setup sure doesn't seem worth the trouble."

As they neared the dam, they crossed the stream. Tying the horses to a post, they headed through the trees and toward the mill. Ten minutes later, they walked around to the front where a pickup was parked along the bank.

"Is someone here?" Emily whispered.

"Nah. That thing sits there more times than not when the copter is coming in."

George looked up and searched the skies. "It usually doesn't come in on Sundays. But it looks like it will today."

"What's this all about, George?"

"I'm not certain, but... I have a feeling that it could be drugs."

He walked over and put an ear to the door, trying the knob. Convinced no one was inside, they were walking around the yard for the third time, looking for the best way in, when a helicopter swooped in over the trees. George grabbed Emily, pulled her to the ground, and they crawled into the underbrush.

When they were safely hidden, he reached over and picked weeds out of her hair.

"Sorry. Didn't hurt you, did I?"

"Besides the busted kneecaps?"

He laughed, swatting more weeds from her hair.

The helicopter landed, shut down, and three men began to carry boxes into the building. Emily noticed that one of them was Harold. When they had made their last trip inside, the pilot left in the helicopter, and Harold locked the door and drove off with the other man.

"I'll go in through one of those back windows on the second floor," George said as they made their way across the yard and around the building. He pointed to the window on the right. Lifting a nail from a shirt pocket, he fiddled with the end and dropped it back in.

"Wait right here. I'm going to fetch something I hauled over last Sunday."

He ran into the trees and came back carrying a sturdy piece of lumber with grooves and long enough to reach the second floor. They stabilized it against the window ledge, and George pointed to a rock.

"Grab that for me, will you. And hold the board."

She handed the rock over, and he dropped it next to the nail.

"Well, here goes."

Emily lowered a knee to the board and held on with a firm grip. When he was halfway up, the dogs began to bark in the distance.

"Please hurry, George. I've seen them before. They're like grizzlies."

When he reached the top, he propped himself up and used the nail to chisel breaks in the windowpane and the rock to knock out a piece of glass. Reaching in, he turned the lock and opened the window. The dogs were approaching as he slipped inside.

"George. I'm coming up."

"I've got you covered," he said, turning back and holding the board against the base as Emily made her way up. She reached the window as the two animals rounded the corner. One of the dogs leaped onto the board and began to claw its way up.

George helped Emily inside and heaved the lumber away from the building. The dog yelped as it landed upright and ran off, the other one right behind him. George closed and locked the window and positioned the rock so that it looked as if it had been thrown through the glass.

Emily looked around, flushed with excitement. They moved to the railing and gazed down to the first floor. There were several machines, cut and stacked wood, a large bin of sawdust across the room, and some other evidence of a working sawmill.

"We'd better hurry," she said, glancing back toward the window, "those dogs have an owner. The guy in the truck."

She followed George along the open area and to the first door. He tried the knob.

"Son-of-a-gun, it's locked."

The next room looked like an office, although the furnishings were sparse, with only a desk, a couple of chairs, and a filing cabinet. Emily watched George check each drawer, then tailed him back to the locked door.

"This has to be it," he said

Lifting the nail from his pocket, he tried to manipulate the lock.

"Doggonit. It's not going to work."

He pulled the nail out and shoved it into his pocket.

"Listen," Emily hissed. "I think I hear something."

She darted to the front window and looked out.

"It's Mr. Schillings in the Model T. And there's the truck right behind him."

She whipped around as he hurried over. "What do we do?"

Outside, doors slammed.

George looked down over the railing at the sawdust bin that ended somewhere beneath the steps.

"We've got no choice," he said, already halfway over.

There was a swish and another as the two landed in the sawdust, stifling coughs and sneezes as they took cover.

Moments later the door burst open.

"I was told this is our best load, so far," one of the men said.

The dogs could be heard in the distance, moving back toward the building.

"Oh, boy, here they come. Probably sniffed it out," someone said, jokingly.

"Not unless you got some in your pocket."

"Somethings sure got them worked up."

"Harold. Get those damn mutts into the cab," Donald grumbled.

When the dogs arrived, Harold went about persuading the animals into the truck as the other men stepped inside and closed the door.

"So," came Donald's voice as the men climbed the stairs," if this load lives up to their promise. This will be just the beginning."

The men's shadows flashed through the cracks in the wood where the two crouched below. They reached the top and continued along the overlook. A minute later, they started to stack boxes at the head of the stairs.

Emily's nose began to quiver. Her mouth puckered and she gasped for air. I... go... nuh... snee... eez," she whispered.

Her spasms continued as the doorknob turned, and Harold walked in.

"Grab this," someone hollered from the head of the stairs.

Harold shuffled up the steps as tears streamed down Emily's cheeks. When he neared the top, her sneeze broke.

"Hey, you getting into the stuff already?" one of the men said as they started back down.

"I was about to ask you the same thing. You got a cold or something?"

"Oh, a little," the man said, suddenly feeling the urge to sniff.

There were several more trips before the last of the group left the room upstairs and rumbled down the steps. Finally, the door closed.

Emily and George waited for the vehicles to drive out of the yard before scrambling from the bin.

"Look!" Emily said, pointing to where sunlight burst through the broken window. "How could they not have noticed?"

"That's it," George said, "you're coming home with me."

"No. I can't. The children. I can't desert them. I'm serious George. Everything'll be okay. I mean, what's so different from last week, or a month back?"

"So, when do we call the police? Do you have any doubts about what's in those boxes?"

"They didn't come right out and say. And since we have no proof. I mean…what do we tell the police? We have to keep in mind that Schillings has a number of friends with the police force. At the very least, I need to find a way to get the children out of there first."

"All right. But I'm going to try to persuade the folks to go uptown to talk to a lawyer first thing in the morning. Hopefully, they'll figure out what to do."

<><><>

*W*hen Emily made it back to Schillings, she was heading to her room to change clothes when she heard weeping from Maria's room. She hurried over, swung the door open, and found the young girl drenched in tears.

"Oh Emily," she wailed, "something terrible has happened. Our uncle Bud died last night."

Emily closed the door and rushed to where the girl sat on the floor next to her bed.

"I'm sorry Maria, I'm so sorry."

She sat and placed an arm around her.

"Your uncle was such a nice man. And he loved you guys very much."

"We love him too. Now he's gone. Just like Mommy."

Another burst of sobs shook Maria's shoulders. Emily pulled the little girl into her arms and let her weep.

"Maria," she said, after giving her some time. "Cry for them. It's good to release the pain. But I just want you to know that I believe Bud and your mother are okay."

Maria stopped crying and looked up. "Really? You do?"

"Yes. I do. With all my heart."

The little girl began to sniffle again. "But we're being sent away, and we won't ever see you again."

"You're leaving? Are you sure?"

"Yes. I heard father tell Pearl that he and Otto are going to the funeral. When Pearl asked if we were going, he said no. He told her to make sure our things are packed because we're leaving."

Emily tried to stay calm, but this was all happening too fast.

"Did he say where you're going?"

"No. Just that someone will be here to pick us up at six tomorrow night. When I heard that, I came up here."

Emily was sickened, and yet she wanted to believe the children would be better off wherever they were going. From everything she knew, it was most likely a boarding school.

"I'm sure you'll go somewhere very nice."

137

"But I don't want to go to a strange place. Especially not without you. And what about our ponies?"

"I'll find out where you are, and I'll go see you. And I'm sure at some point you'll be able to have the ponies brought to you."

Maria was comforted by Emily's confidence. But Emily was troubled not only by the children's loss, but because if Uncle Bud hadn't died, they wouldn't be leaving. She didn't understand why their father refused his uncle's offer to take them in. And now that he was gone, they were being sent away. Something was terribly wrong.

Emily pulled Maria close and kissed her forehead, filled with anger and disappointment toward Mr. Schillings. *"Please God, don't let anything happen to these children. They've been through enough. Please bring them a miracle."*

Whenever Emily set her mind to prayer–which to her grandmother, would've meant more than once or twice a month–there was always an answer. The lesson should have been learned long ago. But like so many times before, it took an event, or several, to waken her.

"Maria? Remember that first day we met in the garden?"

"When you told me God was to infinity."

"Yes. I hope you always remember that."

"I will."

"He listens when you talk to him, you know. My grandmother made sure I knew that. I haven't always listen the way I should. But I do believe."

"Me too."

"You'll feel very sad for a time, Maria. But you and Nathan will get through this."

Emily saw relief in the young girl's eyes. And as much as she wanted to quietly slip away, she would stick around to see the children off and get the license plate number before she left.

That night, after the children were asleep, Emily lay in bed and wrestled with her thoughts. She wasn't convinced that her boss hadn't seen her and George hiding beneath the steps. And now that drugs seemed to be involved, and things were looking more sinister, including what she had seem from the tree branch near the fence line, she had a sick feeling about Peter.

As dawn approached and she still hadn't slept, she got up and dressed, certain what she must do. Fear pumped through her veins as she stepped into the hallway and turned toward the back entry. All was quiet except for the sounds of her shoes tiptoeing across the marble floor. She made it halfway down the stairway when there was a clicking sound like a door...or maybe footsteps.

Standing firm, she looked up, waiting for the next sound. When it didn't come, she hurried down the steps, out the back door, and to the barn.

The moon beamed full as she rode bareback, balancing a shovel and a flashlight across her lap. There was just enough light from the approaching dawn to see her way across the arena and to the riding trails. When she reached the fence, she secured the horse then listened to make sure she was alone before climbing over.

Lining herself up with the lookout tree, she turned on the flashlight. Dry leaves and branches crackled beneath her feet as she walked through the forest, every so often, looking back to make sure she was still on track. Nearing the area where she had seen the action, the hair on her neck and arms pricked like needles. A few more steps, and there it was—the recently overturned earth. Her breath caught in a gasp, wishing she had been wrong.

Dreading what she might find, and in a hurry to be finished, her hands trembled as she laid the flashlight on the ground and began to work the shovel with all the power she could muster. Jab, after jab, after jab like someone gone mad, she drove deeper, heaving dirt aside.

With her arms ready for another hit, she sensed someone nearby. Driving the blade into the ground, she scanned the wooded area. But there was nothing but an eerie calm and the sound of birds beginning to chirp as soft light filtered through the trees and down into the hole she was uncovering.

She raised her arms again and slammed the blade in deep. This time it struck something. She gripped the handle and scraped dirt aside, revealing a blue shirt and part of a hand. A muffled shriek escaped from her clinched jaw as she dropped the shovel and stumbled back.

To her right, hurried footsteps crunched over fallen leaves. For an instant, she froze, then shot through the trees, letting her instincts lead her way. When she reached the fence, she grabbed a post with both hands, stepped up, and hurled herself over, releasing the rope that held Startoo. Mounting the horse with fear-driven agility, she nudged the filly and pulled the reins in the other direction when she noticed Paul heading toward her on horseback.

The roof of the mansion came into view, and Emily realized she had no choice but to jump the fence. She had lined up the horse when Paul caught up with her, grabbed the reins and forced Startoo to a stop.

"What're you doing? She's not ready for a jump like that."

Emily glanced around expecting someone to come out of the forest. Only why would they bother when Paul was there to take care of her. She noticed him look in that direction.

"Listen," he said, turning back to her. "I can only guess why you're set on ignoring me. But I could think of better reasons to resent someone."

She nudged Startoo again. But Paul pulled the reins tighter.

"Look at me!"

His order took her by surprise. Unable to stop herself, she looked into his eyes, surprised there were no signs of cruelty. And yet, after the horrifying discovery just minutes earlier, she feared trickery, like almost everything else since she stepped from the train.

"Well… I think she could've made it," she said, sliding from the horse, hurrying to the fence, and climbing over.

"Emily. I need to talk to you!"

For an instant, she almost stopped and turned to him, but instead, she sped through the grove toward the mansion.

She took off her muddy shoes, left them at the back door, and scrambled up the steps. Finding Nathan already up and dressed, she grabbed his hand and took him to Maria's room.

"Okay, you guys. This has to be quick. I have to leave. But I'll send someone to pick you up."

It was time. She would turn herself in. But first, she had a story for law enforcement.

She placed a hand on Maria's shoulders. "Go down and tell Pearl that you guys are packing up your things. Bring back a snack and both of you stay right here."

"Where're you going?"

Emily glanced at the door. "I don't have time to explain. You have to trust me. Please. Just do as I say."

She gave them each a hug and rushed out.

Once in her bedroom, she pushed the back of a chair under the doorknob. Scrambling around the room and into the closet, she gathered her belongings and stuffed everything into her bag.

There was a tree branch off the porch that would be an easy exit. She was about to head that way when someone tried the knob.

"Open up!" Donald shouted, banging on the door.

"I said, open up!"

She had only taken a few steps when the door flew open and sent the chair flying.

He sailed across the room, grabbed her by the shoulders, and shoved her against the wall, her head spinning from the impact.

"You had it so good. Damn you, woman!"

He punched a fist into the wall, let her go, and walked away as she sank to the floor.

After he left, she pulled herself up and went to try the door. Discovering that it was locked from the outside, she went out onto the porch. It was impossible to know who it was, but she saw a shadow move below. It looked like the end of the line for her.

Her head throbbed, and she was tired from the digging, tired from troubled sleep, and from all the weight she had carried for so long. Ready to give up, she went to lay across the bed.

When she heard someone open the door a few minutes later, she didn't bother to look up.

"Are you okay?" Maria whispered.

Emily's eyes popped open, and she leaped out of bed, grabbed the girl by her shoulders and guided her to the door.

"Please, Maria. Go back to your room. And remember. I love you and Nathan, no matter what."

"We love you too."

Maria hesitated, tears streaming. Emily gave her a gentle nudge. "I'll be okay. Just do as I say."

When Maria ran off, Emily grabbed her bag. She pulled the strap over her head, tucked it under an arm and dashed into the hallway. As she neared the staircase, Donald came from around the waterfall and grabbed her by an elbow. She wrapped her other arm around the railing and yanked it free.

CHAPTER NINETEEN

*D*onald Schillings gazed down at Emily lying near the bottom of the staircase. Paul came from beneath the balcony, lifted her into his arms, and glanced up at his boss before rushing out the front exit.

Dogs were yelping in the distance as Paul carried Emily to the barn. He grabbed a blanket, draped it around her and tucked it in, making sure her bag wasn't pulling on her neck. She moaned and fell limp against his right shoulder as he flung another blanket over her and hurried to the waiting horse.

He gathered Emily's willowy frame into a firm grip and placed a foot in the stirrup. With his left arm wrapped around her, the reins and the horse's mane in his right hand, he mounted the horse in one swift move. Repositioning his hold on Emily, he tucked the blankets in and gave the horse a nudge. They moved quickly from hiding, across the lawn, out the front gate, heading south through the forest.

With the yelping force of dogs in the distance, Paul tightened his hold on Emily and headed down an embankment, across a brook, and up the bank on the other side. They followed alongside a fence until they reached a broken railing. Tucking the reins in, making it easier for the horse as it headed back home, Paul dismounted with Emily secure in his arms.

Stepping over the fallen planks of the fence, he crossed the road and walked to the nearest farmhouse. He made his way across the yard, took the steps up to the porch, and tapped the door with a foot.

An elderly man cracked the door open.

"Please, sir. She needs a doctor."

When the man saw Emily, he swung the door open.

"Oh, for goodness sake. Come in. I'll call an ambulance."

Paul glanced back across the road. "I don't think we should wait for an ambulance."

A woman approached, noticing the protruding gash on Emily's forehead. "I'll get something for that."

She reached for a set of keys on a stand and handed them to her husband. "You'd better run them to the hospital, Sid."

As Samuel settled in the back seat with Emily, the woman hurried to the car. She covered Emily's head with a gauze wrap and helped Paul make her comfortable. Lifting the bag from around her neck and laying it on the seat, she touched her arm.

"I'm sure it's broken."

◇◇◇

*W*hen they reached Saint Mary's General Hospital in San Francisco, attendants rushed Emily to the trauma unit. Paul gave the nurse appropriate information and settled in for a long wait.

Several hours later, Doctor Barnes walked into the waiting area and spoke to a nurse. She handed him a chart and when the doctor had finished looking it over, Paul approached and introduced himself.

"How is Emily doing?"

"Well… Our main concern is a concussion, but we're keeping a close eye on her. And from what I've seen in my years of practice, she seems to be suffering from exhaustion which means rest will be her friend for the next several days. With care, I believe she'll come out of it just fine. Other than that, she has a broken arm and a number of bumps and bruises."

"Say, Doctor Barnes. I'd like to ask you something… I, um… I had to take her on horseback to reach help.

145

Luckily, the horse had a smooth gait. And I was careful to hold her in a way that limited movement. Do you think it might've... That it might have hurt her?"

"I'm sure it didn't help. But it doesn't seem to have done any lasting damage."

The doctor looked at his watch. "I have to go. But just to let you know, we'll keep her in intensive care until morning. She'll be in two-fourteen around ten. Oh, yes, there will be someone outside the door to check your I.D. An aide will be sitting with Emily for the time being. Of course, when you're visiting, she'll be able to leave unless you request otherwise."

◇◇◇

*W*hen Paul walked into Emily's room the next day, he found her lying amongst a mound of pillows and blankets. Her head was wrapped in a bandage, and an arm was in a cast resting on a pillow. A nurse stood at her bedside, adjusting an I.V. She took a thermometer from under her tongue and wrote the information in a chart. Paul waited until she had returned the chart to its spot at the foot of the bed before he approached.

"She looks peaceful."

"I don't think she'll do much moving around for a while," the nurse said. "Her temperature is up a little. But her blood pressure and pulse are what's expected."

"That's good to know."

Once the nurse tucked in the covers and left, Paul moved to her bedside.

A young doctor entered the second-floor nurse's station to make patient reviews. He noticed a cloth bag lying on the counter, although he didn't pay much attention to it as he moved it over to make room for a chart. When something slid from the bag onto the table, he picked it up.

"Carolyn, where did this blue bag come from?"

He set the chart aside and stared at the unforgettable drawing of a girl riding a white dove on the cover of a notebook.

The nurse poked her head around the corner. "It belongs to Emily Rezell in two-fourteen. Some elderly man dropped it off. Said it was left in his car when he brought her in. Poor thing had a bad fall. Oh, and Doctor Barnes was just looking for you. That young lady is his patient.

"Doctor? Is everything okay?"

"I hope so."

He slid the notebook into the bag and rushed up the hallway.

A minute later, he burst into two-fourteen. He exchanged greetings with Paul who was standing on the other side of Emily's bed, gazing out a window. After washing his hands, the doctor moved to the foot of the bed and read through the patient chart. When he had finished checking her vitals, he set the stethoscope aside and turned his attention to Paul as he walked over, slid his hands around the rail and gazed at Emily.

"She hasn't moved since I came in."

"Your concern is understandable. But considering what she's been through, her vitals are in the normal range, and from reading her chart, even better than from an hour ago. I'm sure by morning there will be noticeable changes."

"After a good night sleep."

"Absolutely. Sleep is the best thing for her right now.

"Say... I'm Doctor Michael Foster. I'm working with Doctor Barnes. Emily and I met on a train last year. We spent quite a bit of time together. And she mentioned wanting to find a friend of her mother's. By any chance, is that you?"

Paul glanced at Emily, and back to the doctor.

"Yes. It's me she was looking for. I'm... I'm Samuel Dimsmoore... Um... Paul Samuel Dimsmoore is my official name. She knows me as Paul, although I'm known as Samuel to most. As far as she's concerned, I'd like to keep it that way until I'm able to talk with her. I've already discussed this with the head nurse."

"Yes, of course.

"Hmm. Samuel Dimsmoore. You have no idea how many times I wished I had asked her what your name was. I had no way of contacting her to make sure she was okay and that she found you."

"It was a miracle she found me at all. Because I haven't lived in San Francisco for years. Thankfully, she had my uncle's address and sent him a letter, although without a return address. But while working as a nanny, it seems she tried to reach out to me."

Michael looked down at her bandaged head. "How exactly did she fall?"

"Let me just say that its under investigation. Now, what led up to the fall. I don't know, except that early this morning she came barreling out of the woods. She jumped a fence, mounted her horse, and took off like a scared rabbit. Right after she dismounted and left for the mansion, I saw a man come from the same area and head that way too. I thought about it a little too long. And by the time I got there she was lying near the bottom of the stairway."

"Oh, dear."

Samuel stepped around the bed and Michael followed him across the room.

"I didn't see it happen. Although it didn't look good, him standing there staring down at her."

"Him?"

"Yes, her boss. Donald Schillings."

Michael thought for a moment. "Schillings... Mm. That name sounds familiar."

"From what I hear, he planned to run for mayor of San Francisco."

"Ooh, yes...I do know who he is. This is just unbelievable."

"You can say that again. Here I thought I was doing the right thing...being careful, taking it slow with her. But I messed-up."

"You messed up? Do you mind telling me what this is about?"

Samuel took a seat, and Michael joined him.

"I guess the best place for me to start is when my uncle brought me the letter from Emily. She gave three different dates when we could meet at a place call Mack's House of Food. And she also mentioned that one of the waitresses found a job for her."

"So, you met her at the restaurant."

"Well. I didn't get the letter soon enough to meet her the first time. But the minute I got it I went over. No one seemed to know a thing. Although everything pointed to a waitress named Maxine. When Emily didn't show up on that second date, I confronted her. Still nothing. And when she didn't show on the third date, I tried to force the information out of the woman. She became belligerent. I never gave up, though. Finally, I managed to pry it out of her that she had taken her to a... Well..."

Samuel gave it some thought. "From what I heard... It seems that Emily is suffering from exhaustion. And because you obviously have a meaningful relationship with her, I'm going to tell you something in confidence."

"Of course."

"So... That waitress? She took Emily to a... To a brothel."

"You can't be serious."

"I am. Although it looks like she didn't stay long."

"You said she was a nanny."

"Yes, after leaving the brothel. I talked the waitress into confessing where she was. Actually...I hounded her until she got so frustrated she let it slip."

Samuel sighed again and leaned back in his chair. "One day as Maxine was leaving work, I showed up with bribe money I got from selling my pickup. By then, my impatience had turned to anger and I demanded to know where the brothel was. In her frustration, she blared that Emily was at Donald Schillings. I handed the money over. But as the bus came up the street, she gave me payback for pressuring her."

"And the payback was?"

"I can't remember the exact words she used, but it went something like, *'If you think you're so tough, how about this.'* Then she went on to tell me that Emily called the restaurant while I was there waiting for her. But after she was given my description, she didn't want to meet me."

"You're description? You mean, your color?"

"Yes. But that ridiculous waitress had no idea what drove me."

"I'll have to say... Emily refusing to meet you doesn't sound like the person I met on the train."

"I agree, Doctor, but...."

Samuel tapped his fingers on the armrest of his chair. "You have to have known her grandfather to understand. And by the look on Emily's face when I showed up at Schillings, and by the way she reacted towards me at times, it seemed that the old guy had an enormous influence on her."

"So... You say you went to Schillings and met Emily. Then you left without her, and returned at some point to find her near the bottom of the stairs?"

"No, I went there and stayed. You see. After what the waitress said, I couldn't just show up at Schillings and tell Emily about.... Well, about everything that happened when I was working for her grandfather. And most important, she needed a chance to have a new perspective and to shun whatever misguided values or fears he put on her."

Samuel scratched his head. "I came so close to telling her who I was several times. At the last minute, just before her fall, I intended to, but... Now I could kick myself for not going after her."

"So, how were you able to set yourself up with Schillings?"

"I know that men of his stature are always looking for help. Luckily, I had contact with someone who was able to recommend me for hire as a stableman. Undercover, of course.

"At first, I thought Schillings had rescued Emily. But it didn't take long for me to become concerned over what sort of a man he was. The first clue was when I talked with one of the housekeepers...Gabriel. When I questioned her about Schillings, she became nervous and zipped her mouth. He had asked me to keep an eye on her brother and make sure he wasn't stealing from the outbuildings. That was confirmed. And after talking with Gabriel, I had more questions. When I mentioned Emily, she said she didn't know much about her, except that she was always kind. But she seemed to get into one fix or another."

"Now that doesn't sound like her either."

"I'm beginning to think it does," Samuel corrected him. "I could see her heart and how much she cared about the children. But I have a feeling she was used to living on the edge. Finding herself at the brothel and then at Schillings is proof of that."

Samuel gazed across the room at Emily peacefully sleeping. "She was a wonderful nanny. But at times it seemed she was carrying the weight of the world on her shoulders."

Footsteps came up the hallway, and the men rose and walked toward Emily's bedside as Doctor Barnes walked into the room.

"Doctor Foster, hello," the older doctor said as he went to wash his hands before joining the two.

"You know each other?"

Michael glanced at Samuel. "We do now."

"And... Emily?"

"I met her on a train last year. We spent several nights together."

Michael's face turned red. "Let me explain."

Doctor Barnes chuckled, picked up a stethoscope, and lowered the bedrail.

"There's no need to explain. I know you well enough that none is needed."

Doctor Barnes checked Emily's vitals and both doctors looked over her chart. Later, as they were on the way out the door, Michael turned to Samuel.

"I'll be out of town for several days. But I'll check on Emily when I return."

"Thank you for letting me know. And I'm certain she'll be happy to see you."

CHAPTER TWENTY

Not quite awake, Emily moaned and stirred, troubled by dreams. She opened her eyes as Samuel appeared in the doorway. He acknowledged the aide sitting at a corner window, who, upon seeing him, gathered her belongings and left.

As Samuel walked toward Emily's bed, she sank back into her pillow. Hesitating for a moment, Samuel slowed his pace.

"Listen, Emily. I'm here as a friend. I'm your friend.

When she relaxed, he stepped to the bedside table. "It's nice to see you're awake.

"Do you recognize me?"

She nodded, groggily, pointing to the pitcher of water.

"You thirsty? Here, let me help you."

He filled a glass with water, moved to the bedside, and helped lift her head so that she could drink freely. After satisfying her thirst, Emily lay back on her pillow and drifted off with thoughts of asking him why he was there.

Later that day, Doctor Barnes stepped through the doorway and motioned Samuel over.

"I've got news," he said, taking him by an elbow as they walked into the hallway.

"Doctor? Is Emily okay?"

"Yes, she's fine. It's Donald Schillings. I was informed that someone brought attempted murder charges against him."

"Oh, boy." Samuel glanced at Emily through the doorway. "And to think I allowed her to stay there with him."

"Now don't beat yourself up. From what I'm learning, he's fooled a lot of people."

"Trust me Doctor, I never thought he was a saint.

"So, what happened, anyway?"

"It looks like Schillings may have arranged for a couple of his men to kill a private detective. Luckily, the guy managed to escape. Of course, Schillings denies everything. He says it was a setup to make him look bad. And that he only wanted them to rough the guy up a bit. At any rate, they'll be able to keep him in jail as they do a thorough search of his home and sift through reports coming in."

"It's a relief, doctor. And thank you for keeping me informed."

"I knew it would ease your mind to know he's in jail.

"Oh… I hear you'll be taking overnight duty."

"Yes, and you know I'm more than happy to sit with her.

*O*nce again, Emily wrestled with nightmares. She sat up, gasping for air. Samuel rose from the corner chair and went to her bedside. She turned to the man who had been more of a challenge than anything, from the moment he appeared in the barn doorway.

"Are you okay?"

Emily sighed and lay back on her pillow. "Dreams. Endless dreams."

She adjusted herself and gazed at the man she knew as Paul, fully awake and curious as to why he was there.

"You've been here all along, haven't you." she said. "How long has it been, anyway?"

"I've been here for the most part, and this is your fifth day.

"So, Emily. Do you remember falling down the stairs?"

"No…I don't."

"Well...I found you near the bottom of the front staircase. Donald Schillings was above, gazing down at you."

"That doesn't sound good."

She touched her bandaged head and looked down at her cast. "Must've been *some* fall."

"I'd say so. Do you remember anything? Anything at all?"

She thought for a moment. "Running. I recall running. Or maybe it was the sound. I'm not sure...."

"Wait a minute.... I was in my room, and.... Maria came in. She was....

"Paul! Are the children okay?"

Emily clutched the bedrail and pulled herself up. "Have you gone back to check on them?"

"There was no need. Schillings is in jail. And I was told the children are staying with a nurse who's with the police force."

Emily sighed and settled back against the pillow.

"That's good to know. I was so worried about them. But I'm not surprised about Donald Schillings."

She tried to recall what happened just prior to her fall. But all she saw was the fear in Maria's eyes as the little girl turned and walked out the door.

Emily closed her eyes and concentrated, putting herself at the head of the stairs with Donald. But nothing came to her...except....

Wait a minute. I was riding Startoo across the arena with just enough light to see my way. There were trees, and... I had a shovel....

"Oh, my goodness!

"Paul? Did they find the body?"

"A Body? What, body?"

"Someone wearing a blue shirt. Buried in the trees."

Samuel's voice was raw. "Is that what you were doing? Hunting bodies?"

"Just the one. Out past the arena."

"I heard nothing about that. I doubt the police even know."

His eyes were ablaze as he leaped from his chair and headed across the room. He turned at the door, shook his head and sighed as he stormed off.

Not sure why he had left so angry, Emily picked a magazine off the nightstand, hoping to forget the vision she uncovered in the trees. Finally, she clicked on the television and soon fell asleep.

*W*hen Paul returned later that evening, Emily pulled herself up as he took a seat next to her bed. His eyes were no longer ablaze, but sad.

"They found something, didn't they."

"I'm afraid so. Gabriel's brother, Erwin."

"Oh no. I didn't realize Erwin was her brother. That's terrible. Poor Gabriel."

"It sounds like his body was moved from Schillings' property. Someone found it in a shallow grave near Lobos creek a couple days ago."

Emily sighed and lay back on the pillow. "Poor Gabriel," she said again. "She has to be so upset."

Tears welled and rolled down her cheeks. "Do you know what happened?"

"The theory is that after Erwin's father left his mother with five children to raise, he got mixed-up with the wrong crowd."

"I knew things weren't right with Gabriel from the first. I should've done something."

"What could you have done? Erwin made his choices. It's heartbreaking, for sure. And I'm sorry you had to find him. Though you can't take responsibility for what happened. It's important that you allow yourself time to heal before concerning yourself with anything else."

"But I feel so bad for Gabriel and her family. And poor Erwin. He was just trying to help."

"I know. I know. It doesn't seem fair. And I understand the emotions. But right now, I think you should get some rest."

Emily had to admit this whole thing was draining, and she was finding it hard to keep her eyes open.

"Mm. Maybe I will nap."

"That's the best thing for you. And…it's late.

"So… I'm heading home for the night. But I'll be back tomorrow."

Emily watched him walk across the room, closing her eyes and drifting off before he made it to the door.

*T*he next morning, Emily was relieved when a nurse removed her IV. She had slept without dreams and felt clear of mind. Then she recalled what happened to Gabriel's brother.

Samuel came in as she gazed down at her breakfast, thinking how sad it was that Erwin would never enjoy a good meal again.

"You don't like pancakes?"

"I love them. It just doesn't feel right at the moment."

"The pancakes?"

"No. To eat, after what happened…you know."

"Listen, Emily. I understand it's not easy. But I want you to try to put it out of your mind. There's nothing you can do to change a thing. And something else. If you don't eat, your body won't heal like it's supposed to. And the quicker you heal, the sooner you'll be discharged.

"At least eat the eggs."

Emily pushed the pancakes aside.

"Did they give you an idea when I'll be discharged?"

"The last I heard was three or four days."

"That soon.

"I'm not sure where I'll go."

"No need to worry. That's being taken care of."

Emily was surprised that arrangements were being made for her. Her plan had been to turn herself in. But she wanted to see the children first. She hoped they weren't frightened, being taken away, and unable to say goodbye to her. It was bad enough that their uncle was gone.

"Do you think I'll be able to see Maria and Nathan?"

"One would think so.

"Say… I'm heading to an appointment. And on the way back, I'll stop by and check with Social Services to see if I can find out more."

Samuel was getting ready to leave when an aide came in with a wheelchair and announced that he was taking Emily for an x-ray.

"Give the young lady a minute to take in some breakfast, if you will, please," Samuel said as he headed across the room.

At the door, he looked back at Emily and mouthed, *eat your eggs*, then disappeared up the hallway.

She picked up her fork and mashed up the eggs, wondering what Paul would think if he knew the details of her past and her plans to turn herself into the police… Not only what Paul would think, but everyone else she had come to know and care about.

A nurse was taking Emily's vitals when Samuel returned that afternoon. After she left, Emily noticed Paul looking out the window deep in thought. There was so much about him she didn't understand, and she intended to find the answers. But first, there was something else pressing on her mind.

"Paul. I need to talk to you."

He went to her bed and sat. "Is everything okay?"

"Yes. It's just that several days ago when everything was still a blur, I think I saw... Or maybe it was just that I thought I heard...."

She dropped her eyes. "Oh, forget it. I'm sure it was just a dream."

"You're talking about Doctor Michael Foster, aren't you. The man you met on the train."

"You mean...he *was* here?"

"Yes. And he seems like a nice young man. He's working with Doctor Barnes. I'm sure he'll be back in a day or two."

Emily's spirits soared, knowing Michael was so close. *He led you on, silly girl,* came the voice of doubt. *Remember how he snuck off the train without telling you*?

"He'll be back," Samuel assured her.

"It doesn't matter."

Yet it did. It mattered a whole lot. She rubbed the bandage on her head. "Does this make me look like a mummy?"

"Hm. Just a little."

Samuel smiled, stood, and reached for a magazine from the nightstand. "But I might add, a very attractive one.

"Say, young lady. I hear you got up on your own for a while. And that's good. But I also heard the nurse remind you to take it easy for the rest of the day. So, I'll tell you what." He nodded to the easy chair in the corner. "I'm going over there and look through this magazine while you rest."

He started off, but she reached for his arm.

"I want to talk."

Stepping back, he took a seat. "Okay, what would you like to talk about?"

"I'm trying to understand a few things. Like… Why are you going through all this trouble for me?"

His startled reaction, the creased brow and tightened jawline took Emily by surprise.

"What… Am I going to die or something?"

"No. You're not going to die."

"But why are you here? I'm glad you are. It's just that. As you recall, we weren't exactly buddies back at Schillings."

He rolled up the magazine and used it to tap a palm.

"There is something I've wanted to talk to you about. But… I don't think this is the time. Let's wait until you feel better."

"I feel fine. In fact, I feel great. Except for this disturbing head bandage and my arm wrap. And now you've got me curious. Just…tell me what it is."

"I'm reluctant to bring this up at the moment. But if you insist. And if you're sure you feel well enough."

"Yes. I'm sure."

"So… There was a letter you wrote to Samuel Dimsmoore. Do you still want to find him?"

She raised herself up to get a better look at him. "Yes. Of course, I do."

His forehead gleamed as he rolled the magazine tighter. "This may seem like an odd question, but... Did you tell anyone you didn't want to meet him?"

"No. Why would I do that?"

"Oh, dear."

"Paul? How'd you know about Samuel? Was I talking in my sleep?"

He dropped the magazine on the stand and stood.

"Listen Emily. I don't know why this is so difficult for me to say. But the truth is, that… I'm Samuel…birthname, Paul Samuel Dimsmoore, and I'm—"

"You're… *Samuel*!"

"I know I should've told you sooner."

"Then why didn't you? Oh, my goodness. Why'd you keep it from me?"

"I'm sorry. And maybe it's no excuse, but I was told you didn't want to see me because... Well... Because I'm Black."

"Who told you that?"

"The waitress at—"

"Macks House of Food? Maxine?"

"That's the one."

"Oh, that woman. I was afraid she was going to do something like that. I just knew it!

"But Paul... I-I mean... Samuel. Look at me. I'm not exactly Snow White. And you know what? It sounds like she's the one with the problem."

"Probably.

"But if you recall, your reaction when I arrived at Schillings was not a pleasant one."

"Oh, yes. I do recall that," Emily said, embarrassed. "I'm sorry. And I admit I was upset when you showed up. But it wasn't personal. You see, I expected to be in charge of the lessons, the horses, the whole works. I had it all planned out. And it was a big deal for me. A real big deal.

"Even so... My disappointment was short-lived. It was other things I couldn't get past.

"Let me ask you this. Did Mr. Schillings expect you to spy for him? You know, on his help?"

"Uh... I was hired as the stableman. But there was a little of that too."

"Well, there you are. And don't forget. You weren't always pleasant."

"Don't you see. I was worried about you. Sometimes worry is mistaken for anger."

Emily looked into his eyes and recalled when Samuel stopped her from jumping Startoo over the fence and said he needed to talk to her.

"I can see that."

"One thing that had me concerned was that you did as you pleased, almost daring to be caught. I mean, I didn't expect Schillings to be a murderer or anything like that. But I questioned his ethics."

"So, why didn't you just take a chance and tell me who you were?"

"Believe me, I waited for the right opportunity from the first day. But I was afraid that if you knew…. Well….

"Listen Emily… I tried to tell you several times, even as you ran for the house just before you fell…or whatever happened at the head of the stairs. Another thing, and why I was so concerned was that I saw you take the horse out of the yard…twice. In fact, that last time, I was planning to tell you when you returned with mud on your shoes and pants. Remember? You refused to talk to me and rushed back to the house?"

"I remember. But, what about the traps I found in the barn? Why'd you leave one on the neighbor's property? You could've killed one of their dogs."

"Emily…I found those. Harold was bragging about the fur he caught setting traps across the property line. I guess when he was much younger, he used to hunt with an old guy that lived over the hill. Because of the deer crossing on Schillings' side, he didn't like to set traps there, but now and then he still set them a few feet onto the neighbor's property all the way up to the waterway. I didn't know much about what was going on, but I knew something wasn't right. So, I went over and found as many traps as I could and stored them in the stable."

"I'm sorry. I didn't….

"Uuh. Wait a minute! Y-you're Samuel."

"Yes. That's what I just said."

"But… You knew my mother."

"Yes, I knew her."

Emily tried to process the information that had been such an emotional part of her life.

"So then… Did you know my father?"

"Yes…I know him."

"You mean you knew him. He died too."

Samuel moaned, beginning to pace beside her bed.

"Your father didn't die."

Samuel stopped to gaze at her. "He would've given his *life* to save your mother's."

The shock of his words took her breath. Tears rolled down her cheeks. "How do you know all this? Do you know where he is? Do you know why he left me?"

"Emily, you're getting worked up. The Doctor's not going to like this. Listen. Tomorrow, I promise I'll tell you anything you want to know. Right now, you need to rest."

"No. I can't wait for tomorrow. For once in my life, I want the truth. I want to know about my mother. I want to know where my father is. And I want to know why he left me with my grandfather."

She struggled to hold in a sob.

"Grandfather has always grieved over my mother. It hurt him to even look at me. Do you know what that was like?"

Samuel sank to the chair.

"Oh, Emily. I'm so very sorry. If I'd known you were unhappy, I would never have left you there…."

Blood drained from Emily's face. Her tears stopped.

Samuel stood again and tried to take her hand, but she pushed him away.

"I've wanted so much to tell you. I tried."

"Then why didn't you? Why did you and everyone else lie to me? Tell me that. Just tell me… *Why?*"

Her sobs broke. And Samuel set a box of Kleenex on the bed. She grabbed tissue with her free hand, dabbing her eyes and wiping her nose, dropping the Kleenex, grabbing more, and sobbing as if she would never stop. Each time he tried to take her hand, she pulled it back, until he reached again and held tight.

"Please, listen. I'm not trying to make excuses. But I didn't even know about you until you were three years old. As soon as I heard. I went to see you."

Her sobs stopped, not sure what he just said but wanting to hear more.

"What did you just say?"

"I went to Illinois to see you. You were out in the yard with your grandmother."

"You saw me with...Grandmother?"

"I was standing in a grove of trees next to the driveway entrance. Both of you looked so happy. You were running with the dogs, tumbling on the grass, and laughing. Your grandmother was sitting on the front steps, laughing with you. I just couldn't see taking you away from that. I wanted so much to walk over and talk with you, but...."

He shook his head. "That wouldn't have gone over well. And I didn't want to upset you."

Emily wanted to stay angry. It was as if she needed someone to pay for her pain. Still...she had an overwhelming need to reason with herself. *After all these years, I have a father. He's right here beside me by choice, with the same warm blood running through his veins as the blood in mine.*

"Grandmother and I were happy back then. Us two together always made the best of things."

Emily picked up the tissue box and dropped it back onto the bed. "She died when I was seven."

"Oh no. I'm sorry. I'm really sorry."

"It wasn't that I lived in a state of misery every second. I mean... I had happy days. But...there were times when it was a real struggle. Some bad things happened. And I hated that they kept me in the dark about you and my mother. They wanted me to believe you were dead. Why would they do that? Why'd you leave my mother? And what happened between you and my grandfather? Please. I deserve to hear the truth."

164

"I agree with you. And I'll do my best to give you what you need.

"So... Where do I begin?"

"Grandfather."

"Okay. Let me think. Well....

"I recall this one day that Rachael and I were in the barn. She was trying to convince me that we should elope. When I told her I'd like to sit down and have a talk with her father, she said it wouldn't work. Then she confided to me that she was surprised he had given in and hired me, because she learned from her brothers that years earlier her uncle had joined an all-Black band. And when he was murdered, her father, your grandfather, became filled with unforgiving rage. I knew he wasn't impressed with me from the first, but until then, I wasn't sure why."

"Still... I've wondered many times that if we had eloped, if he would have eventually come to accept the matter of my—"

"That your skin is darker than his."

Samuel looked at his hands. "A lot darker."

"How'd you end up at my grandfather's anyway? And what about you and my mother? How'd you get together?"

"You see, it was twenty-one years ago when I'd been wandering around for about six months hoping to find direction. Someone had just stolen all of my belongings. And I was desperate when I stopped at your grandfather's farm looking for a job. He turned me down, flat-out. And I'm not sure what happened, besides him knowing I asked for little pay, but... one of your uncles picked me up as I was walking alongside the road a few days later."

"It was probably in the middle of harvest, right?"

"I'm sure it was. All I had were the clothes on my back. I lived down by the creek. And one day your mother showed up with food, a tent, bedding, and clean clothes."

Emily grabbed a pillow from the foot of her bed and used it to prop herself up. "I'll bet that made you feel good."

"Yep. It sure did."

"Did you love her?"

"Oh Emily. I loved your mother more than you could ever imagine. She was my first love."

His eyes welled. And Emily reached for a tissue, holding it out to him. He wiped his tears away, gathered up the rest of the tissue and tossed everything into the waste basket, then took a seat.

Emily waited for him to settle back in his chair.

"So... what happened? I mean...how'd you fall in love?"

He turned his head and stared out the window as if he was searching for a glimpse of the past.

"I'll never forget that first time I saw Rachael riding her horse across the field. Her hair was like a halo against a beautiful sunset. I didn't know her name back then... Too afraid to ask. So, every time I thought of her, I thought of her as a ray of sunshine. That's what I called her."

"Sunshine?"

"Yep. And she called me her bello mezzanotte.

"She's been gone for a long while. But she'll always have a place in my heart."

"I've wondered about that many times. Thank you for telling me."

"You know... Several years back I hired a private investigator from Chicago to go out and make sure you were okay. He told your grandfather he was there to buy cows."

"I remember that! Oh, and the guy was on the train. I was so...." *What am I saying? I can't tell him about Claude. Not yet.*

"Emily? Did you talk to him?"

"Uh... No. I wasn't even sure it was him...a-at first."

166

"When he saw you at the farm, he told me you seemed content."

"I'm sure I was at the time. If I had the animals around, and if I could read and dream, I did fine."

"Your grandfather had some wicked faults. But I do understand his anger toward me when he found out that Rachael was pregnant. What father wouldn't be enraged. Still…that's no excuse for neglecting his granddaughter. I knew that Rachael was his pride and joy. And I thought that…."

Samuel moaned. "Well, my thinking didn't help you any, did it."

"You thought he'd feel the same about me."

"Yes. Because you were part of her."

"Grandmother did her best to explain that to me."

"Oh Emily. I wish you would have had her longer. Both her and your mother."

"Me too."

"Say… I wrote you letters. Obviously, you didn't get them."

"There were letters?"

"I sent one to your aunt Francine each year around your birthday. I think you must've been five the first time. Of course, you couldn't read yet. But I hung onto hope that someday you'd get at least one. And when I finally got your letter, I was overjoyed."

"I almost didn't send it."

"It was meant to be that you did.

"You know, Emily. That first time I saw you in the stable. I nearly lost it. Normally I'm level-headed. But this last month or so… My mind has been spinning."

Emily gazed at her father, remembering that first day she saw him standing in the barn doorway, irritated at his arrival and at the same time, aware of how handsome he was. This didn't seem real yet. But it felt good to know what it was like to have a father, and finally know the truth.

167

In some ways, she felt reborn—like with that earthy smell after a spring rain shower as the sun appears through the clouds.

CHAPTER TWENTY-ONE

*E*mily sat with her bed raised, reading a magazine without a thought of her bandaged head and unattractive hospital attire. When Michael walked through the door, all at once, she was aware of the way she looked. She dropped the magazine and pulled the covers up.

"Hello," he said, looking over a shoulder as he washed his hands.

"Hi, Michael."

He walked to the foot of her bed, picked up her chart and glanced up.

"It's nice to see you."

"You too."

He finished reading, set the chart down, and went to stand beside her.

"I just talked to Doctor Barnes, and he said you're healing well."

She rubbed the mummy-like swath on her head.

"Does that mean this'll be replaced with something smaller?"

"It does. As a matter of fact, Doctor Barnes will be here any minute now."

Michael touched an area just above the patch on her forehead. "I see there's a tiny scar from the minor train mishap."

"Didn't you know, I'm collecting them."

"Scars?" Michael chuckled.

He glanced at the door. "Listen Emily, there are some things I've wanted to say. First, of all… On the train. I…I had no right."

She knew he meant the kiss. That beautiful moment she had ran over in her mind a hundred times if not more. She had hoped somewhere in the back of his mind it meant something to him too.

"What about breakfast, Michael? You didn't make it."

"No. No I didn't. But I was planning to. That was until a wire came through saying that my mother had passed away."

"Oh, Michael. I'm so sorry. I had no idea."

She looked into his eyes, those dark beautiful eyes that hadn't changed at all.

"We had hoped she'd get better. But... She knew. We all knew she may not pull through after her heart surgery."

He paused, thoughtfully, gazing at Emily with concern before pulling himself from what seemed an intimate knowledge he wasn't ready to share.

"As soon as I heard the news of my mother's passing, I wrote you a note with a number where you could reach me and gave it to a steward. I got off in Sacramento, where my sister lived at the time. Ever since, I've wondered if you got the note."

"No. I didn't get it. And I'm really sorry about your mother."

"Thank you. And I'm sorry about missing breakfast."

"You have no reason to be sorry. I...um. I thought...."

She shook her head, feeling horrible that she had been angry at him for something he had no control over.

"You know, Emily... After some soul-searching, I realized that our parting probably didn't end the way you were anticipating." He smiled. "You took me by surprise. But... I meant every word I said. In fact, at breakfast that morning, I had planned to talk about us meeting up once you settled in San Francisco. When I had no way of contacting you...it was tough for a while."

Tough? What does he mean? That he missed me?

170

She met his gaze and realized that he really had cared about her.

"Michael. How we parted wasn't easy. But, you have no idea how much you helped me. Just…being my friend."

She longed to say more, but a nurse came in and set about the usual routine. After she had laid out supplies and chatted with Michael, Doctor Barnes swept in as he always did, stopping to wash his hands before approaching his patient's bedside.

"So…young lady. Are you ready for the unveiling?"

Emily assured him she was more than ready.

Once he had removed her binding and replaced it with a mere patch over the wound, he went to the foot of the bed, picked up her chart, and made some notes.

"Everything looks good," he said, reading through entries. "The arm cast will stay on for several more weeks. And if nothing has changed by morning, I'm going to release you from the hospital."

He returned the chart to its slot and headed across the room.

"I'll be in to see you before you leave. Make sure you eat, and drink lots of liquids."

He stopped at the door and turned to Michael. "I'll see you in the boardroom."

"Oh yes, yes, I'll be right there."

When the doctor left, Michael stepped to Emily's bedside.

"By the way…earlier, when you were out having x-rays, I was at the nurse's station when a man named Peter called for you. One of the nurses said he had already tried to reach you several times, so I told her I'd talk with him. He said he was waiting for a plane out of the country and wanted to make sure you got a message."

"You say it was, Peter?"

"Yes, Peter Graham…

"Emily? What is it?"

171

"Nothing. I…I just thought… I'm sorry, go on. What did he say?"

"He wanted you to know that he was with the police when they searched Schillings' residence. At the time, he thought you were still living there. He wanted me to remind you about the conversation you had on the path the night of the ball. That…and the slippers. He may have wanted to say more, but his plane was loading.

The slippers? And the conversation on the path?

The path was where she told Peter about the necklace, and where he had a conversation with Donald Schillings. When she had seen him in the ballroom, he had jokingly referred to Cinderella's glass slippers, and pointed out those she wore that night, belonging to Donald's deceased wife. *Wait! Of, course. The necklace would have to be somewhere in their suite.*

It all made sense. Peter was among those who searched the mansion and would never have been allowed to take anything. But he had just confirmed what she had already suspected. Donald had been holding her necklace. And with him in jail, there was time to locate it before he was released. She would wait for the right opportunity.

"Is this someone you're seeing?" Michael asked.

"No. I've only met him twice. We have Donald Schillings in common. Did he say why he was leaving the country?"

"I assumed it's for an investigation. You know he's a private investigator, don't you?"

"Not until now."

With Peter's unconventional ways, it was obvious why that had never occurred to her.

"Say, Michael? I was just wondering how you're doing with everything. With your internship?"

"Great. I love it here…love working for Doctor Barnes. He's the best. But…it looks like I'll be doing the rest of my training in Ghana with the Peace Corps. Two years."

"In, Ghana? How did that happen?"

"I've been planning this for a while. Well, ever since I heard President Kennedy speak about the Peace Corps while he was still campaigning. I knew right away that I'd join."

"That's really something. I'm surprised. But if that's your calling. I'm happy for you."

"Well... It's been a process. But I'm very excited."

Michael moved toward the door. "Say, I have a meeting to attend. But I'll give you a call. I'll look for your contact number in the file."

Emily didn't know if she was more relieved that the woman who met him at the train station was his sister, or more disappointed that he would be leaving for two years.

Samuel walked in the next morning with a breakfast tray for Emily. She was already dressed and sitting next to a window.

"Good morning," he said as he strolled across the room and set the tray on a stand. "I've been assigned to make sure you eat your breakfast."

She picked up a piece of toast, lifted the lid from a bowl, and looked affably at the mush. "Mm, I love porridge."

"That's good because there're rumors floating that you can't leave until you've cleaned your bowl."

He pulled up a chair, took a letter from a shirt pocket and placed it on the table. "When you finish, here's something for you. It's a letter your aunt Francine sent me."

Emily glanced at the letter as she ate. When she finished, she picked it up.

Samuel,

I want you to know I'm writing this for my niece, not you. And I won't ever accept your part in what happened to Rachael.

What you should know is that she was pregnant and determined to go to San Francisco to be with you. Finally, one day she exploded and flat out said she was packing her bags and leaving. They kept her in her room, hoping to talk sense into her. That's when she climbed from her bedroom window and fell.

Just hours after Emily was born, Rachael died. Of course, your daughter is three years old now. It's easier to pretend the whole thing didn't happen. But I knew Rachael enough to know she would want you to be aware of what's taken place. And that's the least I can do for her.

Francine

Emily stared at the letter.

"Aunt Francine never recovered. I don't think any of them did. But I believe she knew writing you this letter was the honorable thing to do."

"I think you're right. And I'll always be grateful to her for that."

There was a knock on the door and Doctor Barnes walked in. "Good morning. I hope I'm not interrupting," he said with a grin.

Samuel stood and moved the table aside as the doctor came from the basin.

"I think you have a patient that's anxious to leave."

Doctor Barnes picked up Emily's chart, reading as he walked to where she sat.

"Well, it looks like everything's in order. Your vitals are good, and you're healing well. Any headaches? Dizziness?" he asked touching the area around her bandage.

"Nope."

"You can remove the bandage in a few days." He moved his hand down to her broken arm. "The cast will stay on for at least two more weeks," he added, glancing at her empty bowl.

"So, Emily... I don't know if your father told you yet, but we've arranged for you to stay near the hospital. You'll be staying with Donna our in-home nurse. Since she's part of Health Services, and the police force, she's also agreed to care for Mr. Schillings' children until family members are able to pick them up."

Emily turned to her father. "You helped with this, didn't you."

"I know how much they mean to you."

The doctor scribbled in the chart and handed it to a nurse.

"Ok, young lady. Unless something changes, I'll see you in a couple of weeks.

CHAPTER TWENTY-TWO

*T*he children rushed over to Emily as she walked into the house with her father. After introductions and a round of hugs, Maria asked about her cast. Before she could answer, Donna shuffled Emily off with Samuel to drop her luggage in the bedroom.

When they returned, Donna offered Emily an easy chair, and Samuel the couch. Taking a seat across from them, she gave a rundown of what to expect as far as health concerns.

"Oh, and Doctor Barnes told me to make sure you don't run yourself down. That, little ones," she said, looking to where Maria and Nathan were hovering around Emily, "that means she needs lots of rest."

Her attention turned back to Emily. "Of course, I understand they're excited to see you. But if it becomes too much, there are plenty of games to keep them occupied."

"They'll be fine. Once we get a chance to visit."

Emily recognized the books she left at the mansion, sitting on the end table. "Oh, you guys, thanks for bringing these."

Nathan repositioned himself and forced the books into a neat stack. "We thought you might want some reading time."

He glanced at his sister, and back to Emily. "Um, we were...um. We were wondering—"

"Let me," Maria said, impatiently.

"Go on then, ask."

"Um," Maria began, not quite as bold now. "Are we living with you again?"

Nathan leaned his elbows on the armrest staring up at Emily, hopefully. "Can we? Can we stay with you?"

"Well…" Emily looked at Samuel.

"I'll take it from here," he said, turning to the children.

"Maria and Nathan, guess who I talked to? Your Aunt Agnes. And as soon as she returns from Europe, she's coming to pick you up and take you to New York City."

"I want to stay with Emily," Maria moaned.

Nathan folded his arms in a pout. "Me too."

"Okay, Okay," Donna said, waving her arms. "Hold on a minute. I'm sorry kids. But Emily's not in a position to take on a responsibility like that."

Emily pulled the children over and made room for them on either side of her. They looked up at her with those big eyes she had come to love.

"As much as I want us to stay together, Donna's right. But I'll bet if you give your aunt a chance, you'll love New York City. There's a skating rink, and there'll be plays, movies, and amusement parks. And that's only the beginning. I'm sure there'll be stables where you can bring your ponies and ride all you want. You'll have so much to do you won't know where to begin."

The children's eyes lit up as she talked. And their curiosity about New York became an adventure.

Samuel stopped by several evenings later after coming back from the sea. Maria and Nathan had just gone to bed and Emily sat at the kitchen table with her father.

"I thought you might want to hear a little about your family."

"Oh… I haven't thought that far ahead."

"You are interested, aren't you?"

"Yes, of course."

"Well, first there's my wife, your stepmother, Adah. And… You have a sister. Her name is Rose. She just turned sixteen."

Samuel pulled out several pictures of Rose, handing them to her.

"She's beautiful."

"As you are. See…look at those gorgeous eyes, and long neck, just like yours. You're taller than Rose. But you're both slender. That comes from your mothers as I've never been the slightest bit lean."

Emily brushed a hand along her neck and up over her lips, seeing the similarities, and trying to imagine what it would be like to have a sister. As thrilling as that was, she wondered how Rose and her stepmother would feel when she showed up and disrupted their lives. Once they found out about Claude, they would certainly have an opinion.

*D*onna accompanied Emily to the clinic to have her cast removed. Emily was disappointed that Doctor Barnes was called to the hospital for an emergency but pleasantly surprised to see that Michael was in charge.

"So, this is where you're doing your internship."

"Here, and at the hospital. But, as I mentioned, I'll be leaving with the Peace Corps."

"Do you know when?"

"About three months."

"That soon."

"It's been in the works for a while now."

Emily knew she was being selfish for wishing he would stay. Although she admired him for volunteering to go.

"What you're doing is commendable."

"I consider it an honor.

"Say... I've been planning to call you." Michael glanced at the clock on the wall. "I know this is last minute. But so much of the time I'm called to duty. And since you're here, would you like to have dinner with me?"

"Dinner. Tonight? Uh...Yes...I would. But I'll have to check with someone first."

"Sure. And let's meet out front in about twenty minutes."

He finished taking off her cast and left to care for another patient.

Emily knew Donna was a stickler for regimen and hoped she didn't make a fuss, because she wasn't planning to give in easily.

"You know," Donna said when Emily told her about the dinner invitation. "If it was anyone else, I'd think twice. But I'm thrilled you have a friend like Michael. I've only heard wonderful things about him."

Donna smiled and touched Emily's arm. "Go on and have a nice time. But don't forget. You still need you're rest. So, don't make it too late."

*E*mily and Michael found their way to a fish diner down by the waterfront with sounds of seagulls and whiffs of the ocean that was just down the hill from the restaurant.

Michael ordered wine. And Emily didn't realize what she would do until the moment he was ready to fill her glass, and she placed a hand over the rim.

"No thanks."

She drew her hand away, sat back, and watched Michael pour his wine. For a moment, she was ready to tell him why she had sworn off alcohol. But she didn't want to delve into what happened when she drank too much and upset Maria. Getting so personal at the moment would ruin the mood.

"You see, Michael...I'm not twenty-one."

Michael looked surprised. "Oh... I just took for granted that you were. On the train, it sounded like you'd been out of school for several years."

"That's true. I was. But it had to do with living on a farm. I guess you could say I self-taught many of the years that I could've been in school."

"Hm. That's interesting. I would've never guessed."

Michael moved the bottle to the side. "I'll have them take it away—"

"No. That's not necessary. The men in my family like their drink. I'm talking about the hard stuff, not a dinner drink. And I have no problem with that bottle, or your glass of wine sitting on the table."

"Are you sure? Because I—"

"Please, enjoy your wine. I'll just order grape juice.

"So, Michael... I guess I should apologize to you for drinking on the train. It seemed like a good thing to do at the time. And I'd read that under-age passengers on boats and trains, do that sometimes."

"You're right, they do. I did. Wine, that is. The appeal for hard liquor just isn't there."

Emily wished she could say the same.

The restaurant didn't have grape juice, but the waitress brought her a tall glass of iced tea.

They ordered fish, and deep fries. Emily had her first taste of lobster, and with it dipped in butter, she was in heaven. Soon they were talking as if no time had passed since their time on the train.

He talked of his experiences working in the medical field. She spoke of her excitement that she had a sister, and that she would return to school and eventually be a teacher. He talked of Ghana and his hope to do good in the world. And she reminisced about their Prosciutto Gouda in the diner while he joked about his chance to practice medicine on her after cows stopped the train for several hours.

The conversation turned to her arrival in San Francisco. She recalled how she had gazed at the Bay Bridge and wondered what he was doing on the other side.

"That had to have been hard for you to be alone in a strange town. I wish I would've been there for you."

His eyes searched hers. "Listen, Emily, I think I should tell you something. Your father and I had a talk soon after you arrived at the hospital. We were both concerned about your emotional state. And I asked him to explain what happened to you when you first arrived in San Francisco. He told me where Maxine took you."

"So... he did make it to the restaurant. I'm sure she enjoyed that."

"From what I heard, I would agree. Anyway. Your father felt you might need someone to talk to. And since I have training in that area—"

"That's thoughtful of you. But there's no need. Thanks to my grandmother, I was able to make due...."

Moose came to mind and Emily swallowed a lump in her throat. "You see. I used to dance for my grandmother when I was very young. It's one of my fondest memories. And so... I danced to get through that strange place I found myself in."

Emily wasn't ready to tell Michael how she also used alcohol to get through her time at *The Palace*. That would lead to even more troubling things she couldn't talk about.

"You... danced. Hmm. I'm impressed the way you were able to focus on something positive."

"I had no choice."

Emily smiled, wondering how much Michael would have to learn about her before he questioned her stability and maybe even backed away from their friendship.

As it was, later that night, Michael held her hand when they strolled to the beach. He carried her shoes as they walked along the shoreline. And later, on Donna's front porch, he pulled her into his arms.

"It sure was nice to spend time with you. We'll have to do it again."

"I'd love that."

He straightened and gazed into her eyes. She could see he wanted to say something more, and maybe even kiss her. But soon he would be gone for two years. And she knew he was too respectful to take advantage of or hold her back in any way. She wondered if he would think differently if he knew how she felt. Her thought was, no—and how could she not be enamored by him even more.

He took her hand and raised it to his lips, said goodnight, and took the steps down to his car.

She watched him leave, still feeling his arms around her, and the imprint of his kiss on her hand, wishing for more.

*E*mily knew her life was about to take a turn when she saw the look in her father's eyes as he walked into the dining room where Donna, the children, and she sat at the table playing a game of Clue.

He motioned for Donna to take the children from the room. She pulled herself from the table and grabbed a camera from the counter.

"All right, you two. You were just bragging about your somersault skills. Let's go out back and see what you can do."

After Maria and Nathan were safely out of hearing range, Samuel took a chair across from Emily. She had already guessed what this was about. An officer had come to her room and had questioned her. At the time, she had hoped nothing would come of it but knew that her past might be revealed before she could turn herself in. And yet, she hoped there would be some time to spend with the children first.

"You know about Claude, don't you."

"I'm afraid so."

"I didn't mean for it to happen."

"I know you didn't. And don't ever think otherwise.

"Oh, Emily... To think I failed your mother tore my heart out. And I'm sorry. I'm so sorry for whatever you've gone through."

It was almost as if he was trying to take the blame for what she had done.

"You didn't fail me, or my mother for that matter.

"But... maybe I shouldn't have come and brought you into this mess."

"No. Don't say that. I couldn't bear the thought of you facing this alone. You did the right thing. This is where you belong, where you've always belonged."

He looked hard into her eyes, struggling with his next words. "I need to ask you something."

She braced herself, holding her breath.

He moved a hand across the table next to hers. "Did, Claude... Did he ever force himself on you?"

Emily winced, ashamed, nodding that he had.

Samuel's hand clinched into a fist.

"Damn him. Damn—

He rose and walked in circles then sat again.

"I'm sorry. My going off certainly won't help you."

"There's no need to be sorry."

"But I should have listened to my instincts."

When Samuel had gathered his composure, he reached over and placed his hands over Emily's.

Tears streamed down her cheeks.

"It must seem impossible right now, sweetheart. But this will pass. You'll come out on the other side with a weight off your shoulders and your whole life ahead of you."

"In the meantime, what's going to happen?"

"Well... Doctor Barnes was able to talk with a judge. Thank God, the man is aware of the doctor's exemplary reputation. And he agreed to make an exception in your case. That's why you're still here.

"With that being said... The court in Illinois has its rules. And of course, there will be a formal indictment. But once the facts are known, I have to believe the charges will be dropped."

Emily got up and went to the window. "I'll have to go back to Illinois, won't I."

Samuel went to her side. "I'm afraid so. But not until Doctor Barnes releases you from his care."

They stood watching the children.

"You know, Emily. There's no reason to tell them."

"Maybe. But what if they find out another way? That would be worse."

"You have a point. And if you don't mind. Allow me to tell them."

*E*mily said goodbye to her father, went to her room and slept until after dinner. When she awoke and found that the children were preparing for bed, she went in to say goodnight.

She sat at the foot of the bed, feeling like she should say something.

"Sorry that I missed dinner. I—"

"We know what happened," Maria said. "Samuel told us that someone hurt you."

Nathan punched his pillow. "Yeah. And now you have to straighten things out in court."

"Oh, you guys. I'm sorry for letting you down."

Maria sat up. "You didn't let us down."

"You've been nicer than anyone since Mommy," Nathan added, scratching the tip of his nose.

There was a knock on the door and Donna sailed into the room.

"Hate to interrupt, but you children best be saying goodnight."

Maria took a book from the nightstand and hugged it to her chest.

"Just one story, first. Please, Donna?"

"Well…all right. But only one."

Emily hadn't read more than a couple of pages before the children drifted off to sleep. She tucked them in, knowing how much she would miss them when they left. But she was thankful for the time they had together, and that they would be with family again instead of wherever their father had planned to send them.

*T*he moment Emily laid eyes on Aunt Agnes, she had a good feeling about her. She was a striking woman with hair the color of dark chocolate and hints of honey, styled in a bouffant. Her tan suit, purse, and heels matched perfectly.

The children hesitated for a moment before walking over to meet her.

"Hi, Maria," Agnes said, taking her hand. "My, you've grown into such a pretty girl."

"Thanks," Maria said, politely.

"And Nathan." She extended a hand to him. "I don't think you were two yet when I last saw you. So, I don't have to tell you how much you've grown."

"I'm going to be a lot taller when I'm a basketball star."

Agnes patted the top of his head. "A basketball star, huh?"

"Either that or a taxi driver."

"Well. As long as you love what you're doing."

The driver picked up their luggage and headed back to the car as Agnes placed an arm around the children's shoulders.

"You guys ready to go? The plane leaves in two hours."

"I might be a pilot too," Nathan beamed on the way to the car.

185

After the children said goodbye to Emily and Donna and settled in the car, Agnes pulled Emily aside.

"I want to thank you for being so good to them." She looked back at the children. "Their mother will be so happy to see them."

Emily didn't know if she heard right. "You said, their mother? I… I thought she died."

Agnes chuckled. "Flora's alive and well in Texas. She looked back at the children again. "It's their father. I had doubts about him all along. But I do believe that man's a psychopath."

"Do you know why he would want everyone to think she died?"

"I haven't talked with Flora enough to get all the details yet. You see, until just a couple of weeks ago, we hadn't talked in several years or seen each other for over six. We're ten years apart and have never been close. Although we're planning to change that.

"You know, she did mention she tried to keep in touch with Maria, but it didn't go over well."

"Now that's interesting. Because Maria was expecting to have an ongoing relationship with a pen pal. You think it was her?"

"It sounds like something Flora would do."

"But why would she leave the children with Donald in the first place?"

"Let me tell you. It's a whopper, and a tail of intrigue. See, Donald had his eye on the mansion for years, but with all the trouble he caused his uncle Bud, the guy refused to sell it to him. The place is over a century old, willed to Bud by family. He stayed at the mansion now and then for extended visits, but he lived in Texas all his life. Anyway… Bud started coming into our family restaurant and took a liking to Flora. At the time, she was dating one of Donald's friends, Kenneth. When they broke up, Donald swept Flora off her feet, and they married soon after.

"Bud was overjoyed and believed his nephew was a changed man. He was thrilled when Maria was born. And it wasn't long after that he sold the mansion to Donald.

"Then a few years after Nathan was born, things began to change. Flora and Donald unofficially separated. And when she went to Texas to settle our parent's estate, she and Kenneth rekindled their friendship. She returned to the mansion intending to bring the children back with her."

"So, she deserted them for Kenneth?"

"Not intentionally. You see, at one time Kenneth flew cargo from Mexico to New York. When he learned he was hauling cocaine he quit. But now Schillings is using that information to blackmail him. Flora told me she never would've agreed to his demands if she and Kenneth weren't expecting a child."

"But why would Donald go through all the trouble of keeping the children? From what I saw, he never had time for them."

"All I can say is that whatever it is, there's something big in it for him."

Agnes looked down at her watch and headed for the car. "I've got to run, but when I find out more, I'll let you know."

She turned at the car door. "Oh, and when I talked with your father, he gave me his number. I'll have the children call when they settle in."

As they drove away, Donna came out and sat on the front steps with Emily.

"Well? What do you think?"

"I think they're in good hands."

Emily was telling her the news about Flora when a car rumbled up the street. It backfired as it pulled up to the house and rattled to a stop. Emily was surprised when her father stepped out. Donna held onto the rail and pulled herself up.

"You know… Things have a way of working out."

She patted Emily's shoulders and walked inside.

"Hello, sweetheart," Samuel said as he came up the sidewalk and took a seat next to her. "Did Maria and Nathan make it off okay?"

"Oh, yes. And you'll never believe what I found out. Long story short. Donald Schillings blackmailed the children's mother into deserting them. He coerced her into playing dead. Can you believe it?"

Samuel chuckled. "Having his wife play dead is stretching it a bit. But I'm not shocked."

"I know, me either. The children will be so happy, though, seeing their mother again. Their aunt sure is nice."

"That's good to know."

The two sat watching cars pass by until Samuel broke the silence.

"Well... I, um...I hate to break the news. But Doctor Barnes will release you from his care in three days. That means you're in good enough shape to travel."

Emily shivered, and Samuel wrapped an arm around her shoulders.

"I know it sounds drastic. And I wish I could drive you to Illinois myself. But even if I could, they have their protocol.

"And, by the way, I guess I should tell you that since last week sometime, you've been under house arrest."

"Is that why Donna won't allow me to go for a walk alone?" She looked up at a picture window where the woman sat in a chair that overlooked the front yard. "And why the buzzer goes off every time a door opens, and why the windows only open so far?"

"You already guessed then."

"Not exactly. But I knew something was up."

"Oh, Emily. You've been through so much. And it hurts me to tell you this. But...um. It's impossible for me to go along with you to Illinois. I'll be there in a couple of days, though, I promise...that's if you're still there.

Hopefully, they'll straighten everything out and send you back home. If so, I'll be there to ride back with you."

Samuel sighed. "It's my job. They're in a spot. A couple of our men were injured, one nearly drowned."

"That's scary. Were you there?"

"No, I was off that day. Had I been there it may not have happened.

"Anyway, Adah and Rose will follow you and the officer to the airport...at least give you a send-off. Just to let you know. Rose is desperately trying to talk her mother into allowing her to go along with you. I'm on her side."

"I appreciate that."

Emily got up and headed back into the house to cover her disappointment. "How about some coffee?"

"I feel terrible that I can't go with you," Samuel said as he followed her into the kitchen. "But I work for my uncle, and he's already done so much for me. He didn't complain when I took time off to work for Schillings. And then being with you in the hospital."

Emily set two mugs on the table and turned to him.

"I don't know what's wrong with me. I haven't even thought of the sacrifices you've made."

"Listen. Nothing I do for you is a sacrifice. Not ever."

Emily poured their coffee, returned the pot to the stove, and sat.

"Does Michael know?"

"About Claude? I'm sure he doesn't."

"So... Are you going to tell him?"

"I don't know."

"Well... It's clear he cares about you. But, of course, it's up to you.

"Oh... I have something that might perk you up. I'm taking you to church on Sunday to meet your family."

"Really. How many will there be?"

Emily wasn't sure she was ready.

"Of course, your sister Rose will be there. And Adah, your stepmother. Then there's my youngest sister Bernice who just moved back to the area. She's the big star at the moment since she's the only one of the females with a college degree. And... let's see. My mother, your grandmother will be there with my brother Ted and his family. My sister Nell and a few other aunts, uncles, and cousins. You'll meet them all."

"Do they know about…about everything?"

"A little. But for the moment I didn't think they needed to hear the details. They know you were assaulted and that you have to go to court in Illinois."

"And the police trust you to take me to church?"

"Everything's been taken care of. And I don't want you to worry about anything except being with your family. Okay?"

Learning about her new family was exciting. But she was concerned about their reaction when they learned the truth. There was Michael too. They'd had such a great time together. And it was obvious they had strong feelings for one another. But there wasn't a bone in her body that wanted to give him the news.

CHAPTER TWENTY-THREE

Sunday morning, Emily sat at the window waiting for her father. He was fifteen minutes late. And she began to wonder if something had happened to him. Or... What if her troubles were too much for the family.

When he finally pulled up, she said goodbye to Donna and headed for the door. By the time she stepped outside, Samuel was looking under the hood.

"Sorry, I'm late," he said as she walked up, wiping his hands on a rag.

He dropped the hood and went to open the door for her. "Once I whip this old Buick into shape, it'll run like new."

Emily noticed what looked like an updated seat cover as she sat in the car.

"It's not so bad."

Her father had such a good attitude. But something didn't seem right about him driving the rundown car. Donald Schillings was in jail, and who knew how long it would be before he received his pay. She had forgotten about the money coming to her. But when and if she got it, she would give it to her father.

Forty minutes later, Samuel pulled into the parking lot of a small white church. Emily stepped from the car and gazed at the steeple that pointed straight up to God.

As they took the wooden steps to the top, a young boy swung the door open, and the sounds of a choir burst out into the sunlight. Samuel took her hand, and they walked through the entryway and up the aisle. As they neared the pulpit, Samuel motioned her down a row. A woman, whom Emily realized was her grandmother, welcomed her with a nod and a smile.

When the choir finished the hymn, a young woman stepped forward.

Samuel leaned toward Emily. "That's your sister, Rose."

When Rose began to sing with a voice as beautiful and clear as a crystal blue sky, Emily found herself holding her breath and fighting back tears.

After the service, relatives gathered outside to meet the new addition to the family. Some shook Emily's hand, others hugged her and said how happy they were to finally meet her. The whole event took her by surprise. She had never seen such enthusiasm given to one person for just showing up.

Adah came over for a quick introduction. She was an attractive woman, tiny, but looking bold in a bright yellow skirt and matching jacket, and sophisticated, with her hair pulled back, and a small black hat set to the side. As Emily watched her walk away to help prepare food, she thought she was gracious, but she wasn't so sure Adah was thrilled to have a stepdaughter.

"Hi, Em."

Emily looked up to see her sister come down the front steps. Her long white dress flowed around her shins, and her eyes sparkled like a pair of diamonds. They embraced, and Rose cocked her head.

"You're taller than I expected. I knew you'd be beautiful, though."

"And you have the most breathtaking voice I've ever heard."

"You haven't heard anything yet, because every one of us Dimsmoore's love to sing. The Siscolly family does too. Say... Have you met everyone?"

Emily nodded. "I think so. There's so many."

Rose took her by an arm, and they followed a group to the picnic area behind the church. "Let's go down to the water while they put out the food."

The girls took a path to a bench near the water.

"Like I was saying, we do a lot of singing in our family," Rose said as they sat. "You should hear us at Christmas when we all gather at Gramma Dimsmoore's. Last year was the first without Gramps. It sure seemed odd at first. But Gramma said, *'Now, don't you all go feeling bad 'cause he's up there with Jesus and he's probably humming along. And I'm sure as anything that he's happier than he's ever been.'*

"And you know what? It turned out to be one of the best Christmases, ever."

Emily tried to envision the whole bunch together, celebrating. "Your family's so welcoming, Rose. So happy."

"Oh, we are. Not that we don't have our problems. And listen, it's your family too."

Emily was grateful for the show of acceptance. At the same time, she felt unworthy and embarrassed if they knew what happened with Claude. Just as shameful was her time at *The Palace.*

"I guess it'll take time for me to comprehend that I'm. Well… That I'm…."

Before she could stop herself, Emily burst into tears, wanting to spill everything to Rose about Claude and *The Palace,* about everything. She needed to confide in her. But it was too soon.

"For heaven's sake. Don't tell me you're bawling 'cause it finally hit you that you're one of us."

Emily looked up. "What? No."

She wiped tears with the back of her hands, dabbing her eyes with her skirt. "It's just that…that it's so great to be on the good side of life. Right now, I'm not even sure I deserve this."

Rose wagged a finger. "I don't want to hear any of that nonsense. You deserve the best, and don't let anyone ever tell you any different. And as for your so-called *'good side of life*' comment. To some that would be a refutable statement. Not that I believe it for a minute. Our family's been lucky in many ways. And for the most part, we're happy. But listen, Emily...you've lived with Whites all your life, and no matter what shade of brown you are, now that you're lined up with us...well, being Black will be part of your life. Many won't blink an eye, but others will look at you differently. You otta know something about that."

"A little."

"Of course, you do. A person would have to live in a cave not to."

The girls both stared out over the water, mulling over their own thoughts. Emily was proud of her new family and hungered to know them better. It was the upheaval that her past would cause them that troubled her. Her father accepted her, that she was sure of. And from the way it was going, it seemed the truth wouldn't be too much for her sister. But there was no certainty with the others. How could their perception of her not be affected once they knew everything.

"So. You didn't live in a cave, did you?"

Emily turned to Rose then realized she was joking. "No. But I never saw anything firsthand either."

"You learned about slavery at school, though."

"A little. And I read some too, although I only went up through the eighth grade."

"Why is that?"

"Grandfather decided I was needed at home. Chores."

"That's not right."

"When you're living on a farm it is."

"What kind of a man is he, anyway?"

"Well... From what I gather, after my mother died, he was never the same. There were some other issues, a murdered brother. But I have a feeling her death was a catalyst to most of what went on. Anyway, the teacher let me skip the first and second grades."

"Now that's impressive."

"I read everything I could get my hands on. listened to the radio. And whenever my uncle Steven went into town, he picked up a newspaper. And like I said, I read some about slavery. But until I left Watseka, I only saw photos of Blacks."

Rose chuckled. "And now you find you're related to a bus load.

"You know Emily, our great, great, grandparents came to San Francisco back in the 1800's. At the time, it wasn't too bad for them, comparatively speaking, that is. There were support groups even back then. Like many others, our forebearers had pride and determination. And their influence has carried down through each generation. But it's mother with all the push right now. Sometimes I wish she would let up a bit.

"So…you met her, didn't you?"

"Your mother? Yes, I did. She came over, introduced herself, and dashed off to start lunch."

"She never stops," Rose said with a laugh. "Probably why she keeps her clerical position at a law firm. The sad truth is that they take advantage of her. I suppose that's the reason she's always harping at me to make sure I get my college degree."

Rose heaved a sigh. "It's not that I don't want to go to college. But... Oh, I don't know why I'm telling you this. I guess it's that I don't want you to think we're perfect and everything's going to be all killer.

"Anyway," Rose said, jumping to her feet, "The dinner bell rang five minutes ago. And I don't know about you, but I'm famished."

The girls went arm in arm to join the rest of the family for lunch. Emily did her best to socialize, even though all she could think about was her trip back to Illinois and what everyone would think once they learned the details.

After lunch, the girls said good-bye to the family and headed up to where Samuel was pacing in front of the Buick.

"You okay Father?" Rose asked as they approached.

He leaned against the car and folded his arms.

"So…Emily. Remember our discussion about the custody being turned over to the police officer who will travel to Illinois with you?"

"Yes."

"Well, it's in effect at six tomorrow morning, just before your flight."

Rose took Emily's arm. "I tried to talk Mother into letting me go to Illinois with you. But she doesn't want me to miss school. I'm sorry, Em."

"Now, don't forget that Adah and Rose will be there in the morning to follow you to the airport," Samuel added.

He pulled himself from the car and went to Emily, slipping an arm around her shoulders. "I feel sick about this. But as soon as I drop you off, I have to head to the boat. The repairs have to be finished by morning. It'll be an all-nighter as it is."

Rose wrapped an arm around Emily's waste and squeezed. "I'll call you every night."

"You guys. I know what you're doing. But I'm fine. And I've accepted what's about to happen."

No matter how much confidence Emily put forth, she was far from ready. But she couldn't stand to see them feeling guilty and fumbling around trying to make her feel better.

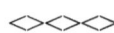

*T*he last few nights without the children had been tough on Emily. She missed them. Knowing her necklace was sitting at Schillings' frustrated her. And she thought of telling her father but decided that getting the necklace back was going to be on her. Her father sacrificed enough. She would deal with it at the right time.

To Emily's surprise, Donna came in as she was preparing for bed and said she had a phone call. At first, she thought it was Michael and was relieved it was George.

He called, excited to tell her that a lawyer had advised his parents to hire their own surveying company and that the results had just come back in their favor. They were getting their property back.

"Of course, with all that's gone on, it'll have to go through the court system, which could take a while."

"At least you've got your land back. And I'm so happy for you."

She thought of telling him about Claude and what she was about to face but decided he had enough to deal with on his own.

"Hey, George. How'd you know I was here?"

"I called the hospital and talked with several nurses until I found one who was willing to help me find you. She set the call up with Donna."

"That was clever. Has anyone ever told you that you should be a detective?"

"My mother. All the time."

Emily laughed. "At least I know who to call if need be."

"You're not so bad yourself."

"Well...if we had no other obligations. I'd go in with you."

"Oh. Me too. In a minute.

"Well, Emily. Donna gave me five minutes. So, I'd better let you go. You get lots of rest, now."

They said goodbye, and Emily returned to bed. She tried to take George's advice. But with the lights out, the stillness was like a cold, heavy cloud weighing on her.

*A*t six-thirty the next morning, Donna came in to wake Emily and told her someone was there for her. Thinking it was Adah and Rose, she slipped on a robe, stepped down the hallway, and looked around the corner. She noticed a police officer standing at the kitchen entrance. Rose was at the front door.

"Surprise. I'm going with you," Rose said as Emily hurried over.

"Don't tease me."

Rose reached outside, picked up her suitcase and set it inside the house.

Emily looked out the door. "Where's your mother?"

"She's already gone, Em. You're stuck with me."

The girls went to the bedroom and Emily dressed and finished packing while her sister laid across the bed. Her journal was with her father for safekeeping. And it felt strange not having it close by. But then she had Rose coming with her.

"What changed your mother's mind about you coming with me?"

"So…Right after you left, yesterday, Grandmother and my mother got into a squabble. Thank God, Grandmother won. What finally settled it was that she took a collection from family members for my flight, Father's too.

"Needless to say, my mother wasn't happy. Like I mentioned, she's always worried about anything that might interfere with my studies. And she's set on me going to Wilberforce. That's the college my Aunt Bernice graduated from. That was the same college Father considered attending before he ended up at your grandfather's farm."

"And where he met my mother," Emily added. "Did he ever make it?"

"You mean to college? Nah. After Father left Illinois, he got to working on his uncle's fishing boat. He's done that ever since. He loves the sea."

"Have you decided what you'll study?"

"I'm leaning toward lawyer, maybe even politics. I'm not sure yet.

"Oh, that reminds me… I don't know if you heard. But a friend of your lawyer's is letting us stay in an apartment above their garage. There's a kitchenette. And they're even bringing up a television. Hey…we can whip up a tuna casserole and a chocolate cake for dessert. We'll watch Wagon Train."

Emily picked up a handful of socks from the bed and deposited them into her bag. "You make it sound like a vacation." She thought for a moment and smiled. "It does sound like fun, though."

"That's the spirit, Em.

"Say, speaking of food. I think I smell bacon."

"Go on and eat. I'll be right in."

Five minutes later, Emily walked from the bedroom with the same bag she brought from the farm. When she set it next to Rose's, she noticed there wasn't a sound from the kitchen. It was too quiet—nerve-rackingly quiet. Her grandmother used to say you could always tell when a storm is brewing by the uncanny calm in the air.

"Better come eat some breakfast!" Donna called.

Emily walked in to where the two women sat at the table. The officer was leaning against the counter drinking coffee.

"Let me get you something," Donna said, moving to get up.

"No need. I've got it."

Donna settled back. And Emily filled a cup with coffee, took a piece of bacon, and went to stand alongside the officer. She figured since they would be spending the day together, why not break the ice. Looking over, she noticed that his nametag read, 'Officer Douglas'.

"Hello, Officer."

When he didn't respond, she wondered why he couldn't, at least, nod, or something. His demeanor was depressing, and she wanted to lighten the mood.

She finished the piece of bacon and tried again. "You know…if you want the day off, my sister will make sure I make it to court on time."

Rose laughed. "On God's honor."

Still, the man didn't move a muscle except to sip his coffee.

Donna got up and put her dishes in the sink. "As far as I'm concerned, there should be another way."

Rose stood and gathered her dishes. "Ain't that the truth. Anyone can see by spending a minute with my sister that she doesn't need this escort service. It's a waste of taxpayers' money if you ask me."

The officer reached back, set his cup down, and pulled himself from the counter. "Time to go."

Donna took Emily's cup and set it in the sink. Rose grabbed her hand, and they all walked to the front door where the girls picked up their luggage.

"You'll do just fine," Donna said, as they headed up the sidewalk. "Just remember all the people that believe in you."

Emily laughed at how tough Donna came across. But in reality, she had a good heart.

"Thanks, Donna. I'll try to remember that."

CHAPTER TWENTY-FOUR

*T*he three walked into the terminal at the San Francisco airport where they would catch a flight to the Midway in Chicago. When their flight departure was announced, Officer Douglas escorted the girls outside, ordering them to stay back until all the other passengers were onboard.

Seeing the plane that was about to take her to Illinois shocked Emily to the core. She had known the day would arrive when she would face what happened with Claude. But now that the moment was upon her, she wondered what happened to the comforting words from her grandmother that had always come to her rescue.

She gazed at the steel bird sitting on the tarmac. It was nothing like the image she had drawn on her notebook with the white wings of a dove holding her like soft pillows. They were both meant to take her somewhere. And while the beautiful white bird on her journal cover could no longer carry her to safety, the one with cold blue stripes running down the middle, waited to transport her to painful memories.

Rose took her hand, and Emily felt the tension and sweat in her palm. It made her sad and warmed her heart at the same time to witness the support her sister gave her. When they were the only ones left waiting to board, Officer Douglas motioned to the girls, indicating that Rose should go first.

Inside, the plane was like a tunnel, cramped, and stuffy. Passengers stared at the trio as they passed. The tension was overwhelming. Emily knew Rose felt it too by the way she whipped around and grabbed her elbow.

"This won't be so bad," she whispered. "I hear there's a snack once we're up in the air."

"That'll be nice."

"The important thing, Em, is that we're sharing the experience together. Don't you think?" Rose bent to get a look out the window. "And on such a beautiful day."

Emily cringed to think how she would have reacted if Rose hadn't come along with her upbeat personality, joking around, and trying to pretend she didn't want to break down and cry.

"All right you two, straight to the back," the officer barked. They exchanged *what-a-grouch* looks and kept walking. When they reached the last row, Rose offered Emily the window seat. Officer Douglas sat across the aisle.

The engines revved, and the plane began to move as a stewardess laid out safety procedures. When she finished, the cabin became silent except for the whine of engines as they taxied up the runway, turned into position, and stopped.

Emily leaned toward the window as they rolled again, quickly picking up speed, the ground passing in streaks and flickers. Her stomach dropped as they lifted and moved from the earth, the plane shaking with a grinding din that seemed would never stop. Finally, they leveled, and the roar of the engines faded to a hum.

Almost immediately, the stewardesses began moving carts up the aisle.

Rose placed a hand over Emily's. "You, okay?"

Emily pulled her gaze from the scene below and sat back in her seat. "I'm going to jail."

"No, you're not."

"I don't know, Rose. On the way up, I realized they must really want me bad." She nodded toward Officer Douglas. "Him, and this plane ride almost all the way across the entire country. Would they go to all this trouble if they weren't set on putting me away?"

"You can't think that way. Listen Emily. Let's talk about something exciting. I know. Tell me more about Michael. You know, your cute doctor friend."

The girls began to talk and even had a few laughs. At times, Emily almost forgot what was waiting for her at the other end.

After a while, they succumbed to lack of sleep and dozed. When the plane made a sudden descent, Emily opened her eyes and leaned to the window as they careened over the landscape that moved closer and closer until the earth was at the window, and the wheels hit the runway with a jolt. The scenery passed in a blur until the plane slowed, and gravity set her up in her seat.

Officer Douglas stood and motioned for Emily to stay seated. When they stopped, there was an abrupt silence, and a strange calm filled the cabin as everyone stood and gathered their belongings.

*T*hey had barely entered the terminal when two police officers approached. One of them stood in front of Emily and the other walked over to Officer Douglas.

"We're here to pick up Emily Rezell."

"She's all yours," Officer Douglas said. He handed over a folder and walked away.

Before Emily knew what was happening, one of the officers asked for her bag, nearly ripping it off her shoulder. The other pulled her arms around to the front and handcuffed her wrists.

Rose tried to work her way in, but it was impossible to get near Emily.

"Stand back, Ma'am," one of them said.

"Well, there's no need to be so rough."

The officers each took Emily by an arm and hustled her toward the exit. Rose followed them outside.

"What do you think she's going to do? Run off after coming this far?"

Emily looked back, attempting a smile as they took her to a police car.

Rose called to the officers. "She's not a criminal! You... You, *imbeciles*," she finished under her breath.

"Don't worry, Emily! I'll call your lawyer before I catch the bus over!"

Rose watched until Emily disappeared inside the police car then closed the door and marched over to Officer Douglas.

*E*mily stared straight ahead as they headed south out of Chicago. She was too shocked to cry. Or maybe it was the anger at the way the men handcuffed her and took her from the building as if she were less than human. Once in the car, the officer sitting in the passenger seat went through her bag before handing it back to her. She felt violated. Not only because he touched her personal possessions, but because they thought she might have a weapon.

She gazed at the two in the front seat chatting as if they were on an outing. It struck her that they were probably acting on the information given to them. Most likely that she had murdered a poor innocent man going about his morning chores.

As they neared Watseka, fear settled in her belly and knotted like a rock. She longed to poke her head out the window and let the breeze whip across her face. Leaning back in the seat, she closed her eyes, imagining a long, cool drink of vodka sliding down her throat and spreading warmth through every cell in her body.

When they came to the corner that led to the grocery store, they took a left and sped to the other side of town, onto Cherry Street, past the courthouse, and into a parking lot.

One of the officers left with her folder, and the other took her inside a building into a small, dingy room with only a table and two chairs. He removed her handcuffs, and left, letting the door close with a bang. Emily's stomach churned as she looked about the room, recalling Claude's warning about what happened to the young and beautiful in prison.

She walked over and sat, folded her hands on the table and waited. Finally, the door opened. A man looking to be in his late twenties burst in, puffing as he scrambled over.

His coat sleeves hung almost to his knuckles, and his shirt buttons were in danger of popping over his ample mid-section. His tie was in disarray, and his sandy hair was tousled and in need of a trim.

"Hello Emily," he said, struggling to catch a breath as he pulled out a chair and took a seat. "I'm Ryan Dillard. Your father hired me to represent you.

"I meant to make it sooner, but I just now managed to escape from the courthouse. And listen… I had no idea things were going to go down the way they did."

He leaned closer and lowered his voice as someone came into the room. "I want to remind you not to say a word about the case to anyone but me. You do understand that don't you?"

"Yes, I do. But…."

Her voice cracked as she glanced about the room again. "I'm not sure how I do this."

"I'm sorry, Emily. Your father explained what happened. And I assure you that I'm doing everything in my power to have you out of here in a couple hours. It's just a matter of going through the process."

He put a hand on the table next to hers. "Are you okay?"

Emily nodded.

"So," he said, standing. "I'm going in for a briefing now. And as soon as everything is resolved, I'll be in to see you."

After he left, the staff member, who had stepped in earlier, waited for the door to close.

"Over here," the woman said, motioning to Emily's bag.

Emily's knees trembled as she stepped across the room. "Th-they already searched it."

"Come on. Let's have it."

The woman took the bag from her, set it aside and led her to an even smaller room for a needless search. Her clothes were taken, and she was given a prison uniform.

Emily barely noticed the hand on her elbow as a guard took her to a cell. The door closed behind her, and she stood gaping at the bleak surroundings. The walls were green bricks, and the cot was cold iron with only a gray wool blanket tucked so tight she figured a person would have to wrestle it free to crawl in. She plodded across the cement floor, laid on the cot, and waited for the next hour, struggling to keep herself together. Fearing that if she burst into tears they would never stop, she concentrated on the sounds of footsteps, the murmurs, occasional tempers, and clanging doors.

She was drifting when she heard the rattle of iron. Her eyes popped open, and she stood, expecting to be released. One look at Ryan's face and she sank back to the cot.

"I tried my best. And I'm sorry, but you're going to have to stay here until court tomorrow."

He pulled out a handkerchief and wiped his forehead.

"This is difficult, Emily. But the judge is concerned because you've been a fugitive for so long. Running is a sign of guilt, you know."

"I should've gone to the police right away. But I wasn't thinking straight. And I feared they wouldn't believe me."

"Your father said Claude raped you. Is that what was happening before he was killed?"

"Well, not at that moment. But he did...before. And he was expecting that...that we would... You know."

"Was he threatening you at the time?"

Emily nodded. "You see... I was in the process of running away that morning, and he tried to stop me."

Ryan walked over and sat beside her.

"Can you tell me how the pitchfork ended up in his chest?"

"It's not what I planned... I was trying to scare him off. And he charged at me. He tripped at the same time my foot caught a loose board. It happened so fast...."

Ryan looked down at his notes. "I see you turned eighteen just prior to the incident. In the court of law, that makes you an adult."

His voice was low and thoughtful. "It seems odd that you'd be running away."

"I know some may not understand, but I think Grandfather thought it was my duty to take care of him and my uncles for the rest of their lives."

"And Claude, right?"

"Him too."

"Was he a relative?"

"No."

Ryan set his notebook on the cot, folded his hands, leaning so that he looked down at the floor.

"Tell me Emily, what it was like living on the farm."

She began to talk, hesitantly at first, not wanting to confuse him, and saying only as much as she thought he needed to know. When she finished, he sat quietly for a few moments. Picking up his notebook, he stood, walked to the bars, and turned to face her.

"It's easy for me to believe your story. And I wish we could just sit down with the judge, end it right now, and send you on your way. But that's not the way the system works.

"Tomorrow in court, you'll be allowed an opportunity to plead your guilt or innocence. I want you to plead 'innocent by reason of self-defense'. There's a good chance you won't have to be jailed during the trial. Although I think you should know that Judge Grosslyn is not the most lenient. And I might add that he was pretty perturbed that you were on the run for over a year."

A door banged in the distance and footsteps approached. The jailer unlocked the cell door, and Ryan stepped outside. He looked back through the bars.

"I'm going to give it my all."

When he left, she lay back on the cot and listened to the footsteps fade away.

CHAPTER TWENTY-FIVE

*E*mily was able to change into her street clothes the next morning before being taken to the courtroom, where they sat her at a table with her counsel.

Ryan waited for her to sit. "Try to relax. And remember what I told you."

The last people she wanted to see were her grandfather and uncles. Yet she couldn't help but to check over a shoulder. The room was almost empty, and it didn't take long for her to see they didn't show. Rose smiled at her. But Emily saw fear in her eyes.

The courtroom was called to rise. And Judge Grosslyn, a tall man who looked to be about sixty, walked in and took his seat at the bench. Ryan had warned her about the judge, and she searched for something positive, laugh lines around the eyes, something soft. But there was nothing of comfort, only stiff, dark hair, combed to the side, harsh feathery eyebrows, and a set mouth.

When everyone had taken their seats, the judge addressed the courtroom and turned to Emily.

"I ask that the defendant rise."

Ryan took Emily by an elbow, and they stood together.

"Miss Rezell," the judge said, "What is your plea?"

"I...I..." Her throat tightened and she ran the words over in her mind.

Ryan leaned to her. "Louder. Speak louder."

"I... I plead innocent, Your Honor, by reason of self-defense."

The judge took a minute to evaluate documents. Emily's muscles were so tight she felt that if someone tried, they could snap her like a twig. The room was still as he set the papers aside and looked up.

"Because of the serious nature of Claude Thorn's death, and the fact that you've been a fugitive for over a year, I have no choice but to order that you reside in custody until after the trial."

Rose gasped. There were murmurs, sharp breaths, and creaking wood from a baffled handful in the room as they turned in their seats.

Emily clutched the tabletop, imagining herself fleeing from the building. Ryan placed a hand on her back and consoled her until someone pulled her away. At the door, she turned and looked at Rose.

That's when she noticed someone leaning from behind and talking to her sister. There was something vaguely familiar about the young woman, although Emily couldn't place her.

*T*ears that Emily had been holding back, flowed down her cheeks as she changed back into her prison uniform. She wondered how it could be that the tiny cold room with the hard cot was to be her home for now. No matter how many times her thoughts had taken her here, she could not have imagined the hopelessness. The only thing she could do was to lay and wait and be thankful it wasn't as Claude described.

When Ryan came, she sat up to make room for him on the cot. Declining her offer, he leaned against the bars. He was a mess, cheeks ashen, forehead glistening with sweat, and his eyes filled with concern.

"I tried my best to talk the judge into reconsidering. But he stands firm with his decision. He feels it's in the best interest of the court to keep you here. On paper it looks bad. A violent death with a pitchfork through the chest, leaving the scene of the crime, a cover-up, and being a fugitive for over a year. Each one of those could lead to hard time. But the one the prosecution will hone in on is being a fugitive. He will say it proves your guilt and that anything you say can't be trusted."

"Does the judge know about Claude? About what he did?"

"I told him. Although, you must realize he's read the police report that puts Claude as the victim. The moment the police saw him, they believed it was cold-blooded murder. At first they thought it was Steven."

"That's ridiculous."

She looked around the dismal room. "What am I supposed to do?"

"Did you tell any of your friends about Claude?"

"No. The last time I had friends around here, I was fourteen. I doubt they knew he existed. So, no. Besides, one of them died. And the other moved to South Carolina."

"Anyone else? Anyone at all that you may have spoken to about Claude?"

"No…no one."

"That's too bad.

"Listen, Emily. It's not advised that the defendant take the stand. In most cases I agree. But when I attended law school, a very intelligent professor said there are times when we should prepare our clients. I think this is one of them. It's your decision if you take the stand. I'd never force you. But I think I should warn you that the prosecutor is going to come at you with everything he has. It's his job to prove you're guilty. If you win, he loses. Sauer is a prosecutor for a reason. He doesn't like to lose. And he's been on this case since the beginning."

"What if the person is innocent?"

"It doesn't matter."

Ryan gazed at her in deep thought. He began to walk back and forth from one end of the cell to the other.

"The report says you hated Claude because he kept the cat population down."

"But he did. He did kill cats, mostly kittens."

Ryan glanced up, still walking. "And the prosecutor will say, you don't murder someone for killing cats."

"I didn't kill him because of the cats. I... I didn't mean to kill him."

"I'm sorry for sounding harsh, Emily. But I'm *trying* to make you see what you're up against. We need to prove to the jury that Claude severely injured you, that he raped you. Give me something more than, he killed a few cats."

A few cats? What are you saying? One is too many.

"I talked my uncle Steven into taking kittens to an animal shelter in town. But I don't think any of the men thought much of what Claude did. The thing is, Claude seemed to enjoy it."

She watched Ryan circle around and stop in front of her. "Go on," he said. "It's important that you remember the worst. The very worst."

He continued his walk, and she closed her eyes, filled her lungs with air, and slowly let it out. Even though the memories made her shudder, she had no choice but to gather every ounce of strength and speak of things she didn't want to remember—things she had covered in scribbles of pain, or so far back in her mind that she would need a chisel to set them free. She squeezed her arms across her chest and forced her thoughts to a place frozen in time.

The memories came like blades through her heart, one by one. And finally, she was ready to claim them, ready to tell the horror that she had kept inside.

"Once, Claude stuffed a litter of kittens into a gunnysack and headed to the creek. I was so angry, nothing could've kept me from trying to save them. As I followed him, he stopped and put in a stray cat. He just snatched it up as it walked by and stuffed it in with the rest. I heard them. I... I saw them trying to escape. It was so...hori...."

Emily leaned forward with her head on her lap and sobbed.

"That's it. Feel the rage. Allow yourself the anger. You don't want this to be your home for the next ten fifteen years, do you?"

She sat up shaking her head. "*No.*"

Ryan lifted a handkerchief from his shirt pocket, sponged his forehead and began to pace again—his feet tap, tap, tapping across the concrete floor.

She followed his movements back and forth, realizing this man was suffering too so that he might help her. All at once, she no longer cared about the tears streaming down her cheeks and flowing like rivers into her mouth and down the front of her uniform. She could not have stopped them if she tried. Wiping each cheek on a shoulder, she pulled the box of tissue closer and continued.

"When Claude approached the creek, I crept as close as I could, ducked behind bushes and watched as he threw the sack into the water. As soon as he left, I ran over, waded in, and pulled it out.

"I was so happy, so relieved they would live. I dropped to the ground and was untangling the rope when I heard footsteps. I looked up, and Claude was glaring down at me like I was the one doing something wrong. I tried to run with the sack, but he caught me and flung it aside. I heard the kittens crying as he grabbed me by the hair and drug me to the water. He pushed my...my head *under until I nearly drowned.*"

Emily stopped to catch her breath and force back sobs.

"He pulled me up and made me watch as he *drowned the kittens one by one.*

"...After he left, I gathered them up, and...."

Her shoulders shook and she allowed the sobs to free the pain she had kept inside for so long.

Ryan went to sit beside her, placing a hand across her back.

"Emily, that's a terrible story… Just horrible. But I'm glad you told me. It's been there for a while, hasn't it? Are you okay?"

"Mmhm."

"I'm sorry I had to put you through this. Claude did some things that are... Well, they were despicable and cruel. Unthinkable.

"But let me just say something for your peace of mind. You're the one that suffered the most. The cats didn't know what was going on. They weren't in pain."

He sat for a few moments until her sobs subsided. Pulling his hand from her back, he stood.

"If you decide to testify, I want you to let yourself go in the same way that you did right here. Whatever you feel the need to say, do it without holding back. I won't ask you about the rape right now."

He touched her shoulder. "I'll see you tomorrow."

Ryan started toward the bars and Emily called to him.

"Mr. Dillard? I…I should probably tell you something. It's about a place I worked when I first arrived in San Francisco."

He stepped back and took a seat. Are you talking about *The Palace*?"

Emily nodded. "Mmhm."

"As far as I'm concerned, there's no reason to bring it up in court. It has nothing to do with why you're here. And your father already explained the situation to me in confidence just in case it ever came to light. We'll hope for the best."

Ryan gave her knee a pat and stood.

"I'm sure those who saw you there have already moved on to other things. Or maybe they don't want their own secrets revealed."

After he left, she lay on the cot and listened to the curses, banging doors, hurried footsteps, and the ones slow and averting.

Sometime late in the afternoon a guard pushed an envelope through the bars. Emily brought it back to the cot and pulled out a letter.

Dearest Emily,

When you feel helpless like you must feel now, just know that you have those who love you unconditionally. Father and I will always be here for you. Please find peace in knowing that things will get better, and that you will smile again. Everyone will know the truth in time. And you will be free.

Forever your loving sister, Rose

CHAPTER TWENTY-SIX

*W*hen the day of the trial arrived, once again, an officer brought Emily in through the side door and escorted her to the counsel's table. The courtroom was almost full this time. There was no need to look for Grandfather or her uncles; Ryan informed her that they would be witnesses for the prosecutor.

Emily watched as twelve strangers with her future in their hands walked in and took their seats. Her gaze settled on a middle-aged man hunched in a mass of shoulders and neck. He placed a pencil over an ear and looked directly at her.

A chill washed over her, and she turned away, searching for someone or something that would give her hope. But even the common seemed odd—the updo as stiff as porcupine quills, the gray hair in tight curls, creaks of old wood, and shuffling feet.

The room became silent as the bailiff stepped forward and asked everyone to rise. Judge Grosslyn appeared in a dark flowing robe, spoke a few words, and took a seat at the bench. He directed the lawyers to begin, and Prosecutor Sauer stood and stepped to the podium.

"Your Honor. Ladies and gentlemen of the jury. Claude Thorn worked at the Rezell farm for over twenty years, only to be murdered by the boss's granddaughter. While he lay dead with a pitchfork in his chest, Emily went to the house and made breakfast. Now who does that. An innocent person? I think not. After breakfast, she attempted to cover up the crime by burning her bloody clothes, the blood of Claude Thorn. Then she caught the first ride out of there and took a train to San Francisco. To make matters even worse, she was on the run for over a year. Ladies and gentlemen. Does that sound like someone who is innocent?"

The prosecutor gazed at the jury giving it time to sink in. "It sounds like someone who's guilty, doesn't it. She'll try to tell us all kinds of horrible things about Claude. But as the trial progresses, you'll see that she has not one person to back up her claims. Not one. So, ladies and gentlemen of the jury. Before the end of the trial, I will prove that Emily Rezell drove the pitchfork into Claude Thorn's chest out of hate."

*W*hen the prosecutor had called Emily a murderer, Ryan had gripped his armrest before he found his guard and settled back to wait his turn. But the moment Sauer finished his opening statement, he leaped to his feet and hurried around the counsel's table with vengeance.

"Every defendant is presumed innocent until proven guilty," he said, moving past the podium. He stopped in front of the prosecutor, his eyes sweeping across the jury members. "I hope when I prove Miss Rezell's innocence, that there's an apology for the wrong that's been done here today."

He tapped the counsel table and stepped toward the jury. "Ladies and gentlemen, by the end of the trial I will prove that Emily Rezell was the victim, and Mr. Thorn was the perpetrator. By the end of the trial, you will learn that Claude Thorn had a split personality. On one hand, he was able to put on airs that gave him likeability. On the other hand, he could be sadistic in nature. Those having his temperament can be perfectly nice to one person. But for those they see as weak or downtrodden, they allow evil to take over. I can't say for certain what went on in his head. But I am convinced that his barbaric actions caused his own death. And I am confident that by the end of the trial you will come to this same conclusion."

When the lawyers had finished their opening statements, Prosecutor Sauer stepped forward. Emily knew with his good looks, stylish dark hair, and perfectly fitted suit, that he had something extra going for him right from the start. But she hoped the jury would see beyond his appearance and piercing words.

"The state of Illinois brings Mr. Rupert Rezell to the stand."

Emily couldn't take her eyes off her grandfather as he made his way to the front where he took an oath.

The questions came one after another.

"Mr. Rezell. Did you tell the police that Emily was late making breakfast the morning Claude died?"

"I... I may have."

"The police report says you did.

"And isn't it true you told the police as you drove your tractor from one field to another, that you saw Emily standing next to the burn barrel with smoke rising?"

"As I recall. The police asked me who used the barrel last."

"And who did you say it was?"

"...Emily."

"Why was that unusual for her to use the burn barrel that day?"

Grandfather hesitated.

"Why was that unusual, Mr. Rezell?"

"Because we only burn once a week."

"And?"

"And...we had just burned the day before."

"Didn't the police find remnants of a blouse and skirt inside the barrel? And didn't they belong to Emily?"

"…Yes."

"And isn't it true that Emily fled to San Francisco less than an hour before Timothy found Claude's body?"

"Yes."

"Thank you Mr. Rezell. I have no further questions."

When it was Ryan's turn with cross-examination, he moved to the stand and gazed at the old man. Emily wondered if he was reflecting, maybe trying to place him in the world she had described.

"Did Emily ever give you trouble?"

"No, not really. At least not much."

"In other words, she was a good kid."

"I'd say so."

"Did she cook and clean for you and other members of the household from a very young age?"

"Yes."

"How long did Claude Thorn live on your farm?"

"Twenty some years."

"Claude did some drinking, didn't he."

"He liked his whiskey."

"There're reports that say using alcohol lowers a person's inhibitions. Would you agree?"

"I'd say so."

"The report also states that using too much alcohol can result in reckless decisions. Would you say that is also true?"

"Drinking too much can do that."

"And isn't it true that Claude drank alcohol at least four or five days out of the week, if not more?"

"Probably."

"Were Claude and Emily ever alone in the barn together?"

"They had their chores to do."

"I'll take that as a, yes.

"Could it be that Claude raped Emily while they were in the barn togeth—"

"No! Of course not."

It seemed the old man was offended that anyone would think something like that would happen in his barn.

"But… There was time for him to do just that, wasn't there?"

"Your Honor," the prosecutor said, rising from his chair.

"He's leading the witness."

"Sustained."

"Okay… So… Let's say if you had known that Claude raped Emily. Would you have been upset?"

"A hypothetical question, Your Honor," came the prosecutor.

"Overruled. Go on. Answer the question."

"Yes... I would've been."

"Could it be that Emily was hiding Claude's violent behavior toward her?"

Emily wanted to scream at her grandfather—
Yes, yes, yes, Grandfather, yes.

"I can't say."

"But there is a possibility."

"Your Honor. He's pressuring the grandfather and the jury with unsubstantiated, bushwa."

"Sustained."

Ryan stepped toward the stand and gazed at the old man. "Mr. Rezell. Have you ever been so pained by something that it was difficult to put into words?"

Rupert's jaw tightened. "I have."

"Thank you, sir. That will be all."

Prosecutor Sauer brought Emily's youngest uncle to the stand. She prayed he would be wakened to signs that he ignored in the past.

"Mr. Timothy Rezell," the prosecutor began. "You told me that you and Claude had a good relationship. Isn't that true."

"Yes."

"Let me ask you. What kind of a worker was the deceased?"

"He did his job. Well...I mean, he'd been having headaches those last several years. But other than that. He put the work in."

"Did he complain about being worked too hard?"

"I never heard any complaints."

"Was he ever violent toward you?"

"No."

"Did you ever see him be violent toward anyone else?"

"No."

"Did you ever see Claude Thorn, force himself on the defendant?"

"No."

"Did you ever suspect anything nefarious was going on between Emily and Claude?"

Emily held her breath when Timothy glanced at her. It was as if he was trying to think back. He seemed unsettled. Ryan told her that the prosecutor had already questioned the men, and there were set answers he would expect from them.

"Mr. Rezell?"

"Uh... No. It never entered my mind, sir."

"You're the one that found the deceased, aren't you."

"Yes."

"It must've been traumatic for you. Floor covered in blood. A body. Could you imagine someone hating him that much?"

"...No."

"The person had to have been filled with venom, wouldn't you say?"

"Well... It looked that way. But—"

"Did you ever see Emily angry at Claude?"

"Umm...Well...."

"You're under oath, Mr. Rezell. Did you ever see Emily spew rage at Claude."

Emily cringed because both of her uncles happened on the scene just as she exploded at Claude after he threatened Kidders' life if she wouldn't go to the loft with him.

Timothy set his gaze on Sauer and shook his head. "I'm not sure it was rage."

"She was angry, though."

"...She was."

"What were her exact words? And remember, you're under oath."

Timothy looked pained.

"Mr. Rezell. What did she say to him?"

"As I recall. She said...she hated him."

"That will be all, thank you."

It was Ryan's turn with cross examination, and Emily willed Timothy to look at her again.

"Your grandfather said your niece was a good kid. Do you agree?"

"Yes."

"Anger was brought up. Have you ever been angry, Mr. Rezell?"

"Plenty."

"Did Emily do anything that would make you believe she was capable of murder?"

"No."

Emily was relieved when Ryan decided that was a good time to dismiss Timothy, leaving that thought with the jury. She expected Prosecutor Sauer would call Steven to the stand, but instead, he brought up a police officer.

"Officer Jenkin, thanks for coming in.

"You were the first to learn that Emily was with Claude when he died, right?"

"Yes, sir."

"Would you please tell the court how that came about?"

"Well...after the deceased was found in the barn loft, and we realized two members of the household had left the property, I was called to track them down."

"I see you found Steven soon after. Tell us what happened."

"When Steven said he dropped Emily off at the movies, and when he went to pick her up, she was gone, I suspected he may have killed them both. There were backups nearby and I sent them to look for Emily's body."

"Did you arrest him?"

"No, sir. He was a suspect. I was still questioning him."

"What sort of questions did you ask him?"

"I asked if he had gotten into an altercation with Claude that morning. He said, no. That he hadn't seen him since the day before. Then I asked if there had been any funny stuff going on with Emily. He said he'd mentioned to her that she was acting peculiar. But all at once, Steven got this startled look on his face and asked if Emily was okay. About then a detective showed up and said that the wife of a police officer had picked up a young lady with Emily's description in Kankakee and took her to the bus station. That's when I realize we were after the wrong person."

When the officer was dismissed, and Ryan declined a rebuttal, Steven was brought to the stand.

"Mr. Rezell," Sauer said after Steven took his oath and sat. "What was your relationship like with Claude?"

"We had our squabbles."

"You just heard the officer's statement. Would you mind elaborating on Emily's demeanor the morning Claude died?"

"It's been a while."

"The statement you gave that day says you told Officer Jenkin that Emily had been acting strange that morning."

"That was before I knew what happened."

"Mr. Rezell.... I'll repeat. Did you tell Officer Jenkin that Emily had been acting strange that morning?"

"I'm not sure I said strange, but I do remember something like that."

"Did you see her in the barn that morning?"

"Yes."

"Was Emily acting troubled, or fidgety when you saw her that morning?"

"…Yes."

"How about during and after breakfast? How about as you left for Watseka? Was she acting, nervous?"

"…As I recall, she was."

"Okay, Mr. Rezell. Let's talk about a statement you made just hours after Claude's body was found. You said you had seen Emily upset with him. Is that correct?"

"Well, I—"

"Sir. I asked you that day if Emily had ever become angry with Claude. You said, yes. Is that true?"

"I suppose I did."

"Did Emily ever take a swing at the deceased?"

"Well... I don't know if she expected to hit him, but there was once."

"So, she has a little temper. She lost control."

"Not as a habit."

"Sir. Emily lost control that day when she swung at him, right?"

"Well, yes."

"Thank you. That will be all."

Ryan stood for his turn and walked toward Steven.

"If you're angry enough to want to hit someone. Where would you land the punch?"

"In the jaw."

"When Emily took a swing at Claude. Can you tell us where it was aimed?"

"From what I recall. His arm."

"How tall was Claude?"

"Mm. Over six feet."

"Thank you. I think we get the picture."

"Let me ask you. Approximately how many times did you see the defendant and the deceased alone in the barn?"

"Well...uh. Over the years, I couldn't say for sure."

"So, it was more than twenty or thirty times?"

"Oh, yes. At least."

Mr. Dillard stopped in front of Steven and studied him. "Did you know anything about Claude drowning cats?"

Steven thought for a moment. "As I recall, yes."

"And what were your feelings about that."

"I never really thought about it. It happens."

"Did you ever drown a cat?"

"No."

"Why not?"

"Well...I just wouldn't do that."

"Which of the men in the family was Emily closest to?"

"I'd have to say, me."

"Did Emily ever talk to you about her personal problems?"

"No."

"Let's say she was afraid of Claude, afraid of what he would do to her. If she had refused to go into the barn and do her chores, would there have been hell to pay?"

"Yes."

"So, let's say Claude was harming her. She wouldn't have had a choice but to go into the barn and do her chores."

The prosecutor half rose from his seat. "Your Honor. Once again, Mr. Dillard is digging for clues where there are none."

"Sustained. Strike that from the record."

"The point I'm trying to make is that with all we've learned, Emily was likely holding things inside. Do you agree?"

"It seems that way."

"Thank you. No further questions."

On that note, court ended that day. And, as before. Emily turned at the door and put on a brave face for Rose before she was taken away.

CHAPTER TWENTY-SEVEN

*C*ourt was in session, and Emily expected her father would take the stand. Ryan had been talking to his assistant and turned to give her an update.

"You're father just called to say he's been held up."

"What? Is he okay?"

"Yes, he's fine. Just flight delays. But listen, I have some promising news. A woman filed a report on behalf of the defense several days ago. It's all set, and she'll take the stand in a few minutes. But first, I'm going to put your sister on."

When Ryan called Rose to the stand, she was able to tell the court what a big heart Emily had. And that she was recently a nanny for two young children who thought the world of her.

"I heard you had a telephone conversation with the children's tutor. Would you mind speaking on her behalf?"

"Not at all. You see, she was very impressed with the way Emily came in and changed the children's attitude and even brought up their grades. And my father...our father, he personally witnessed her dedication to her job and to the children. And I've seen first-hand how she cares about the feelings of others. She's not...." Rose glanced at the prosecutor. "She's not what he said."

"Thank you, Miss Dimsmoore, for allowing those who don't know anything about the defendant except what they've heard in the news and the courtroom."

As the prosecutor stepped forward, Emily could see he was itching to lay into Rose.

"You've known your half-sister for how long?"

"Uh... a little over a week."

"A little over a week?" Sauer glanced at the jury with raised eyebrows. Several of them struggled to hide smiles.

"Do you consider Emily to be a truthful person?"

"I do."

"That's interesting. Because I'm trying to figure out from what experience you're drawing your trust in the defendant. Let me ask you. Before my opening statement, did you know that your sister was holding the pitchfork that went into Claude's chest? In other words, did she confess this to you?"

Rose glanced at Emily and back to Sauer.

"Let me ask you again Miss Dimsmoore. Did your sister confess to you that the pitchfork she was holding ended up in Claude's chest?"

"Well...n-no. But—"

"The truth is that she was never going to tell anyone. The truth is that she had been fleeing the law for over a year when you met her. And it was only when her name showed up in a San Francisco newspaper that finally brought the attention to the police. Isn't that, right?"

"Isn't that right, Miss Dimsmoore?"

"...Yes."

"Thank you. That will be all."

Ryan stepped forward with determination.

"You said you've known Emily for a little over a week. How much time did you spend together?"

"I'd say at least twelve hours."

"So, you were just getting to know each other. What did you talk about?"

"I told her about myself, and about the family she never knew she had—a father she thought was dead. Her mother died within hours after her birth. And her grandmother died when she was seven. I learned how that affected her. And I learned she wasn't able to attend school until she was nine. Even though she loved going to school, she had to drop out after the eighth grade to help on the farm. I know that bothered her greatly."

"Thank you Rose."

After Rose was dismissed, Sauer brought up two character witnesses. If anything, they made Claude look like an all-right guy. Even Ryan could do nothing to bring a smidge of negative from these men.

After a court break, and once Emily was brought back in, Ryan took stage.

"I call Mrs. Melanie Houser to the stand."

Emily noticed that Melanie was the woman she saw comforting Rose right after the judge ordered her to jail.

The young lady was trembling as she took her oath and sat, looking down, only glancing up when asked a question.

"Miss Houser, did you know the deceased, Mr. Claude Thorn?"

"Yes."

"Would you please explain the relationship you had with him."

"We didn't have a relationship. At one time he was a friend of my father's. And he went out with my sister for a time."

Finally, Emily knew who she was. It was the sister of the red-haired woman who might've straightened Claude out—that's if he'd had any sense.

"From what I hear, it wasn't quite that simple."

Melanie cleared her throat, patting her chest.

Ryan stepped closer. "Will you please tell us what you came to say."

Taking a breath, she looked at Ryan.

"My sister and I were swimming at the creek. She had to leave for a babysitting job."

"After she left, then what?"

"Well... I was getting ready to go back to the house when Claude showed up."

"So now you're alone with Claude. Would you please tell the court what happened next?"

"What happened was that...."

Her eyes darted to Emily and back to Ryan. She leaned forward, her voice barely audible. "Claude raped me."

There was mumbling throughout the courtroom until the judge slammed down the gavel.

"Let me remind you to keep your emotions to yourself. Either that or stay home."

Ryan waited for everyone to settle.

"Miss Houser. Would you please tell the court how old you were when this rape took place?"

"I was fourteen."

There were gasps and more mumbling until the judge slammed his gavel again and threatened to clear the room.

"You're one in a million," Ryan said, "and thank you."

He nodded and took a seat as the prosecutor stood for his turn.

"Miss Houser," Sauer said when he stepped forward.

"After this alleged rape. Did you go home and tell anyone what happened?"

"...No."

"You've never told anyone?"

"...No."

"There's something that has me puzzled. I'm trying to figure out why when someone rapes you, you decide that it's not important enough to tell even one person. And yet you show up years later and tell a crowd of people just that. I don't buy it. There's something you're not telling us. Is it revenge? Jealousy? Or maybe it's notoriety? Is that it?"

"No."

"I have no more questions."

Prosecutor Sauer turned to the judge and asked if he could step to the bench. Their conversation lasted for several minutes before Ryan was called to join them.

After the judge heard from both lawyers, Ryan looked discouraged as he returned to his seat.

"That's it for today. Mr. Sauer was going to bring Melanie's sister to the stand, but he wants more time for discovery. Court will be adjourned for several days."

He glanced back as Melanie left the courtroom. "What in the world does he think she would gain by making up a story like that? Clearly, it's not notoriety."

Court convened three days later, and Emily was relieved to see her father sitting next to Rose. Just knowing he was there gave her courage.

The judge had finished his introduction and turned the floor over to Prosecutor Sauer. He called Melanie Houser to the stand.

"Miss Houser. Several days ago, I questioned your reason for taking the stand. I couldn't decide if it was revenge, jealousy, or notoriety. My conclusion is that it's all three. Let's talk about revenge today. You mind if we do that?" He motioned to the jury and audience. "Just... discuss a few things here in front of the court."

Melanie's frustration seemed to have put a fire beneath her, and her gaze swept across the room and straight back to him.

"Your father and Claude Thorn were friends at one time, weren't they?"

"Yes."

"Will you please tell the court what happened the last time your father stopped by the Rezell farm?"

"Well. They... They were—"

"There was a big argument, wasn't there."

"...Y-yes."

"What was the argument about?"

"I don't know all the details. But there was some kind of a conflict over business."

"Okay. So, let me refresh your memory. Your father claims that Claude convinced him to put money into an investment that went belly up. Isn't that correct?"

"...Yes."

"And even to this day. Isn't your father trying to get his money back, insisting that Rupert Rezell was part of the scheme? Isn't this all true?"

Melanie's eyes filled with tears, her fire gone. She dropped her head, nodding. "Yes."

"Thank you. That will be all."

"Does the defense care to question the witness?" the judge asked Ryan.

"Yes, I do, Your Honor," Ryan said, taking the floor. He placed an elbow on the podium. And Melanie met his gaze.

"Did you know about the argument between your father and Claude before the incident at the creek?"

"Yes."

"Were you personally affected by that conflict? In other words, did you hold anger toward Claude at that time?"

"No. I didn't."

"And is there any reason why you were, or would be jealous, let's say, of Claude, or your sister?"

"No. None."

"Would you call yourself a loner?"

"I would."

"So, you don't do a lot of gossiping. Gossiping, as in spreading lies and unnecessary banter."

"No."

"The prosecutor says you came here for notoriety. Is that why you're here?"

"No, sir."

"And why did you decide to come forward."

Melanie nodded toward Emily. "For her, and... To set things straight."

"Thank you, Melanie. That's honorable of you. You're free to go."

Ryan sat and the prosecutor stood and announced his next witness.

"I call Mrs. Charlette Houser-Clark to the stand."

Emily was mesmerized as she watched Claude's former girlfriend walk to the stand and take an oath. Sauer looked pleased as he began.

"Is Melanie Houser your sister?"

"Yes."

"At any time, did you see Claude act inappropriately toward Melanie?"

"No. I don't recall they ever talked."

"You told me that Claude was once your boyfriend."

"I did."

"How did Claude treat you?"

"Just fine."

"Were you in love with him?"

"I thought so at the time."

"What happened to your relationship?"

"Well…when I was visiting the Rezell farm one day, my father came by and demanded I leave and never see Claude again."

"And did you see him again?"

"No."

"Did you understand why he was angry with Claude?"

"Not, really."

"Do you believe Claude raped your sister."

"First I heard of it."

"Do you think Melanie is lying?"

Charlette shrugged. "Who knows."

"So. In other words you think she could be lying."

Ryan stood. "Your Honor, he's trying to put words in her mouth."

"Sustained."

"It seems to me that sisters would know if the other was lying about something like that. Don't you think, Mrs. Clark?"

"Probably."

"Thank you. I have no further questions."

When Ryan chose not to question the witness, Emily turned to him.

"Now how are the jury supposed to believe Melanie after that?

"You know... I was there when their father came to get Charlette."

Ryan thought for a moment. "It's clear that those sisters have a puzzling relationship. And from my experience, sometimes it's best to just let things play out."

Emily turned to her lawyer. "Remember when you asked if I wanted to spend the next ten, fifteen years in jail? Well, I don't. And I've made a decision. I want to take the stand.

"Uh... Are you sure?"

"I'm positive."

"Okay. I'll set things in motion."

The judge ordered a recess. And when they returned, Ryan called Samuel Dimsmoore to the stand.

"Mr. Dimsmoore. How did you know Mr. Thorn?"

"We both worked on the Rezell farm."

"And how long was that?"

"About a year."

"So, you must have spent many hours with him."

"Yes, sir."

"Did you know Mr. Thorn before you started working for Rupert Rezell?"

"I'd only seem him once at a farm where I stopped to look for work."

"Did you ever suspect that Claude had behavioral problems?"

"I did."

"Was there a particular incident that led you to that conclusion?"

There was a clatter as the courtroom door flew open. A man hurried up the aisle, handed papers to the prosecutor, and rushed back out.

Ryan waited for the commotion to stop before turning back to Samuel.

"Go on. Tell us about that incident?"

"Well. It was an argument between Rachael and Claude."

"What were they fighting about?"

"I can't say for sure. But I heard her ask Claude what was happening to him. Then she went on to say that she hadn't forgotten what he did. And if he didn't change his ways, she would tell her father."

"Did you ask her about what you heard?"

"Yes."

"What did she say?"

"She told me not to worry, and that she had taken care of everything. I didn't want to think the worst, so I put it aside, until...well, until this whole thing with Emily."

"At the time, did you think it was rape she was talking about?"

"Your, Honor, came the prosecutor. "He's leading the witness again. Mr. Thorn was probably doing something non-threatening like smoking one of Mr. Rezell's cigars."

"Sustained."

"Ok. Let's go back to when you saw Rachael scolding Claude. Was she angry?"

"She was upset, yes."

"What was her relationship like with Claude?"

"Well... Rachael was nice to everyone. She was normally a happy-go-lucky, singing in the barnyard, happy. It had to be something big to get her upset."

"Did she ever say anything else derogatory about Claude?"

"Once. After the altercation with him, she made an off-handed comment."

"Do you recall what that was?"

"It's been a while, but one day she questioned whether her father should keep him on. She said that Claude had been changing since he first came to live with them."

"Did she say anything more?"

"Just that Claude's parents both died in a car accident. And that Claude had been in a coma from a head injury for several weeks after the accident. I know she took pity on him."

"In other words, you believe she let him off easy because of pity."

"Yes."

"Thank you, Mr. Dimsmoore. That will be all."

The prosecutor declined his chance to question Samuel. Instead, he stood and walked around the table, picked up the papers the runner brought in, and asked the judge if he could approach the bench. The judge read through the documents and called Ryan to the bench.

There was a heated discussion. When Emily heard Rachael's name, her father's, and her grandfather's name as well, it became clear that whatever they were arguing about, something unusual had just happened. She looked back at her grandfather and uncles. By the looks on their faces, they knew more than she did.

Finally, the judge slammed down his gavel and adjourned court for the day. Ryan and the prosecutor were still talking when Emily was taken from the courtroom.

*B*ack in her cell, Emily paced the floor until Ryan showed up. When the jailor opened the door for him, he walked in and leaned against the bars.

Emily went to him. "What was that about?"

"I don't know how to tell you this, except that. Well...
When your grandfather found out your mother was
pregnant, he pressed raped charges against your father.
There's a warrant out for his arrest."

"After all these years?"

"I'm afraid so. Warrant's don't have an expiration date.
They're active until there's an arrest or charges are
dropped."

"I'm telling you. My father didn't rape my mother."

"That may be true. But, unless your grandfather drops
the charges, and the judge agrees, I can't say what will
happen. I'm sorry. But the judge's hands are tied."

Emily walked to the cot and sat. "Grandfather will
never give my father a break. He blames him for my
mother's death. And he's been angry since the day she
died."

Ryan put a hand through his hair and sighed.

"Alright. Let me see what I can do."

He started to leave and looked back at Emily.

"Your grandfather may hate your father. But he and
your uncles didn't seem all that anxious to have you put in
jail."

"*W*ell, it's done," Rose said when Emily entered the
visiting room. "They booked Father. He's in jail."

Emily slumped to a bench. "I'm so sorry."

Rose sat next to Emily. "You know it's not your fault.
Yes, it's upsetting. But let's be honest. Our father did get
your mother pregnant out of wedlock. Besides, who's to
say the police wouldn't have caught up with him at some
point. The important thing is that he didn't rape your
mother. Just like you didn't murder Claude.

"Listen...let's make something warm to drink and talk
about what we'll do when all of this is over. It will be over,
you know."

The girls tried to think of brighter days when this would be just a memory. They decided to write their father a letter. When it was time to leave, Rose stopped at the door.

"I've lived with Father all my life, and I know that right now he's more concerned about you." She waved the letter. "This is all he needs."

"Rose. When you see Father, tell him that I love him."

CHAPTER TWENTY-EIGHT

*T*he courtroom was filled with reporters from radio and television stations, newspapers, and the curious, waiting for Emily to take the stand.

Ryan's new jacket and trimmed hair didn't go unnoticed. He stood and walked around the counsel's table, at least ten pounds lighter than the day he paced across Emily's prison cell.

"Your Honor. I'd like to call Emily Rezell to the stand."

Emily knew she was taking a big chance, and her knees felt like rubber as she walked to the front, took an oath, and sat.

Ryan approached the stand.

"Please state your full name for the record."

"Emily Alexis Rezell."

"You took care of the men in the family from an early age, didn't you."

"Yes."

"You not only cooked, cleaned, and washed clothes, you planted gardens, canned, milked cows, and helped out with the animals, didn't you?"

"Yes."

"Did you mind taking care of the men?"

"For the most part, no."

"How did it make you feel, working day in and day out?"

"I guess...like I was doing something worthwhile. We all worked hard."

"And working is not a bad thing, is it."

"So... How long did you know Claude Thorn?"

"Ever since I can remember."

Ryan began questioning Emily about the way Claude kept the cat population down. The room was silent as she describe following Claude as he walked to the creek carrying a sack of squalling cats. There were gasps and murmurs as she described trying to save them and how he almost drowned her. The judge only had to reprimand the crowd once.

Ryan went to stand next to Emily. "It's obvious how much that still hurts. But there's something more traumatic we haven't discussed yet. I'd like you to tell the court about the first time Claude raped you."

There were several surprised glances and mumblings in the audience, then silence.

Ryan leaned in. "Take a good breath. And start by telling us how old you were."

Emily did as he said and began.

"I was thirteen, about to turn fourteen in September. School was out for the summer, and I was in the hay loft playing with a new batch of kittens. When someone came up the steps, I didn't think much of it until Claude stood over me. He squatted and stared down at the cats curled up on my lap, smelling like whiskey.

"With one scoop, the kittens landed on the floor. When I picked up the one trapped beneath the others, he plucked it out of my hand and tossed it aside. I tried to scramble away but he grabbed one of my legs and *yanked me back*."

Tears burst from Emily's eyes, remembering that moment. She wiped her palms across her cheeks, took a breath, and continued.

"He had me by the roots of my hair and was holding me down. I fought to get away. But I couldn't move. When he... When he forced himself on me, I screamed. I screamed so loud. But... He held *a hand over my mouth*."

Emily covered her face and sobbed, her shoulders heaving as she struggled to rein herself in.

Ryan went to her. "Are you going to be okay?" he said, quietly.

"Just give me a minute."

He put a hand over hers. "Take as much time as you need."

Emily closed her eyes, took deep breaths, and prayed for strength. When she had calmed, she looked up at Ryan and nodded.

"We know how difficult this is for you," he said, gazing about the room and back to Emily. "Let me ask you. Did this ever happened again?"

"Yes... Many times, for years."

"Why didn't you tell anyone?"

"He said he'd kill me if I did. Besides, I didn't think anyone would believe me. Or... maybe they'd blame me, like he said."

"Reliving that terrible time had to be very painful, Emily. And I want to thank you for bearing your soul."

Ryan stepped closer, lowering his voice so only she could hear. "You did good. And I'm going to stand here for a minute until your calm... Okay? Just remember. Don't let Sauer get to you."

When Emily was ready to continue, Ryan sat, and the prosecutor stepped forward.

"On the morning of Claude's death, "Did he try to stop you from leaving the farm that morning?"

"...Y-yes."

"Did he confront you about a family heirloom you took from your aunt's house after she died?"

"Well, I—"

"It's a simple yes, or no. Did you take a necklace from your aunt's house? And did Claude confront you?"

"Yes."

"Is this why you killed him?"

"No."

"Did he threaten to tell your grandfather that you had the necklace?"

"...Yes, but—"

"Did he threaten to tell your grandfather that you were leaving?"

Ryan had warned Emily about Sauer's tactics, but she was shocked by the way he came at her, trying to cause confusion. She hadn't mention the necklace to Ryan because she had no idea the prosecutor would use it against her.

"Miss Rezell. Did Claude Thorn threaten to tell your grandfather that you were trying to sneak away?"

"Yes."

"Did you hate, Claude?"

Emily didn't know what to say. She probably had hated him at times...at least hated what he had done to her. But if he had stopped what he was doing, she would have forgiven him. She had....

"I hated what he did. And at times, maybe I felt that way."

Ryan jumped to his feet. "This is ridiculous Your Honor. The man is badgering the defendant. She's already made it very clear what happened."

The judge nodded to Sauer.

"Sustained."

"Okay, then, tell me. Were you holding the pitchfork as it went into Claude's chest?"

Emily opened her mouth to defend herself, but nothing came out. She couldn't lie and the truth made her sound like she meant to kill him.

"Miss Rezell. Were you holding the pitchfork when it went into Claude Thorn's chest?"

"...Yes."

"I could barely hear you, Miss Rezell. And I doubt anyone else did. So, let me ask you again. Were you holding the pitchfork when it went into Claude Thorn's chest?"

"Yes."

"After you killed him, why did you run?"

She looked at the prosecutor, the jury, and back to him. "I was scared."

"Of course, you were. You were afraid of being caught. Isn't that right?"

"I..." Emily looked down at her hands.

"Miss Rezell. Were you afraid of being caught?"

"Yes."

"That will be all."

He took a seat, and Ryan stepped forward. There was fire in his eyes.

"Would you describe to the court the minutes before Claude died?"

Emily gazed into Ryan's eyes, drawing courage from him.

"Claude was either going to force himself on me, or I would have to give in. He had already dragged me up to the barn loft, slammed me against a pole, threw me to the floor, *and kicked me.*

"I-I was trying to trick him, so I'd have time to get away."

Emily had asked Ryan why no one mentioned the matter of Claude's jeans. He told her that the prosecutor knew it was a touchy subject. And to ensure no one would bring it up, Sauer insisted that someone who was covering up the crime and fled the scene could surely have positioned the jeans wherever they pleased. Ryan knew, as far as the jury was concerned, it could go both ways, and if not in their favor, that could be a fatal blow. He told Emily to let the information come out naturally. She knew this was the moment.

"I had to think fast about how to get away from him."

"Would you please tell the court what happen."

"Knowing Claude, I had no choice but to trick him, to make him think I was giving in."

"Giving in?"

"Yes. That I would…lay with him.

"Right after I convinced him of that. I knew time had run out for me. And everything became a blur as I went at him trying to scare him off with the pitchfork. But he was so enraged he wasn't getting what he thought, he came at me saying he'd kill me. That's when he tripped at the same time my foot caught a loose board. We collided. That's what happened. We collided. It was an accident. I never would have killed him on purpose. Never."

"Thank you for clearing that up, Miss Rezell. That will be all."

Emily was surprised the prosecutor didn't come after her with a rebuttal. Instead, there was a short break. But when it was time for the closing statements, Sauer was merciless.

"Let me ask you ladies and gentlemen of the jury," he began. "Why would Miss Rezell run for her life if she wasn't guilty? The truth is. She wouldn't have. And remember, she eluded the police for over a year. As it's been stated, the only reason she's here is because someone recognized her name in a San Francisco newspaper.

"Emily Rezell had over twelve and a half months to step forward and tell the truth. Instead, she comes up with this absurd lie she tried to pull off today. Where is the proof that Claude raped her? Oh, yes, there was a weak claim from Miss Hauser that was hastily proven ridiculous. Not one soul knew anything about what Miss Rezell claims was going on. Not even her grandfather and uncles. Ladies and gentlemen, it's clear that Emily deceived and tricked her way across country hoping to never be seen again. This young lady, a great actress I might add, held hate in her heart for the deceased for reasons not worthy of the death penalty he received. You see. The last straw was when Mr.

Thorn tried to stop her from leaving with the family heirloom. You heard her. She said so herself. And as we conclude this trial, there is no other option but to prosecute her and make her pay for her sins. Now all I ask is that you look to your conscience and do the right thing."

Ryan was calm and confident as he stepped forward.

"We all heard and saw how Emily struggled to talk about the first time Claude raped her. How he held her head under the water until she nearly drowned, how he forced her to watch him drown the cats she so desperately tried to save. And can you imagine the pain she endured, year after year with Claude demanding she satisfy his needs? Maybe no one else knew what was going on. But there is proof if you listened to her story, if you listened carefully to every word, if you looked into her eyes and saw the pain. It's clear that Claude had a cruel and evil streak with not an ounce of guilt to stop him."

Ryan walked over and tapped the table where Emily sat. "This young lady ran because there was no one she felt she could turn to. She lacked the support anyone in this room would need under such harsh circumstances. And she had always planned to turn herself in. In fact, she was about to do just that before she was injured. Sometimes a person needs just the right timing to deal with something as traumatic as what she endured. And now ladies and gentlemen of the jury, we have a chance to right the wrong that was done to this young woman. Thank you for listening with an open heart."

After the jury was dismissed and filed out for deliberation, Emily was taken to the changing room and to her cell. Looking around her dingy living quarters, she wondered how she could wait for hours, or maybe even days to hear the verdict.

Sitting on the cot with her head in her hands and her elbows on her lap, she prayed for mercy. After a fervent prayer, she got up, paced the room, then walked to the bars and listened for footsteps, afraid they wouldn't come, and afraid they would.

Remembering the prosecutor's searing statements, once again she prayed for mercy. Finally, a guard came for her. Her chest ached with the weight of a mountain as he brought her into the courtroom and to the counsel's table.

Judge Grosslyn finished with formalities, asked the defendant to stand, and for the clerk to record the verdict. There were only faint whispers and creaking of the weathered building, but inside Emily's mind, voices droned like a rumbling sea.

Suddenly, the sea became silent.

"The State of Illinois verses Emily Alexis Rezell. Verdict. We the jury, find Emily Alexis Rezell *not guilty of first-degree murder*."

Cheers exploded, and Judge Grosslyn stood, nodded to Emily, and told her she was free to go. Most everyone in the courtroom applauded the innocent verdict and Emily did her best to ignore the few who verbalized otherwise.

She turned to Ryan and gave him a hug. "Thank you. Thank you for everything."

Rose pushed her way through the crowd and embraced her sister. "Come on, Em. Let's get out of here."

Emily looked back at Ryan. "Can I leave?"

He smiled and shooed them out. "You deserve to walk out that front door, a free woman. But make sure to stop at the office to sign papers."

Rose took Emily by an arm and guided her through the crowd of curious onlookers and reporters who spun out questions.

"Will you write a book?" someone asked.

"Do you wish you hadn't picked up that pitchfork?" came another.

"Please everyone," Rose said, "you heard her story."

"Miss Rezell," someone called. "How do you feel about walking out a free woman?"

Emily looked over a shoulder. "Thankful. I'm very thankful. And happy it's over."

Of course, there was the journalist who came from Chicago with an agenda, hoping to get front page.

"Miss Rezell. Which do you regret most, the fateful event that took place in the barn loft in rural Watseka, or your stint at *The Palace* in San Francisco?"

Rose squeezed Emily's arm. "Ignore him. If you refuse to respond he'll probably throw it in the trash. The big story is that you've been acquitted."

Emily hoped she was right, and relieved that no one had brought up *The Palace* during the trial. She hadn't told Rose about it yet and didn't know how she could without disappointing her. It was troublesome that someone got a hold of the information and thought it was newsworthy enough to mention. She hoped Rose was right and the story would die before it began.

As the girls turned for the exit, Miss Tucker stood three feet away. She approached them and took Emily's hands.

"It's so nice to see you again. Hasn't it been at least ten years?"

"Yes, at least."

Miss Tucker took a few moments to gaze at her former student. "Oh, Emily, I've thought about you often. I'm…so sorry for everything you went through. But I'm very proud of the way you've held up."

"Thank you. I was wondering about you…if you'd come."

"You may have known that I moved to Minnesota. And I just got news that you were here two days ago."

"Well, I'm sure glad you made it. You know… I've thought about you many times throughout the years. And I want to say that because of your influence on my life, I'm in the process of getting my teacher's certificate."

"That's wonderful. Congratulations. There is no better reward for a teacher than to hear something like that."

Miss Tucker hugged Emily, said goodbye, and turned to Rose.

"You take good care of her now."

"I will. And it was nice to meet you, Miss Tucker."

"Wow, good stuff," Rose said, taking Emily's arm again.

"What about your father, Emily?" someone called.

She turned toward the voice. "My mother and father were very much in love. He's innocent. So, I'm sure he'll be out soon."

As Emily and Rose made their way through the crowd, someone caught Emily's eye. She almost turned away until she realized it was Daniel. He was taller, and more mature, but he had that same presence about him that she recalled so well.

"Let's head this way," Rose said, tugging her from his view.

Emily leaned for a better look and caught sight of him again. This time she could see he was making his way over.

"Wait. It's someone from school."

Rose released her as Daniel walked up.

"Emily. I'm glad I was able to catch you before you left."

She didn't realize she had been holding her breath.

"Hi Daniel. What a way to meet again…after all this time."

"I wouldn't have missed it."

A pained expression crossed his face. "I wish I had known."

Emily's eyes welled. "We were young. So very young."

He nodded and a tuft of blond curls fell to a cheek as it had many times before, his beautiful green eyes bright, though holding years.

She almost reached over to brush his hair aside, but Rose held out a hand.

"It's a pleasure to meet you."

"Nice to meet you, Rose. And I'm very happy Emily found you."

"Me too."

"I couldn't ask for a better sister," Emily said, meeting his gaze.

"Well… It was good to see you again, Daniel."

"Yes, it was…very nice.

"Bye, Emily."

Someone walked up and said her name. It was a woman she had seen before but couldn't place, possibly from one of her shopping trips with Steven

"I believed in you all along," she said.

"Thank you."

Rose pulled Emily along as she looked around, searching for Daniel, wishing she had asked if he had moved back to Illinois.

"Hey, how come you never told me about him. Was it serious?"

"I was only thirteen, well, nearly fourteen. And…yes, it was serious."

She looked back as they headed for the exit, hoping to get another glimpse of him. But Daniel was gone.

Rose led Emily out the door, down the steps, almost dragging her across the lawn, both of them laughing. When they reached the adjoining sidewalk, she slipped an arm around her shoulders.

"Okay, let's go sign those papers and make a run for it."

All at once, Emily realized that she was really free for the first time in her life.

"Once we get to the apartment, how about we make something to eat," she said to Rose. "I'm ready for some home cooking."

"Exactly what I was thinking. And after we'll go see Father. We'll bring him dessert."

CHAPTER TWENTY-NINE

"*T*hat's the worst idea I've heard in a long time."

"Come on Rose, back me on this. Father has done so much for me."

"I agree. He still won't go for it, though. But, okay, I'll do it for you."

The girls brought their father rolled oat cookies filled with nuts, coconut, and topped with vanilla icing. They spent nearly an hour visiting with him before Emily had the nerve to bring up her plan.

"I'd like to ask you something. And let me explain before you say no."

His eyes narrowed. "Go ahead, I'm listening."

"I want to stay here until you're released. I'll get a job packing groceries, sweeping floors, washing dishes, or whatever it takes."

"Sounds good. But the answer is, *no*."

"Can't you just think about it? I talked to the couple who rented us the apartment. They agreed to let me stay as long as I want."

"They did. I was there when they told her."

Emily gave Rose a thank you smile.

Samuel gazed at her as if contemplating, then stood and took each of his daughters by a hand.

"Listen… I'm warmed by your concern for me. But I won't allow you to stay behind. You're going back with your sister."

"But I don't want to leave you here."

"You…little girl," he said firmly, turning to cup her face in his hands, "you need to get back in school."

He kissed her forehead and pulled both of his girls close.

"I'll be home before you know it. This is something that should've been taken care of years ago. And you know, I have to say that, putting aside your grandfather's misguided beliefs, he had all the right in the world to be angry at me. Maybe this is what it'll take for him to forgive me.

"Come on, girls. One more hug."

Emily and Rose curled up in his arms, each kissing him on a cheek before heading out the door.

"Something good will come of this, you'll see," he called to them.

Rose laughed. "If there was a prize for the most optimistic person in the world, I do believe the prize would be his. Hands down."

*W*hen the girls arrived at the San Francisco airport, Aunt Bernice was waiting for them.

"Where's Mother?" Rose asked as they settled in the car.

"Working late. She said there's cold chicken and potato salad in the fridge. Unless you want me to stop and pick something up for you."

"We'll manage," Rose said from the back seat.

Bernice glanced over a shoulder. "How's your father doing?"

"He's fine. Brave."

Emily gazed out the window. She didn't blame the family if they were upset with her. And as supportive as Rose was, she knew how hard it had to be for her to come home without their father.

When Bernice dropped the girls off at the house, Emily was pleasantly surprised. They lived in a modest home set around a grove of trees a few hundred feet off the main road, not more than five or six miles from the church.

There was a piano in the corner directly across from the front door. Gold-speckled wallpaper glistened with rays of sun seeping through ivory-laced curtains. The dining room was simple, with a long, dark wood table and chairs to match. A china cabinet sat against the far wall between two windows.

Through an arched entrance, the kitchen was bright with various shades of yellows, delicate green trim, and frilly curtains tied back with ribbons.

Emily followed her sister upstairs to their bedroom. She gaped in awe at the white walls with paintings of long-stemmed flowers coming up from the moss green baseboards.

"Rose. This is beautiful."

"It only took me a week to do the painting.

"So… The bed on the left is yours. Father went out and bought it for you right after you got out of the hospital. I went up in the attic and brought down the bedspreads and rugs Grandmother made from pieces of leftover fabric."

"It's like a fairytale in here," Emily said. She noticed two desks on either side of a long narrow window.

Rose pointed at the one on the right. "That's yours."

Emily went to try out the chair, felt the unscratched surface of the desktop, and opened the middle drawer where she found pencils, pens, and other supplies.

"I never expected anything like this."

"Tomorrow, I'll take you up to the attic to see if there's anything else you want to bring down. Oh, and the chest on the right is yours. The clothes basket is in the closet. And there're extra hangers on the right."

When Rose had finished showing Emily their bedroom, they headed downstairs for dinner.

"How late does your mother work, anyway?"

"It's supposed to be five. But they always seem to find reasons to keep her there. Too bad they don't pay extra for that."

"So…I've been wondering how she feels about me moving in."

"She accepts that you're part of the family now."

Something about Rose's tone wasn't as reassuring as Emily would have wanted. Back at the farm she worked hard and knew the men needed her no matter what. Here, she didn't know how she could ever make amends for the upheaval she caused.

Rose handed Emily a plate with chicken and potato salad. "Don't looked so worried. Really, she's fine about it."

"I just don't want to be a nuisance."

"Well, you're not. You're my sister and this is your home."

A car pulled into the driveway, and a minute later, Adah came in through the back door.

"Whew, what a day. Sorry for being late."

"It's nice to have you home, honey," she said, giving Rose a hug. "I missed you."

She set her purse and keys on a counter, turning to Emily.

"You get settled, okay?"

"I did. And thanks for letting me stay."

"Well, of course. You're part of the family now."

Emily caught Rose's smile.

"By the way, Emily," Adah said, pointing to a shelf where the phone sat next to the door that led up the staircase. "There's a number from some guy named Michael."

Emily went over and tore his number from the pad and folded it into a pocket.

Rose glanced up from where she was cleaning off the table.

"You should call him."

"I'll wait a bit. I'm still hung over from court. And besides, what do I tell him?"

"The truth."

After the girls washed and dried the dishes, they said their goodnights, and went upstairs to bed, tired from their early morning rise.

Saturday morning, the girls ate breakfast, cleaned their room, and walked the half a mile to the shopping center. Having access to stores and restaurants was still new to Emily, and she felt like she was on vacation. They stopped at Whiz Burger's, picked up ice cream cones, and walked around, window shopping, and strolling through stores.

They had just left a shoe store when Emily noticed a car lot across the street. When a blue and white Chevy caught her eye, she stopped and grabbed her sister's arm.

"Rose."

"What're you looking at, Em?"

"The blue and white car. That's it. That's the one."

Rose dropped the rest of her cone into a garbage can, and the girls walked across the street.

Emily checked the tires on the car, the windshield wipers, opened the doors, checked the interior, and sat behind the wheel.

"Yep, this is the one I want."

Rose looked at the price tag. "You realize it's nearly two thousand dollars."

"Gee. That's not what I wanted to hear."

Material things had never been important to Emily, and her whimsical mood took her by surprise. Part of it was that she hadn't forgotten the freedom of riding in Delilah's car, nor the disappointment of being stuck at Schillings without a way to meet Samuel. And having her own car would mean she wouldn't have to ask others to drive her around.

She looked across the street. "Let's go back to Whiz Burger. I'm going to fill out an application."

"You know, Mother doesn't allow me to work during the school year."

"How about weekends?"

"What about church?"

"Okay… Friday nights and Saturdays."

"Well…it won't hurt to try."

The girls went back to the burger joint. And Emily filled out an application, this time, using her experience at the farm.

"You worked at a farmhouse?" the manager asked as she looked it over.

"Um…yes, I did. My grandfathers. For several years."

"That's impressive. I sure enjoyed visiting my uncle's farm when I was young. Farming's a lot of work.

"So…three years, huh?"

"At least." It was more, but Emily was afraid the woman would think she was lying.

"It just so happens there's an opening for a cook at the end of the month. I'm still working on the schedule. But I'm sure the part-time will be fine. I'll give you a call."

On the way home, the girls figured that if Emily worked Friday nights, Saturdays, and part-time during the summer, between classes, it would take her almost two years to pay for that car.

"Wonder how much an older version would cost."

"Well. If you like that model, you'll have to wait a few years."

Emily chuckled. "It was fun while it lasted. I'm still going for the job, though, if your mother's okay with it."

◇◇◇

*E*mily was reading a book at her desk when Rose came in and stood, looking out the window.

"What's up, Sis?" she asked, marking her place, and setting the book aside.

"Oh, it's something I've been thinking about since I heard you were coming to live with us. We'll talk later. Right now, mother wants us to finish washing clothes."

The girls carried the wicker basket down to the laundry room and filled the washing machine. They were folding clothes when the telephone rang. Rose ran into the kitchen and picked up, hollering to Emily.

"It's Maria on the phone."

"Guess what Emily," the little girl said when Emily got on. "Our mommy's not in heaven. And she's coming here to live.

And you know what? We have a little brother."

"Oh, honey, I'm so happy for you guys."

"Guess what else? Guess who came to drive us?"

"Who?"

"You have to guess."

Emily thought for a moment. "You mean, Bruce? Bruce is out there?"

"Yep, and he's driving us to the airport tomorrow to pick up Mommy and our little brother. They're all going to move up here with us.

"Hey, Emily? Auntie wants to talk to you."

Emily heard Agnes's muffled voice asking the children to step from the room for a few minutes.

"Well, you were right," Agnes said when she got on the line. "Donald did have an ulterior motive for keeping the children with him."

"I'm afraid to ask."

"It's a doozie. Remember, I mentioned that Bud refused to sell the mansion to Donald until after Maria was born. I can't say for certain how it came about, but since Flora was officially claimed deceased, it looks like Donald planned to have Maria sign the mansion over to him when she turned eighteen."

"Oh, no. That's terrible."

"One positive for Donald, though. He's cleared of that young man's death. It was one of his employees. He's still facing charges for attempted murder, though. And I think because the man was working for the police department, the judge denied bail. Anyway. Everything will be tied up in court for some time."

"Maria told me her mother and new brother will be there tomorrow."

"Yes. Looks like they've been thinking about moving this way for a while. So, it'll be great. You know... I could never be as compassionate as Flora is being. But because Donald is the father of her children, she's working on getting him the appropriate help."

"That's good. I hope it all works out."

"Oh, and that reminds me. There's something I'd like you to tell Flora. It's about when I was injured. For a while, my memory about the fall failed me. And it's not that Donald was completely innocent. But...he didn't push me. I have no idea what the children know, or what they may hear in the future, but I want them to know the truth. So, can you please pass along the information to Flora."

"Certainly. I'll make sure she gets the news."

"Thank you. And you have no idea what a relief it is to know that the children will be with their mother soon. I couldn't be happier for them."

"They're ecstatic. Maria and Nathan have taken a liking to this area. We found stables where they can ride there ponies when they're brought out. And they're excited about getting a summer home at the beach.

"Oh...I guess I should tell you that the bookkeeper sent out the checks for Schillings' employees."

"Really. Wow."

"Amazingly, enough, she's trustworthy. Anyway. It sure was nice talking with you again, Emily. And good luck with everything.

"Say... Here come the children. They want to say goodbye."

Maria and Nathan confirmed how happy they were, and how much they looked forward to seeing their first Broadway show when their mother arrived. When Emily heard that, for whatever burden she had carried for them, it dissolved into pure joy.

After she hung up, the girls finished the laundry and started dinner. Adah had been in her bedroom most of the day sewing a suit for work. She came in as they were setting the table, made a turn for them, and posed.

"It looks store bought. Just beautiful, Adah."

"Emily's right, Mother. And it makes you look sophisticated."

"Exactly what I was going for."

Adah looked at the basket of folded clothes on the counter and the food on the table.

"Thanks, girls, for finishing up the wash. And for dinner."

When they pulled up to the table and filled their plates, Rose broke the news to her mother.

"So...it looks like Emily has a job in a few weeks."

"You realize we have a strict curfew around here."

"We already discussed that. And Emily told them she can only work Friday nights, and Saturdays."

"I hope that's okay, Adah. I was planning to ask your permission."

"Well...with all that's happened these last few months. It's not a bad idea to bring in some extra cash."

The reminder that Samuel was in prison because of her gave Emily a jolt. Adah missed her husband and had to be upset he wasn't home. Not only that, but she had a difficult job. It didn't pay well even with all the overtime she put in.

"Of course, I'll pay rent with the money I earn."

Adah laughed. "Samuel would never go for that. But I appreciate the offer."

After dinner, the girls washed dishes, gathered their laundry, and headed upstairs for the night.

When everything was put away, Emily sat on her bed and kicked off her shoes. "Okay, now, what'd you want to talk about?"

Rose sat across from her. "So... I've been doing some thinking."

"You're making it sound serious."

"It is."

"Should I be worried?"

"No, not worried. But... See, I've been thinking that...um... That since you've been raised White all these years, that you should continue to live White."

"Mm? How and...*why* would I even think it would work?"

"It might. And it sure would be easier on you."

Emily frilled up her dark curly hair, pointed to her dark eyes, and fluttered her hands around her face. "I'm not what you'd call exactly pale, you know.

"And remember the first day we met, you said now that I'm with you, my color will be as obvious as night and day."

"But with your hair pulled back, and with makeup on, you really can't tell what nationality you are for sure. There's a girl at school whose half Polynesian. She runs with the popular crowd."

"You want me to pretend I'm Polynesian? That's not exactly White."

"Oh, Emily, it's hard to explain, but you could pull it off."

"Hold on. You're saying I should pretend you're not my sister. Nope, it's not going to happen.

"It can't be that bad for you."

"Sure, not everyone's out there just waiting to give me a bad time. It's just that...."

Rose groaned, plopped to the bed and rolled to her side, resting her head on an arm. "Uh. You don't understand."

Emily sank to an elbow, facing her. "You're right. I don't. You have a good life. And you're happy. You said so yourself."

"Yes, that's true. And there is a group who's exceptionally welcoming, especially lately. I think some of that's got to do with the drama teacher who came in last year. He's darker than I am. Anyway, I've found the closer you stick to the drama kids, the better off you are."

"So, you belong to the group, I take."

"No."

"Why not? Let's join."

"Easier said than done."

"What does that mean?"

"It's nothing to worry about. Right now, I'm more interested in helping you."

"But I've already been helped. Look at me. I'm free, and I have you and Father. And your mother has accepted me. Rose, this is what I've always dreamed of."

"Okay, understood, and that's all great, but...."

Rose sighed. "Let me ask you this. How will you feel if someone calls you a name like you've committed a crime against them, when in reality, you've done nothing. It makes you want to retaliate. But you can't. Well, you can, but I wouldn't."

"I was in jail, remember? I was raped. It couldn't be worse than that. And I've been called plenty of names, I'll have you know."

"See? You've been through enough."

"So. How do you deal with it, Rose?"

"I've learned where to go, and not to go, who to avoid, and who to trust. You see, we have our routines, and everyone has their own place. Sure... Some of the students choose to take their lunches outside, smoke, and do whatever they do. Others sit in a corner with their heads down reading or studying because they feel out of place for whatever reason. But the difference is that when gym class is over, all the Whites take the first showers. And at lunchtime, Blacks take the back table, and we have our own spot during assembly. Honestly. There have been a few exceptions. But... That's just the way it is."

"Rose. Do you wish you were White?"

"Well...I've wondered what it would feel like. But I've been taught to have pride in my heritage, and I do."

"Then why do you want me to deny mine?"

"I just can't bear the thought of someone putting you down after all you've been through. People can be very cruel."

"What if someone guesses?"

Emily slipped from her bed, grabbed a pillow and walloped Rose. "It won't work, Sis. It's a bad, bad idea."

She slammed another blow, and after Rose recovered, she sat up and grabbed the other pillow.

"Okay. But just remember. I warned you."

Rose brought her arm back and slammed the pillow hard enough that it knocked Emily back on her bed.

They laughed so hard Adah hollered up that it was time to turn in for the night.

*M*onday morning, Adah came during lunch-hour to drive Emily to school for her one o'clock SAT test. Samuel's car was in the shop, and Rose caught a ride to school with a friend that morning. Emily offered to take the school bus, but Rose wouldn't hear of it. She said that unless it was a last resort, she would never take a school bus again, and that she didn't expect her sister would either. There was money put aside that allowed the girls to take the city bus when needed. But the downfall was that it wasn't a direct route and almost took twice as long.

Emily gazed at the blue and white Chevy as they passed the car lot. She thought of her long walks to school from the farmhouse. Not that she minded walking as she found excitement even when it rained or snowed. Nevertheless, no one had offered to take her. And here, Adah had gone out of her way for her. She brushed back her hair that was fluffed into a mass of curls and turned to her stepmother.

"Thanks for bringing me to school."

"Oh sure," Adah said, "my lunch hour, anyway. Your first day. That's always scary."

Unlike the straight gravel roads through the flatlands of Illinois, the paved roads were smooth and wound around. When they reached the last bend, the road swooped down into an area nestled in a valley. No more than five or six blocks over, they pulled up to a curb.

The school building was impressive with five stories of red brick. Emily opened the car door and climbed out, taking it all in.

"When you see Rose, tell her I'll be about twenty minutes late picking you guys up."

Emily turned back and stooped to see Adah.

"I'll let her know. And thanks again."

Closing the door, Emily walked up the sidewalk, excited that this was now her school. She scrunched her hair to ensure there would be no doubt that Rose was her sister. As she reached the building, she made herself as tall as possible, took the steps up, and went inside.

The floors spread out in front of her, dark as the night skies, and speckled with thousands of white spots. Combat green lockers lined the walls.

All was quiet. *Now which way to room one forty-five?* The hall straight ahead was empty. So was the hallway to the right. She heard a door close to her left and turned to face a girl walking toward her.

"Can you tell me how—"

The girl looked straight ahead, sailing past as if she was in a trance.

"What're you looking for?" came a voice from behind. Emily turned to one of her own.

"I'm looking for room one forty-five. Where they give the aptitude test."

"Oh, sure," the girl said pointing, "Go back that way, take the first left. See the numbers up there? Go straight up the hallway to the end. It's on the right."

Emily thanked the girl, headed to the corner, and took a left. A moment later, a bell rang. Doors flew open and students burst into the hallway. She tried to get out of the way, but it seemed everyone was going as she was coming. There were bumps and knocks from each side, a few smiles, and curious looks, but still no name-calling. Until....

"Oh look, a new girl," someone gasped, putting on a production, "a bleached Negro."

Emily looked back over her shoulder and caught the eye of a blond male. He made a comical face and pointed at a group of girls. She shook her head, gave a grimacing smile, and continued down the hallway.

A minute later, when she walked into room one forty-five, at least fifteen students were waiting. No one spoke as she found a seat two rows over. She had never been nervous when it came to tests. But by the serious looks on the students' faces, she wondered if she should be.

Ten minutes later, a man walked in with a suitcase. He introduced himself and explained the rules and procedures before taking a seat. The SAT would be spread out into two days. And once they finished their tests, they were asked to quietly take them to the front and leave.

Emily was third to finish that first day. But just to be sure, she decided to look over the test again before turning it in. After looking up the answers later, she was thankful she took the time; if not, she would have missed several questions.

The next morning, she crunched her hair again, finding that she loved the style. When she was nine, she became aware of her full, curly hair and found ways to tame it. But now that she understood that Timothy's wild hair and hers came from different places, she embraced her identity.

She washed the breakfast dishes and went to catch the city bus. As Rose warned her, it was a long ride with transfers, although she spent her time studying.

Emily hadn't forgotten about the questions she nearly missed on day one and felt a surprising angst as the tests were being handed out. It turned out that with the hour of studying while on the bus that morning, she was assured several of the questions she hadn't been certain about were correct. When she left the room, Rose was waiting for her.

"How'd it go?"

"Better than I thought it would."

"I'll bet you aced it."

"I think I did okay."

They were walking up the hallway, when the blond male Emily had seen the day before, came alongside Rose.

"Who's your friend?"

Rose glared at her sister's hair, contemplating. Emily gave her the eye and poked her head around.

"I'm her sister, Emily."

"I'm Rob. Nice to meet you."

He smiled at Rose. "Why didn't you tell me you had a sister?"

Rose took Emily by the arm and hurried her to the front door, calling on the way out, "Because it's none of your business.

"Bye, Rob."

"Why were you rude to him?"

"I told him goodbye."

"Well, I think he's cute."

"Yeah, you and thirty other girls. The big shot in drama class."

"Ooh, I see. So…come on. Let's join the drama class?"

"No. I have better things to do."

"Like what?"

"Like studying, preparing for college, and making something of myself. What's with all the questions?"

"You want me to pretend I'm White, which is ridiculous. And when this cute White boy talks to us, you were rude to him. You're being such a party pooper."

"Well… What's with your hair…floozy!"

The girls looked at one another and burst out laughing.

Rose turned serious. "Listen, I told you about the drama class. They want variety…Black, White, martian green, you name it. They want me to be in a musical."

"What? And you don't want to?"

"No... I don't"

"But, why not?"

"It's complicated and I don't want to talk about it."

"Okay. But—"

"No."

Emily wasn't giving up but decided to wait.…

*T*hat night after they finished washing the dinner dishes, the girls went upstairs and prepared for bed.

"Rose?" Emily said, pulling back the covers and crawling in. "Tell me why you don't want to be in the drama club. And why don't you like Rob?"

"Rob's fine. I just don't want to be in the drama club. What's wrong with that?"

"Oh, come on, Rose. I know there's something you're not telling me. Here, there's a group of people that'll accept you as you are. And you turn your back on them. Besides, you sing like a meadowlark."

Rose thought for a moment. "Okay. I'll tell you, but from here on out I don't want you to bug me about it, promise?"

"It's a promise."

Rose rolled onto her side, resting on an elbow. She picked up a pencil from the nightstand and tapped it on the bedcover.

"So, about two months ago I spent the night with a friend of mine. She's in the drama club. Her parents went out to dinner and a movie, so we had some kids over. Rob was one of them."

"Hmm... Interesting."

"But then someone suggested we play spin the bottle. The very first spin pointed to Rob, and he had to kiss the girl to his right."

"Oh, so he kissed another girl and you're jealous."

"No. He kissed me."

"And the problem is, what, exactly?"

"Em. You promised."

"Okay. I'll shut up. But you have to finish the story."

Rose pursed her lips and sat up. "It's two-fold. First, there's this girl named Darcy...she's White. She has a crush on him."

"So, do you like him?"

"It doesn't matter. Do you know what would happen if I went after him? You promised you wouldn't push me on this."

"All right. But—"

"But nothing. There's that other thing too. I don't have time to play around if I want to get into the right college. It's not just for Mother, but for me too. And besides...."

"Besides what?"

"Well...when he kissed me. I felt this...I don't know, undesirable rush."

"Undesirable?"

"Yes, undesirable, not something I want. Not now, anyway. Still, after the kiss, we sort of flirted. Darcy was already jealous. But when she found out about the kiss, she and a friend of hers came after me. They called me names and spread lies about me. I finally told her I wasn't interested in him. And that's the way I want it to be. End of story."

"But—"

Rose picked up a pillow and threw it at Emily.

"End of story. Now it's your turn. What about Michael? Did you return his call?"

"No."

"Why not? Is it Claude?"

"Frankly, yes."

"From what you've told me about Michael he sounds like a gem."

"He is. And it would be hard to find anyone as kind as he is. In a way, he's too good to be true. Honestly, he's above me."

"I understand why you'd say that, but it's not true. You should stake your claim before someone else does."

Emily threw Rose's pillow back at her. "Are you kidding? You, who turns away from this cute guy to please some mean White girl."

The girls laughed and joked with each other until Adah came knocking at the door.

"You're being awfully noisy up here."

"I'm sorry, Adah."

"Sorry, Mother."

Adah walked over to Emily and handed her a letter.

"It's from Schillings' lawyer. Your father received one two."

Emily had been told she would receive money, but it didn't seem real as she opened the envelope and pulled out a check for twenty-four hundred dollars. She read it through to the bottom and held it up to Adah.

"This is for everything you guys have done for me."

"Oh, no…no. Your father would never accept that."

"But—"

"No. If I took that from you, he'd kill me."

Adah pulled an envelope from a pocket and gave it a shake. "I don't expect it'll be half of what he should have earned, but he'll be mighty relieved to finally get this.

"You know, girls. You were talking about the car for Emily? Neither of you want to take the school bus, the city bus can be a pain. And you hate to depend on me. Not that I mind driving you around, but I've been reprimanded a few times for being late. So… Why not buy that car you want, something that won't break down at every turn. It'll come in handy for college."

Rose sat up. "You should buy it, Em. I already have my license. You can go out next week and get your learner's permit."

"Oh, and I'm sure your father will insist on putting you on our insurance."

"Mother's right. And the car will come in handy for work too."

Emily had no words. She could have received a million dollars and wouldn't have been more shocked or excited.

Adah headed for the door. "It's up to you. Get some sleep and we'll talk tomorrow."

Emily set the check on the nightstand and lay back on her pillow. "You know…I really want that car."

"Then you shall have it."

Rose reached over and turned off the light. "Night, Em."

"Night, Rose."

*F*or all the bad that happened in Emily's life, things had officially turned for the better. Thrill number one came within days when she and Rose found a bank close to home. Emily gazed at the check one more time before flipping it over and signing her name. Thrill number two came as she opened a savings account for her college funds. And thrill number three arrived as they left the bank and headed to the car lot. They had already informed them that she was buying the Chevy. And when they arrived to pick it up, it was out front waiting for her. Thrill number four was riding in her own car with Rose driving, knowing that very soon she would be behind the wheel.

*B*y Emily's second week at the restaurant, the manager was so taken by her cooking skills, she gave her a twenty-five-cent per hour raise.

Rose had been teaching her to drive in the shopping center parking lot, and up and down their driveway. Finally, the day arrived when Emily drove her own car to school with Rose in the passenger seat.

Emily thought she had done well with the SAT tests. But when the results came back, she was delighted by her score. And because of the excellent results, the school board decided to put her in the twelfth grade, with arrangements that allowed her to take classes toward her college credits. She had already decided to attend San Francisco State University where she would receive a teacher's certificate. Her goal was to finish high school and college before she was twenty-four. There wouldn't be much time for socializing. But to put everything she had into her dream of becoming a teacher, the hard work didn't seem like a sacrifice.

Many were aware that Emily was Rose's sister, but no one seemed to take special notice, or at least she hadn't a clue if they did. For the most part, her sister's warnings seemed to have been needless. It wasn't until she found herself alone in the hallway with two contemptuous female students that she had to defend herself. She knew one of them to be Darcy.

As the girls came up behind her whispering and giggling to themselves, Emily recalled how Darcy and her friend had called Rose some pretty awful names, spread lies, and forced her to give up a boy she liked.

"How come you're not dark like your sister?" the loudmouthed one asked Emily.

"I know," Darcy cut in, "her mother had an affair with her master. So how does it feel to be a bastard?"

Anger pulsed through Emily's veins, but she managed to ignore them and picked up speed toward the exit. They followed close behind her.

"Say, miss whitewash. What does a Black woman, and the master of a cotton farm make?" Darcy said with a guffaw of laughter.

"Uuh, let's see," came the loud-mouthed one again.

"Oh yes, a bitch's brew."

They thought that was hysterical until Emily had finally had enough. She swung around and set her eyes on Darcy.

"What does it feel like to be a moron?"

She was shocked by her retaliation, but it wasn't just about her anymore. It was about Rose too. To think these girls talked like this to her sister made her angrier than she had ever been. She moved closer, towering over them.

"There's something you should know. You're no better than anyone else. And you'll do yourself a big service by taking that to heart. The sooner the better. And by the way. There *was* no master."

Emily took a breath and turned away. She felt a burst of joy as she walked out the front door. In a way, she felt sorry for them. As she drove home with Rose, she explained what happened.

Rose couldn't stop laughing. "I'm sorry. And it must've been horrible. But it's about time someone stuck up to them. Maybe I should've done it myself. Only once I let go, all I can say is that I wouldn't have been as reserved as you were."

"So, dear sister. Now that Darcy's been put in her place. Don't you think it's time to go get your guy?"

"Oh, no, you don't. I don't even care anymore. Let her have him."

"Really? After all that? Are you sure?"

"Yes, I'm over him."

"Say. Did you ever call Michael?"

"Not yet."

Well... You'd better hurry, or he may give up. Mother said he called twice when we were in Illinois."

"It's hard for me to forget, you know...everything. So how can I expect him to?"

"Think about it this way. As you recall, you were acquitted. Twelve jurors believed in you. And let's say Michael decides not to see you again once he hears your story, then he's not the man for you. At least you'll know."

*E*mily was grateful for so many things in her life—especially for her father and Rose's unconditional love and support. She appreciated Adah for accepting her into her home and was grateful for all she had done for her. Except for the fact that her father wasn't home yet, she thought things were going well. Then one day, as she took the stairs down to the kitchen, she overheard Adah talking with her friend, Lou.

She was telling the woman that Samuel had to sell his pickup in order to work for Donald Schillings. And that he had finally received payment from him. Although, it wasn't as much as he would've earned on the boat. Lou reminded her that since he was in jail, he wasn't earning a dime.

Emily didn't want to hear anymore and tiptoed back upstairs. She sulked for days. Finally, Rose asked her what was wrong.

"Nothing, really. I'm just trying to…."

Emily stopped and considered whether or not to tell Rose. "Well…the fact is, that I overheard your mother and Lou talking. Why didn't you tell me that Father sold his pickup because of me?"

"That woman. Listen, Em… You have to know that Lou can be a real *'B'* at times. So don't take what she says to heart."

Emily knew it wasn't only Lou condemning her, but she decided to keep that to herself.

"I'll try not to think about it."

"Good. Because Father will be home soon and all will be well again."

Emily held onto hope that when her father came home, the problem would iron itself out. That's what her grandmother used to say. *'When troubles come. Give it time to iron itself out.'*

"Guess what, Emily," Rose called as she came up the stairs and into the bedroom. "I think it's Michael on the phone."

Emily dropped the book she was reading, hopped off the bed, and ran down the stairs, pausing for a moment before opening the door into the kitchen and picking up the phone.

"Hello?"

"Emily. It's Michael."

"Hi. It's nice to hear from you."

"I've tried to call several times."

"Sorry. It's been a balance of school, work, and…my new life."

"You've got a job. That's wonderful."

"Say…I called to see if you want to go back to the fish diner with me."

"Well…let me see, hmm. They have the best fries and lobster."

"And a beautiful view," he added.

"They're not overly pretentious."

"And it could be our place."

"That sounds wonderful, Michael. And I'd love to go."

"How about Friday, at five?"

"Oh… I work Friday evenings."

"Is Saturday open?"

"I get off at four. I'll be ready by five."

Emily hadn't exactly lied to Michael, but she held back information. And she knew if they were to continue a relationship, she had to tell him the whole truth about why she hadn't returned his calls. The night she revealed much of what happened with Claude to Shayne at *The Palace,* his reaction was what she needed to hear. But with all the alcohol flowing through both of them, who knows how he really felt, or how much he even remembered. Her relationship with Michael was on another level. It was real, and there was hope for something lasting. She struggled as to how and what she would say to him.

Later that night as Emily and Rose sat on the front porch, Emily confided in her sister.

So, Rose. You know that I'm thrilled to be going out with Michael again. But if we're going to be seeing each other, I have to tell him about my life back at the farm."

"I've been thinking about that too."

"How in the world to I tell him?"

"You know. I've heard that by writing a letter about a touchy subject, one has time to think through what they want to say, no words blurted in frustration, and no chance of tears to influence a flash decision out of pity. Not only that, but the receiver has more time to process the information in a calm, rational setting. I've tried it more than once and found it to be the best route."

"That makes sense."

Emily knew the emotional challenge she faced if she relived events from her past in front of Michael. And she decided to use Rose's suggestion. That evening, she took a notepad to bed and spent several hours writing down exactly what needed to be said.

*D*uring their meal at the fish diner that Friday night, Michael's comment about it being *their* place seemed appropriate. Emily hoped the sentiment continued, even after he read the letter. But with each conversation that brought warm glances, laughs, or special memories from the train, she was reminded that he would leave on the cusp of learning the secret she had kept from him. If only they had more time.

"So, Michael. How're things going with the tour to Ghana?"

"Just great. And... We'll be leaving in a little over a month."

"That's just around the corner. You must be excited."

"I am. But I've been so busy preparing, it hasn't seemed real until now. But everything is set. And I've been thinking... Hoping, that we could spend more time together."

"I'd love that."

Now that he was about to leave, Emily felt a shift in their relationship. There was an intensity between them, as if they needed to take advantage of the time they had left.

After dinner, they walked up the beach, excited to enjoy the sunset. Michael pulled her around in front of him and watched the beautiful scene over her shoulder.

"The ocean will always be a reminder of you," he said, kissing her cheek.

"That's how I feel about you. Remember on the train when you said you'd love to be with me when I got my first glimpse? Well...I always think of that as I look at the sea."

After their pleasant night, when Michael took her home and she reached in the doorway for the letter, there was a moment of hesitation before she picked it up and handed it to him.

"Here. This will explain why I didn't return your calls."

"Oh... Is everything okay?"

"Yes. Everything's fine. But you see. When I met you on the train, I was carrying a secret. And it's important that you know."

Emily watched him leave up the driveway, praying it wasn't the end of their relationship. Even though Claude's death was an accident, it was brutal, and she cringed at the thought of Michael knowing this detail about her life.

The phone caught Emily's eye as she entered the kitchen, and she wished Michael would call immediately after reading the letter. But when she took a moment to think rationally, she was sure that, at the very least, he would think things over for a few days before contacting her.

She was in the laundry room getting clothes out of the dryer when the phone rang. Glancing up at the clock, she dropped the blouse she was folding on the dryer and hurried into the kitchen, taking a good breath before answering.

"Hello sweetheart," her father said.

"Oh, Father, hello. How are you? And where're you?"

"We're at a port in Catalina. I know it's late, but I hoped I could catch one of you before you retired for the night."

"I'm sure Ada and Rose are in bed. Would you like me to see if they're awake?"

"No, no. Since we're on land I just thought I'd make a quick call. How are you? You sound a bit under the weather. You okay?"

"I'm fine. Just a little tired. But it's nice to hear your voice."

"Same here. Well. It's late. I'll let you get to bed. But make sure to tell Ada and Rose I said hi."

"I will. Goodnight, Father. I love you."

"And I love you too, sweetheart."

Hanging up, she was happy her father called, but disappointed because for a moment she thought it was Michael. She gathered her clothes from the laundry and climbed the stairs. Near the top, the phone rang again. She set the clothes on a step and sailed down the stairs.

"Hello?"

"Emily," I hoped you wouldn't be in bed."

"I was heading that way. But I'm glad you called."

"As you probably guessed… I read your letter… Several times. There's a lot to digest in there. But first, I want to say how sorry I am for everything you've gone through. It's unbelievable what some people endure and still stay sane. Makes me realize how good I've had it. Yes, it was and still is painful losing my mother. But, she had a good life, and I have faith that she's okay. And I'll see her again."

"I'm glad you feel that way, Michael. It's a comfort to know."

"Yes, it is."

There was a pause as Michael took a breath. Emily's heart sank.

"So, um… About your letter. As far as what you've gone through, seemingly, most of your life. I've seen enough to know that you'll have to deal with those demons from time to time. And I can't even imagine how difficult it was for you on the train after that awful scene in the barn, feeling you needed to keep it to yourself. To get through that intact shows your strength.

"So… um… I just want to say that it pains me deeply to think of that young girl you once were. But I'm proud of the young woman you've become. And Emily. Thank you for being so honest."

A rush of joy flooded through her, and she knew that Rose was right. Michael was truly a gem.

After that night, their passion became even bolder. He barely spoke of her letter. She had put so much mental effort into fighting off memories of her past that his outlook on the subject was a welcome relief. He had always been gracious and understanding, and she should have known. But her past had a habit of telling her something different.

Knowing their time together was temporary, Emily cut back her work hours and studies. Michael had already packed his bags, and he was prepared to leave. With their schedules wide open, they began to spend hours on the phone, sometimes well into the night. She would unwind the extension cord and take the phone into the laundry room so they could talk in private. One evening, he came over, and they sat on the back porch and talked until almost dawn. It was so unlike him. Adah came upon the two, and she wasn't happy. He apologized. Emily did too. But that didn't slow down their desire to be together.

There were many dinner dates. At first, they took their usual walks on the beach. One night, they decided to try something new and found a secluded spot at a lookout point where they parked his car and talked, until their talking turned into more. It was Michael who suggested they visit Fishermen's Wharf the next evening. And the following night, they took a pleasant walk up to Coit Tower to see the view of the city lights. Whatever they were doing, and no matter how perfect their time together was, his two-year trip to Ghana was never far from their thoughts.

<><><>

*M*ichael's departure came quickly. Too quickly. In four days, he was leaving for Ghana at 5 a.m. He called to tell Emily that he had a surprise for her that Saturday night.

"I'm sorry that it's such short notice. But something remarkable just fell on my lap.

"Oh, and… Wear your prettiest dress."

"Sounds exciting. But… How about a small hint?"

"Nope. I want you to feel the suspense."

They talked on the phone for several hours that night, saying words that expressed love without saying it outright. Emily thought of inviting him over, imagining they would go for a ride, maybe up to the lookout. She knew he wanted to. But something told her it was best they didn't see each other that night. It was clear that, on other occasions, one of them had been strong when the other was weak. This night was different.

"Rose," Emily said, as she walked into their bedroom after saying goodnight to Michael, "we need to go dress shopping tomorrow."

"Ok…what's it for?"

"Michael's bent on showing me the surprise of a lifetime."

"Lucky you."

"You realize that Saturday will be our last date before he leaves for Ghana. He'll be on the plane at five the next morning. And we won't see each other for two whole years."

"That calls for something special. You and that dress have to shine. So. Here's a plan. Let's go to San Francisco, to Union Square."

The next afternoon Emily drove her Chevy on the freeway with Rose beside her, guiding her to Union Square. They walked through a number of shops before finding what she was looking for. It was a sleeveless, black chiffon dress that had v-folds at mid-calf, front, back, and sides. Not even the most expensive dress Miss Bea purchased for her could compare.

*S*aturday afternoon, Emily showered, put on her new dress, and pulled her hair into a partial updo in back. The night called for extra makeup. And once she applied finishing powder, Rose ran down to get a camera.

"Remember, when you're out tonight, you're making a memory that you'll cherish for the rest of your life."

"Rose. Why does that sound so final?"

"Two years is not final, Em."

Michael was waiting at the front door as she came through the dining room. He gasped when he saw her walking toward him.

"Emily. You're absolutely…*gorgeous*."

When they got into the car, he patted the seat, and she moved next to him.

"So, how long does the surprise continue to be a surprise?" she asked.

"What… Aren't you enjoying the intrigue?"

She laughed. "I am. I really am. It's just that I can't imagine what you've got planned. How about a tiny hint?"

"Okay, how about two. We're driving into San Francisco. And we'll start off with dinner."

She rested her head on his shoulder for a moment and squeezed his arm. "I was hoping that's where we'd go."

San Francisco was a big part of their relationship, and she had a feeling this night would top them all.

When they reached their destination, Michael pulled into the Fior D'Italia restaurant. The place was delightful, and they thoroughly enjoyed their conversation, and the seafood pasta. As they finished their dessert of Sherbet ice cream, he pulled out an envelope.

"Do you remember when you mentioned there was somewhere you longed to go? We were driving along the Embarcadero. You were gazing out over the city."

"Mm…let me think….

"Oh, Michael! An opera? Are we going to an opera?"

He handed her the envelope. "This is a synopsis for Madame Butterfly."

"I've read reviews. Several times," she added as she opened the envelope and pulled out the synopsis, and a list of the lingo.

"Oh, this will be helpful. Thank you. I'm so excited. You have no idea."

The opera house was more magnificent than Emily could have imagined. Their view of the performers from the Grand Tier was superb, and the live music was like nothing she had ever heard. She had fallen in love with opera. And when Michael took her hand during the third act, she knew it wasn't only the opera that had her falling.

They left the opera and drove to their spot on the beach just as the sun was setting. Emily slipped off her shoes and nylons, left them in the car, and Michael took her hand as they headed to the beach and walked up the shoreline for as far as the rocks allowed. Shades of crimson and yellow spread across the horizon, and under the April moon, they stood by the rumbling sea and clung to each other. Neither wanted the night to end, but she was late for her curfew and Michael took her hand, and they ran up the beach to his car.

Back home on the front porch, he slid his hands up her arms and around her shoulders, gazing into her eyes.

"After this night. I can truthfully say that, right now, I wish these next two years had just ended."

She dropped her shoes and nylons to the porch, struggling to hold back tears. "Me too, Michael. Me too."

"Oh, Emily—"

His mouth found hers with the lust of a sailor's last kiss, her hands clutching his suit jacket, feeling the heat of his breath, and the curves of his lips on hers. Finally, their shocked desperate gazes as they pulled apart brought them to their senses, their eyes speaking words they could not say.

He held her to his chest once more, her fingers memorizing the soft threads of tweed as she clinched her eyes to keep from sobbing and begging him to stay.

"I'll sure miss you," he said.

Tears she had fought rolled down her cheeks. "And I'll miss you."

He held her a moment longer, his warm cheek against hers, then turned away, and walked down the steps to the car. At the door, he stopped and gazed up at her as if he was fighting not to run back into her arms. But it was time to go.

Emily stepped down and sat on the porch watching his car move up the driveway and disappear as the high from the most beautiful night crashed around her. The realization that she wouldn't see him for two years brought fresh tears streaming down her cheeks, her mind playing tricks because it wasn't a hopeless situation. He was doing an honorable thing. Yet the honorable thing was not her. And how could she not wonder if the lust he felt the last few weeks was more about him leaving to a strange land than it was about him falling for her, as she had fallen for him.

Pulling herself up, she gathered her nylons and shoes off the porch and went inside, the sudden loss taking her back to memories of Daniel on that stormy day that soaked her to the bone and broke her heart.

Emily locked the door and headed to the kitchen, feeling like those last minutes at Schillings' when she lay on the bed ready to give up, worn so thin she didn't think there was a splinter of light to grab onto.

That's where her mind took her as she went to the kitchen closet and dug out a jug of rum she had noticed tucked away.

<><><>

*T*he next morning, Emily sat up in bed, hung over, noticing that Rose was already up. There had been a conversation between them the night before, if only she could remember what it was.

Sliding into a pair of slippers, she stood and walked to the window, gazing out and knowing she had to snap out of her depression. Something meaningful and exciting had abruptly ended, and she knew it would take time to adjust. She would have to fight this loss just like she had with every other loss. And with all she had to be thankful for, and the exciting work before her, waiting and pining, and drinking was not something she could do if she wanted to fulfill her dreams.

Michael would think about her, write a few letters, and miss her. But time would pass. He would be busy in Ghana while she tended to her schooling. So, instead of thinking of the worst or dreaming about what should or could be, she would focus on what would help her. And if, by chance, she and Michael's relationship turned into something more one day, she didn't want to waste time on what made her sad, but would make sure on her own merit, not to be discouraged or bitter from the waiting.

After dressing, she tucked in the bedspread and sank to her knees, pulled the bottle from under her bed and returned it to its spot.

The coffee pot was still warm, and as she filled a cup with the brew, it occurred to her that Rose and her mother were in church. After the service, they would have lunch at Grandmother Dimsmoore's. And since her father was at sea, she had all day to herself.

By now, Emily knew that Rose wouldn't hold anything against her, and she knew how lucky she was to have her in her life. The best way to show her appreciation was to never let a moment pass. She would write Rose a letter, not exactly a confession, some, but for the most part, an apology.

With her mind made up, and already feeling better, she made toast, topped with peanut butter and jelly, made a fresh pot of coffee, and headed upstairs.

CHAPTER THIRTY

*L*ate one afternoon, Emily walked down the steps of the school watching for Rose who would pick her up at the curb. She saw a familiar face walking toward her. It was such a shock that it took a few moments to realize that it was her grandfather. He was slightly bent over, with his right hand holding his side. She stopped in front of him and got a whiff of alcohol.

"What're you doing here? And how'd you find me?"

"Didn't you know? This is where your grandmother and I met. We lived here for years."

"Yes, that's what I was told." This was also where her mother was born, although Emily had a feeling he was still in denial.

She noticed a car sitting at the curb. "Did you leave the farm?"

"No. It's Martha and my 50th wedding anniversary this weekend. I decided to come out and stay at the Fairmont…the one off Mason. That's where we stayed for our honeymoon."

Emily was touched. Although she didn't recall Grandfather being so sentimental.

"I'm surprised you came all the way out here."

About then Rose pulled up in the Chevy and stepped out, her head poking over the car.

"You okay, Em?"

Emily started up the walk toward her car, Grandfather trailing behind her.

"Martha and I had planned this trip for years. But then she…."

"Sorry, Grandfather," Emily said, glancing back. She knew how much her grandparents had loved each other, even with all the trials of grief.

They continued up the walk in silence, he a few steps behind.

"Okay," he said, in the gruff tone she had been accustomed to, "it's not just about our anniversary. I need that jewelry box."

"What?" Emily turned to face him. "The jewelry box? Why?"

"You can have the necklace. It belongs to you. But I need that antique box."

"Leave her be, Mr. Rezell!" Rose said, rushing over and taking Emily by an arm. "Haven't you hurt her enough?

"Come on, Em, let's go."

Rose coaxed Emily to the car and shoved her inside. Slamming the door, she ran around the front, hollering at her sister to push the lock. Sliding into the driver's side, she peeled from the curb.

"Why's he here?"

"It's my grandparents' anniversary."

"So?"

"They met here. He also wants the necklace box. Something about it being antique. You know...my necklace that was stollen?"

"The one you say is at Schillings."

"Yes. And I think we should drive over now before grandfather leaves town. If we find it, I'll take the antique box to the Fairmont and offer it to him for dropping the charges against Father."

"That man should've already done that!

"But... Oh, Emily. It would be... So wonderful to have father back with us.

"You know... I think maybe our prayers have just been answered."

Rose got teary-eyed, then bucked up.

"So...are you certain the necklace is at the mansion? And is it even safe to go there?"

"I'm Ninety-nine percent certain the necklace is there. And as far as being safe. I'm sure it is. A detective personally willed me to go. If someone stops us, I'll tell them that he contacted me and said I should go there to pick up my things."

"Who's the detective?"

"Just someone I met...."

"...Okay....

"Can you just tell the police the necklace is there, and let them pick it up for you?"

"That could take months. Besides, what if Schillings says it's his and it ends up in court? I can't afford a lawyer, and even then, who knows what would happen.

"And Rose, we need to get father out of jail."

"Yes, yes, I agree. So, let's go. Which way?"

"Well, it's less than an hour away...up north. I recall turning right just beyond a gas station. It has a Ferris wheel in back. You can't miss it. We'll drive through a forest maybe twenty some miles before we take the second right and drive another ten or so miles before taking a left, pass two exits before taking another right and then a final left. His place is about a half a mile from there."

"You count turns?"

"Yes, I do.

"Listen... We can't miss his driveway. The gate is green, a deep mossy green, and very large.

"You know how to get to Highway 101 North, don't you?"

"Yes, of course."

"So...we'll head up 101 for about twenty miles and start looking for that gas station."

Rose slowed the car, turned left, and headed towards San Francisco, and 101.

"I still don't get why Schillings would be part of a dumb scheme like steeling your necklace."

"First of all. It's an Heirloom. Plus, I'm almost certain someone else instigated the scheme. And of course, you have to take into account that he blackmailed his former wife into playing dead and also blackmailed her husband."

"Ha. I see your point."

*T*he gate was wide open when the girls turned onto Schillings property and headed up the long driveway. Emily had no idea what to expect when they reached the mansion—who was there, or what they would find. And when they pulled through the last gate, she was relieved there were no cars parked out front.

"Wow! When you said mansion, you meant it."

As they climbed the front steps, they looked around, surprised no one stopped them. At the front door, Emily turned the knob and pushed it open. They slipped inside and made sure they were alone before scrambling up the stairs.

Emily glanced at Rose, nervously. "It's to the left, and around the corner."

A minute later, they approached Schillings' suite and Emily tried the door. But it was locked.

"Darn. I was hoping that since the police raid, it would be open.

"Come to think of it," Emily said, as the girls walked back up the hallway, "I'll bet there's something we can use from Nathan's bedroom. He has all sorts of gadgets. If not, we could try a window from the porch outside his suite. But, then we'd have to break a window. I really don't want to do that."

As they rounded the corner, they nearly ran into Gabriel. She squealed, looking as surprised as they were.

"Emily! What're you doing here?"

"I might ask the same. After the way you were treated, I sure didn't expect to see you."

"I haven't been until today. I came to pick up some of my things. Pearl asked me to help out. She's getting ready to move back home."

Emily was relieved to see the young girl had a little more fight in her.

"Say, I heard what happened to your brother. I'm really sorry."

"I still can't believe he's gone."

Emily grasp one of her hands and held it in hers. "How are you doing? Is everything okay?"

"It's tough, but... We just found out Mr. Schillings has to pay my family a settlement."

"Good. That's real, good. You deserve all you can get.

"I've said prayers for you. Hope that's okay."

"Yes. I appreciate that."

"So...I hate to change the subject. But I'm in a hurry. And, well... I need your help, if you would. It's about a necklace that belongs to me. It's an inheritance. Mr. Schillings was holding it for me. I don't know...probably as collateral, or some such thing."

"Sounds like something he would do," Gabriel said, glancing back at the staircase.

"Okay, so I'll see what I can do. But you should know. Pearl's roaming the place. There's a key in her room. I'll try to get it for you."

Gabriel rushed off and the two waited near Donald's quarters. Not more than ten minutes later, they heard footsteps. Thinking it was Gabriel, they were shocked when Pearl stepped around the corner.

"For crying out loud. What're you girls up to?"

"Mr. Schillings didn't tell you?" Emily said, walking toward her. "He was holding a necklace of mine. Of course, he hadn't planned on going to jail. So, I've come to pick it up."

"Well, that sounds like malarkey to me. Why don't you gals hightail it out of here."

She swung around and headed for the stairs. "Come on, hurry it up. I'll walk you to the door so I can make sure it's locked this time. Dumb girl, must've forgot to lock it again."

At this point, Emily was desperate, sure the woman would ruin everything. Pearl would never budge from her position. And she had to do something drastic.

They rounded the corner, and the older woman stopped to shoo them ahead. "Get going. I don't have all day."

As they neared the area where the bedrooms were, Emily whispered to Rose. "That door near the stairway. I'll run over and open it. Shove her inside."

"Stop gabbing, you two," Pearl said from behind.

They neared Nathan's bedroom when Gabriel came up the stairs dangling the key. When she saw Pearl, she stopped in her tracks. While the other two concentrated on the girl's gaping surprise, Emily rushed to Nathan's door and swung it open. Rose finally realized what was happening and grabbed Pearl, who might've gotten away, except that Gabriel got over her shock and joined in.

Emily retrieved a pair of Nathan's handcuffs from the nightstand. She pulled out the key, setting it on the stand as the girls wrangled the woman through the doorway.

"To the end of the bed, Rose."

Once they brought Pearl to the bed, she fighting all the way, Emily secured her to the bedpost.

She looked up the length of the post that reached well over six feet. "Sorry, Pearl. But it won't take long," she said, patting her on a shoulder.

Pearl wasn't interested in her apology and tried to shake her hand off.

"Don't think you're getting away with this," she called as the girls left, closing the door behind them.

"Here," Gabriel said, looking pleased as she handed Emily the key to Schillings' suite.

"Oh, thank you. You're a lifesaver."

"You want me to stay watch for you?"

Emily had already started up the hallway. "If you don't mind, that would be great. We'll be back as quick as possible."

When they entered Donald's quarters, they were shocked at the extent of the ransacking the police left behind.

"Why would they leave such a mess?"

"I think that's just what they do," Rose said, beginning her own search. "This place is still quite impressive."

Emily began to look in drawers, closets, under couches, chairs, in cabinets, and behind shelves, while Rose went to search the other rooms.

"Emily, you should see the view of the water. He even has a telescope."

"I'll bet it's not to look at stars," Emily hollered back.

When she decided to check out a hallway, she discovered a stairway.

"Rose come quick, there's an attic. It's wide open."

It seemed that the attic had once been a cozy retreat, with rows of windows that brought in sunlight. But now cabinets and drawers were pulled out to the max, all gone through. A few had given into the weight and lay half hazard on the floor. There were half-empty boxes strewn about, clothes, and odds and ends everywhere.

Emily noticed a closet full of women's clothing, some hanging, and the rest on the floor. Amongst the piles of clothes, there were heels, flats, a pair of moccasins, and several colorful pairs of slippers like those she wore to the ball—and the reason she had ended up in Schilling's attic. This had to be the place Peter meant for her to look.

She continued walking through the room, searching through drawers, and another closet, then stopping for a few moments at an easel with a half-finished painting of a lake scene. Throughout the room, pictures lay on the floor or hung lopsided on the walls. Off in the corner were a couple of statues and a sewing area. Moving about, she rummaged around, reaching to put things back in order, becoming discouraged.

When something caught her eye, she went to the middle of the room and stood with her arms folded staring at the back wall.

"Are you giving up?" Rose asked. She shut the drawer she had been poking through and went to stand beside Emily.

"What're you looking at?"

"It's the paneling. I have a feeling that somewhere in that interesting design, there just may be a door that leads to the other side."

She moved closer and begun to walk alongside the wall, starting at the left, running her fingers inside each groove. "If I can just find the right spot."

"What makes you think there's a door?"

"Maria told me there used to be an attic opening above her closet. I can tell by looking at the size of this area that her bedroom is well beyond this wall. I've read several accounts of eccentrics building secret rooms in their homes. One thing for sure, whatever's behind this wall, it's something that's meant to be hid."

Rose joined in, helping to check for inconsistencies. As they neared the right corner, Emily felt around the intricate grooves of a wood paneling.

"I think I found something here. All I need is some kind of a hook."

"The sewing machine," Rose said, already hurrying over. She brought back a handful of tools.

Emily tried several before finding one that worked. When there was a clicking sound, she gripped the panel and pulled out a section like one would a drawer. The girls ducked their heads and looked into a room filled with hundreds of boxes.

"Well...I'll be. Looks like George knew what he was talking about."

Rose stepped back and let Emily through the opening. Using the gadget she still held in her hand, Emily slit one of the boxes down the middle. Flipping the lid open, she pulled out a plastic bag filled with a white powdery substance.

"Is that what I think it is?"

"I've never seen any before. But, from what I've heard and read, I'm pretty sure it's Cocaine."

Emily dropped the bag back into the box and gazed around the room, imagining how excited the police would be. She stepped back through the opening and they left the makeshift door open and wandered across the room.

"There's something I'm missing."

"Em? You ready to tell me about that guy who told you to come here?"

"His name is Peter. And I'm sure he found the necklace. But it's obviously not up here. So, it looks like we'll have to continue looking downstairs. It could take hours."

For at least the tenth time, Emily went over the message Peter left her. Because of how secretive he had been, she had a feeling he had done something that would be frowned upon by the police department, knowing the end result would be the same, but with less red tape and quicker.

Again, Emily went over Peter's words, this time, repeating them to Rose. And like before, his message pointed to Schillings' quarters, and the slippers.

"Something just occurred to me, Rose. Maybe, he wasn't using the slippers as a point of location. But instead…it is about the slippers."

Emily rushed to the closet and dropped to her knees. One by one, she picked up the slippers and pushed a hand inside. Nothing.

Rose walked over and stood above her.

"Why would Peter have left the necklace at Schillings' in the first place? You weren't living here any longer."

"That's right, I wasn't.

"Oh, my goodness! I know where it is," she said, leaping to her feet and heading for the exit, Rose right behind her.

"Where're we going?"

"I have a feeling the necklace was here, and when the police searched the place, Peter saw it and took it to my old room."

"So, Em. Do you mind telling me who this Peter guy is?"

Emily sighed as they left the attic and stepped into the entry. "I know it probably doesn't make sense that I didn't tell you about him. But….um.

"Remember after the trial when someone asked me about the barn, and…a place called *The Palace*?"

"Yeah? But I had no idea what that person was talking about."

As they took the winding stairs down, Emily explained in simple terms about how she ended up at Miss Bea's brothel and met Peter. It was easier telling her without having to face her directly.

At the bottom, Rose gave her a hug. "I'm sorry, Em. Don't feel so down about it. It's not like you went there on your own. And listen…you don't have to tell me anything more about it unless you want to. On the other hand, tell me everything."

Emily nodded. "I knew you'd understand. But it's more than that, even more than I can figure out for myself.

"Okay… So.. It's out there. Let's pretend it didn't happen and go find the necklace."

The girls rushed from Schillings' suite and headed to Emily's old room and to the closet. Emily saw the heel of each slipper beneath the shoe rack. She pulled them out, dropped the lightest one, and removed the necklace box from the other.

"Oh, Rose, this is it!" she said as she opened the lid.

"Em! It's stunning."

Emily lifted the necklace from the box and laid it across her hand. "Can you believe it? And I thought it may be lost forever."

She looked around the room. "I'll bet Peter figured out this was my room and offered to search in here, that is, if the police even searched beyond Schillings' quarters. "Either way, I knew I could trust him from the moment I met him."

Ready to return the necklace to the box, Emily saw a small tab she hadn't noticed before. She handed the necklace to Rose, gave the tab a pull and lifted the velvet lining. Beneath, was something bound within a piece of silk. Both girls gasped as Emily uncovered four diamonds.

"So, this is what Grandfather is after."

Rose picked up one of the diamonds. "These are real."

"Are you sure?"

"Look at them. Mother and I have spent afternoons looking at jewelry, just for fun. And I've seen some worth thirty thousand. These are real."

"I'm sure this is what my aunt Francine was talking about the day I went over to see her during a snowstorm. My great uncle won these gambling.

"Oh, poor Grandfather," Emily added. "No wonder he came all the way out here. He must've been desperate"

Rose took another look at the diamonds. "Um. I wouldn't exactly call him poor. And why would someone gamble away diamonds?"

"It was Chicago. I've read horror stories about the gambling that went on. Someone probably had a dozen more of these."

Emily replaced everything and closed the lid.

"Okay. We'd better go."

They went back into the hallway to where Gabriel patiently waited. She seemed to be enjoying the curses coming from Pearl.

"I see you found it."

"Thanks to you. I really do appreciate this. And once again, I'm so sorry about your brother."

The girls were ready to leave when they heard another round of cursing from Pearl.

"I'll go down and find Otto. He's out in the garages," Gabriel said. "He can let her out. It's probably not safe for any of us to go in at this point."

"So, is Otto leaving too?"

"Not yet. He's planning to stick it out until the place is sold."

"Would you do me a favor and tell him, thanks for everything."

"Sure. I'll tell him."

Emily went to Nathan's old room and knocked on the door. "Pearl? Someone'll be up soon to let you out. Good luck."

The girls headed down the stairs, Gabriel up the hallway as Emily and Rose left out the front door.

While Rose drove, Emily took a notepad and pen from her school bag and wrote a thank you letter to Peter. When they arrived in San Francisco, they pulled into the police station. Emily left the letter with the receptionist then went in and had a talk with the chief of police about the boxes they found.

By the look on his face as she spoke, Emily realized the seriousness of what she found. At least her old boss would have plenty of time to focus on getting the help coming his way. And he was about to find out how lucky he was to have had someone like Flora in his life.

*T*he next day, Emily and Rose drove to the Fairmont motel. Emily looked around for the car Grandfather had driven to the school, hoping he hadn't left. Seeing there were several that could be his rental, she went inside to the front desk.

"I'm here to see my grandfather. His name is Rupert Rezell."

"I'm sorry, my dear. But Mr. Rezell was taken to Saint Francis hospital by ambulance last night."

"Saint Francis?"

"Here," the clerk said, scribbling the address and a quick map of the streets.

"It's just up the road. Take a right out of the parking lot. Then you'll turn left at the second stoplight and drive about two miles. You can't miss it."

Emily hurried to the car and read the directions to Rose as she drove up the street. No more than ten minutes later, they pulled into the hospital parking lot.

When Emily walked into her grandfather's room, he glanced up. As she moved to stand beside his bed, he dropped his gaze to the bulge of his feet. She could see he was sober and not in a talking mood.

"Hello, Grandfather."

At times like this, a couple swigs of alcohol would change his mood for the better. But it looked like those days were over.

"The nurse said it's your liver. Cirrhosis."

He grunted.

"Grandfather. I know you've had some heartaches. And I'm sorry. But the fact is… It hasn't been easy for either of us.

"You see... All of my life, anyway since Grandmother died, all I wanted was for you and me to have a good relationship."

His mouth twitched, but he didn't try to stop her.

"Something else. My father says he doesn't blame you for being angry at him. But I'd like you to explain how you could hate him for being a few shades darker than you are. It's just color, Grandfather. Like crayons. We're all the same. I'm Black, and I'm White. I'm part you, and part my father.

"And one more thing… Can you tell me how any of it is an excuse to hate your own granddaughter?

"Listen, Grandfather. I'm begging you to take a good look at why you've held this grudge for so long. Please. Do it in the memory of my mother. I know she loved my father with all of her heart. She died because of her love for him.

"The thing is. I know that I'll see her one day. And I believe you can too."

She took a breath, feeling empowered.

"No one can ever take back the pain and loneliness I felt much of my life. But now I'm going to do something that every single human can do, no matter what color. And that's to say I forgive you. And I do. I forgive you, Grandfather."

Trying not to burst into sobs, she cupped a hand over his. Pulling a cloth sack from a pocket, she turned his hand over and placed it in his palm.

"Here's your diamonds. I'm just asking one thing. Please drop the charges against my father."

Emily didn't want to embarrass him any longer and turned to leave. When she reached the door, he called to her.

"I don't hate you. Never did."

She turned around to face him. When their eyes met, she held her breath not wanting to spoil the moment with tears.

"Thanks for telling me, Grandfather."

<><><>

"*I* feel so much better," Emily said to Rose when she returned to the car. "You'll never believe what he said to me."

"Well? What was it?"

"He said he didn't hate me."

"And?

"That's it? You're happy as a lark because he said he didn't hate you?"

Rose shook her head.

Emily made a face and smiled. Obviously, her sister would never understand.

"He's going to have to stop drinking. At least I hope he does."

"You sure don't expect much, do you."

Emily shrugged. "Actually, I do. And what he showed me was something. I told him I forgave him. That meant something to him. I could see it in his eyes. He wasn't in a talking mood. But I could see that he listened to every word."

"Well…that's good, of course. And forgiveness is important for the soul. But just don't let him hurt you again."

"I have a good feeling about this one, Sis."

<><><>

*A*dah's best friend, Lou, came to the house expecting Adah would be home from work. The two were planning a night out with the girls. Rose was upstairs doing homework, and Emily answered the door and offered to make Lou hot tea while she waited.

Emily recalled how this woman had egged Adah on, reminding her how Samuel wasn't making money while in jail. Even though that was true, she had to force herself not to feel anger.

"Here's your tea, Ma'am," she said, placing the cup on the table.

She was about to go upstairs when Lou asked her to sit. Emily hesitated before taking a seat across from her.

You must feel pretty awful that Samuel's in jail."

"Yes. I do. I feel terrible. But I'm sure he'll be getting out very soon."

"Adah was devastated, you know. Did you apologize?"

"I let her know how guilty I felt. And I offered to pay rent."

"Well… It sure was selfish of you to bring this family such a burden."

"You don't know a thing about my life," Emily said, standing.

"I know enough."

Footsteps came through the back entry, and Adah appeared in the doorway.

"Lou! Outside!"

"You know what this child did, Adah. Why do you put up with it?"

"Lou. I said, out!"

Lou walked out through the back. Emily expected Adah to leave with her. Instead, she closed and locked the outside door and came back into the kitchen.

"I'm sorry, Emily. I want you to know that I don't agree with her. And I should have stopped that kind of talk long ago."

"I realize I've put a burden on you, Adah. And I am sorry."

Adah went over and turned the burner on high, pulled down two cups, and dropped a tea bag in each.

"You know what? Yes, it's been difficult. But you're Samuel's daughter."

She glanced over. "He's always loved you. Even before he loved me.

"Let me give you some advice. No matter where we go in life or who we are, we step on toes. Even if it's not intended, someone gets hurt. But more times than not, our toes get stepped on. There are those who back stab us, lie, and cheat us out of promotions, or try to take away our happiness because of jealousy. No matter where we go, someone turns on us. You want to know the crux of it all? In the end, whatever we're hit with, we win by being honest. Truth is everything.

"So, Emily... I've been unfair to you because of things that have happened to me in the past. And I was wrong not to trust you."

Adah poured the hot water into the cups and brought them to the table, sitting across from Emily.

"The thing is.... We win by building relationships with truth and forgiveness. I learned that in church. Sometimes it takes me awhile. Are you hearing me?"

"I am. And...thank you."

"Listen, Emily. I know you had a rough life. You deserved so much better. As far as I've seen, you've got the inner strength to succeed one day. But it takes time and patience.

"And one other thing. I don't know if we'll ever be best friends. But I will never do anything to damage you and Samuel's relationship, nor your relationship with Rose. Not now, and not ever."

"Thank you for that, Adah. And I'm very sorry for any pain and inconvenience I've caused you. I should've made that clearer. And I just want to say how much I appreciate what you've done for me."

"Well, thank you. And I admit it wasn't easy, but I'm glad I had enough sense to do a bit of attitude adjusting."

They exchanged smiles, and Emily stood.

"I could probably do some of that myself."

Emily was on top of the world as she walked up the steps to her bedroom. No one could ever replace her mother and what they would have shared, but she was thankful for the new relationship she had with Adah.

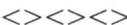

The atmosphere in the house had changed since the two women had their talk. Emily could see in her stepmother's eyes that all of her resentment was gone. It was amazing how much better life felt when that one important person in her life, who didn't care much for her, suddenly did.

Samuel called while the girls were eating breakfast. Rose took the phone from her mother and held it so she could share the headset with Emily.

"We're both here, Father."

"I miss you girls," he said. "I just wanted to tell you that, and that I love you."

"We love you too," they said in unison.

"Like I told your mother, there's a hearing on Friday. I have a good feeling. So does Ryan. Oh, and Emily. Steven reached out to me last week and I was able to talk with him for a few minutes. He sent you something. So, check the mail. If you don't get it today, it should be there by tomorrow."

"You know what it is?"

"Yes. But I want it to be a surprise. You'll like it, I promise."

Emily could barely sleep that night, excited because, one way or another, it looked like her father would be home soon. And whatever she was about to receive in the mail, she knew it would be something meaningful.

Saturday morning, Emily got up early and looked out the window. She didn't have to go to work until two. And she hoped the mailman would arrive before she left. If she strained her eyes just so, she could faintly make out the end of the driveway where the mailbox sat.

Adah invited the girls to go grocery shopping. But Emily knew all she would be thinking about was if the mail had arrived.

"I think I'll pull out a book and sit on the front porch if you don't mind," Emily said.

Rose gave her a knowing grin as she left with her mother. Emily watched them disappear up the road before going upstairs to retrieved the acorns she picked up the day she went to the water with Nathan. She already confirmed the perfect spot with Adah, where she could keep an eye on their growth from the bedroom window. When she finished planting the acorns, she picked out a book and went to sit on the front porch. Keeping her ears peeled for the mailman, she glanced up now and then from her reading.

Finally, an hour later, the mailman pulled up to the house. Emily took the steps down and picked up the bundle of mail. The package at the bottom was for her. She left the other mail on the kitchen table and took hers up to the bedroom. Pulling the box open, she picked up one of the letters from the stack her father had sent throughout the years.

"*My Dearest Emily,*" the letter began, the way they all did. Tears rolled down her cheeks as she read one after the other. She loved the stories he told about her mother.

Later, Rose walked in, laid across her bed, and listened as Emily finished reading the last one.

"Whew. This could make a person weep for days. And then again, if I were you, I might just be angry."

"I was at first. But I'm not anymore."

"It's easier that way, isn't it."

"Aunt Francine could've thrown the letters out. I'm not even sure why she kept them. But I think she always knew what needed to happen at some point. Maybe in there lies the answer."

CHAPTER THIRTY-ONE

*O*n Monday afternoon, Emily went back to the hospital to see her grandfather, but when she walked into his room the bed was empty. She rushed down to the nurse's station, heartsick that she probably lost him just when something good had happened between them.

"I came to see Rupert Rezell. He's not in his room. Did he—"

"He checked out of the hospital yesterday. Are you Emily, by any chance?"

"Yes."

The nurse handed her an envelope. "He left this for you."

"Thank you, Ma'am."

Emily took the letter, found the nearest chair, and sat.

Emily,

I'm an old man who drank hard and lived like a fool, who hated himself as much as anyone. Actually, I haven't had booze since entering the hospital. I already feel better. Longest time without a drink in years. It sure clears the mind.

I'm not proud of what I did to my sister. But here it is. Carl and I loved to go out gambling. Francine hated that. This particular night there was a once-a-year bash in Chicago. Carl always said he'd hit it big. Well, he did. The diamonds. No one but me and Carl knew about them. Anyway, he said he'd split the profits with me if I'd hide them at my house until he could figure out what to tell Francine. I hid them in the necklace box.

304

When Carl died, I thought I'd let them sit until Francine was gone. She didn't have the ambition to do anything worthwhile with them anyway. When she died, I searched high and low for that box.

Melanie's father has been threatening to take the farm for years because of that investment he made with Claude. He's more determined than ever. Now I'll be able to pay him enough so he'll leave me alone. I think I'll even fix up the place a bit. No matter what's happened or how I feel about things. You did take care of us for all those years. And when I sell the diamonds, I'm going to send you money for college.

I want you to know that after you stopped by, I called the authorities and told them I wanted to drop the charges against your father.

"Huh, just like that. And he didn't even sign his name."

Emily was elated as she folded the letter and walked up the hallway and outside where Rose promised to meet her. As she sat on the front steps and waited, she recalled how excited she was about coming to San Francisco.

Nothing turned out exactly as she planned. But she had always clung to her grandmother's words that had been repeated to her over and over until the day she died, each of them written in her journal. Emily thought of one of her favorites:

> 'When trials get you down, something good waits around the corner. And don't forget, my Little Bella Bambina; each time we're met by one of those trials, there's a lesson to be learned.'

Maybe the road ahead would be winding because life is never a certainty. But Emily knew that no matter where she was or what happened, her family would be her anchors. Like her grandmother said, *'All we need is that one person whose love and support never waivers.'*

ABOUT THE AUTHOR

Kathleen lives in Washington state. She began her writing career over thirty years ago in a countryside home in North Dakota. The process of writing her first novel, the September Wind series, has its own story that could fill at least a novella. It won a second-place award from Gardenia Press for a manuscript with the title An Empty Forest when she was still a budding writer (she was chosen for the award just before GP moved from non-pay to pay). She is working on a novel called The Thread That Holds Her (memoirs of a writer), about the journey she may not have taken if she had known where it would lead.

Scrooge and the Romance Effect is a collection of short stories, which includes *Haunted*, a story that took first place in a writing contest. *Knapsack Journey Home* (October Will Never Be the Same) is about life and the loss of her middle son, Chad (Chaddieboy). *Poems of Glass* is a thirty-five year collection of poetry and prose. She's working on several other books, and short stories.

September Wind book III will be out March 31, 2026.

NOTE: I recently learned that I have Hydrocephalus and will need surgery. It seems like trying to get surgery now days isn't like it used to be. And I am sincerely hopeful that I will be able to finish book SW book III by the due date. The first draft is finished. But, of course, there are the grammar edit's and other changes that will lengthen the process.

My sincere thanks to all the readers.

Website: New website coming in 2026

 Amazon:
https://www.amazon.com/September-Wind-Book-Kathleen-Janz-Anderson-ebook/dp/B0C2KV3L5C

YouTube - Memorial Video for Chad:
https://www.youtube.com/watch?v=JWcQaU65Cxk&t=809s

Chad's Facebook memorial
https://www.facebook.com/KathleenAnderson1514

Twitter
https://twitter.com/KatJanzAnderson

Instagram
https://www.instagram.com/kathleenwritesfromtheheart/

www.ingramcontent.com/pod-product-compliance
Lightning Source LLC
Chambersburg PA
CBHW060404260626
47160CB00006B/2429